'A poignant story about t[...] and looking for a sens[...] intense.' Kat Ellis, author of *Harrow Lake*

'*The Wanderer* is a gut-wrenching, epic love story that I could not put down. I was addicted and rooting for Ryder and Maggie from the start.' #1 *New York Times* bestselling author Natasha Preston

'A beautiful book about loss, longing, and love. Josie Williams paints a touching picture of two teens, separated by life and death, battling loneliness to find love for the first time. An original and beautiful story – thoroughly enjoyable!' N.J. Simmonds

'A heartbreaking love story with a ghostly twist; I fell in love with Ryder and Maggie and felt every longing glance and stolen touch. Just gorgeous.' Cynthia Murphy, author of *Last One To Die*

THE WANDERER

THE WANDERER

Josie Williams

Firefly

First published in 2021
by Firefly Press
25 Gabalfa Road, Llandaff North, Cardiff, CF14 2JJ
www.fireflypress.co.uk

A CIP catalogue record of this book is available from
the British Library.

1 3 5 7 9 8 6 4 2

ISBN 9781913102661

This book has been published with the support of
the Books Council of Wales.

Typeset by Elaine Sharples

Printed and bound by CPI Group (UK) Ltd,
Croydon, Surrey, CRO 4YY

For Braxton

PROLOGUE
~ RYDER ~

The human mind is most open in those few precious seconds when the body is on the cusp of death. I've always found it ironic that the time when you're most awake is just as you're about to fall into everlasting sleep. Someone like me, a wanderer, lives for those fleeting moments of a person's passing, because it's only then that we exist to anyone other than ourselves or the other trapped souls that roam the Earth.

Of course, it gets depressing watching people die, seeking out their last breath, willing their demise, just so I can feel something, but after five long years of wandering alone, unacknowledged and unnoticed, I *need* that connection. That split-second rise of the eyebrows, the narrowing of the eyes, or – my personal favourite – the 'who are you?' is enough to make me feel alive again and remember that, although I don't exist anymore, I *did* once.

Maybe I should start off by introducing myself. My name is, or used to be, Ryder Edmonds. Technically, I'm seventeen years old, but I'm not though, because, well, I'm dead. A moment of lost concentration on my behalf while white-water rafting with my family was all it took. The result wasn't pretty. From what I remember of it, my end was quick and painless.

What wasn't quick and painless, though, was my transition.

You see, I hadn't done what I was supposed to. I didn't move on and step into the unknown to begin my next journey – whatever that may have been. It all happened so fast, I was too distressed to think through the consequences of my actions – or, more accurately, my inaction.

One second I was falling from the boat and feeling the punch of cold water swallow me whole and fill my lungs, and the next I was stood stock still at my mother's side, looking down at my lifeless body, noticing how my once-tanned skin now looked grey, and how my lips had a blueish tinge to them. My mother began to shake as my two older brothers, my dad and the instructor all tried desperately to revive me on the muddy banks of the River Tryweryn in north Wales.

Deep down I knew I was already dead. How

could I not know? My own body was at my feet. I watched as they pushed on my chest and forced air into my lungs – it wasn't exactly something one could misconstrue. A ball of horror settled into my stomach, weighing me down. I'd never felt terror like it; it hit me like a freight train, smashing into me and turning my world upside down.

That was when the brilliant shock of light appeared behind me, so bright it almost burned my eyes as I turned to look. It was dazzling, blinding – but somehow it was majestically beautiful. The warmth of it coated my skin, wrapping me up in a feeling of safety and protectiveness, washing away the abject terror I'd felt building inside me moments before. The glow was full of love, radiating a sense of home, peace and serenity – just like one of my mum's hugs.

I could only guess at what this meant – some sort of afterlife. I could feel it, feel the pull of it, the irresistible call of the light and what lay beyond. I knew I was supposed to go ... but when I glanced back to look at my wailing mother, I knew I couldn't leave her. So instead, I turned my back to the light, hoping that if I pretended everything was fine I could somehow will it out of existence. The pull from the glow had been immense, ignoring it had been almost impossible. It was the hardest thing I'd ever done. At one point I almost lost the battle, but I kept my eyes on my mother and fought it with all of my strength.

It was a decision I've regretted every single moment of every single day since.

You see, the light didn't wait around for me to get over my shock and think it through properly; it lingered for merely a minute or two, and then it was gone, and I was left standing there on that bank, watching as my family gave up and cried over my body.

No sooner than the light disappeared, than so did the warmth; in fact, so did every physical feeling that I had ever known. I no longer felt the cool breeze that moved my mother's hair, or the sun that shone down overhead, I couldn't even feel the slick mud or sharp rocks beneath my plimsoll-covered feet.

That was the first indication that I'd messed up. The second indication was when my eldest brother, in his rage and sorrow, picked up his oar and threw it directly at my chest. I'd flinched, like any normal person would do, but I needn't have bothered because the oar sailed straight through my now non-existent body without so much as a rush of wind, and clattered loudly to the floor behind me. That was when I knew I was totally, utterly and royally screwed.

CHAPTER ONE
~ RYDER ~

Around two thousand people die every day in the United Kingdom alone; that amounts to a staggering six hundred thousand lost souls per year. I'd never really thought about mortality much before. You don't question your existence – when you have one. It's when you cease to exist that you begin to question everything.

Most souls, the lucky ones in my opinion, move on to their next journey. Some, like me, don't do what they're supposed to; they fight the light and then get stuck here, alone and unnoticed amongst the living. I'm not sure if there's a technical term for what I am – I refer to myself as a 'wanderer' because that's pretty much all I do all day – wander aimlessly. Wanderers are the souls of the dead that, for whatever reason, don't go into the afterlife. They reject the light, like I did. Some people would call us ghosts, lingering spirits, spectres, spooks or phantoms. We've had many names over the years, but wanderer is my personal favourite. It's less … scary.

There are many of us trapped here. I see them occasionally, walking amongst the living, or sitting watching life pass them by. You can tell they're dead by the soft, shimmery edge to their bodies, kind of like an ill-formed dream or memory that you're trying to recall. We look just … *off* somehow. Also, let's not forget our funky clothes. Doomed to forever wear what we died in, people meander about in pyjamas, hospital gowns, sports gear, you name it. There's even this one guy who hangs around in the city centre by the theatre wearing some sort of Elizabethan get-up, throwing Shakespearian quotes and insults at the oblivious passers-by. I've always wondered when exactly he died, I'd ask him, but he's stark raving mad, and last time I tried to spark up a conversation with him he chased me off, trying to wallop me with his cane. The other wanderers tend to keep themselves to themselves, too angry at the world and their predicament to socialise. Most of them stay close to their old homes, or follow their families around, or just stare off into space as they try to go about their old routines.

Not all wanderers feel the need to do what I do. I only know of one other: my best friend, Jade. She's a little younger than me; she died a week before her fifteenth birthday, but she's been dead a lot longer than I have. Jade is the only wanderer I've met who shares my pain and regret for not passing over to the other side. She's also the only one who feels the need to be validated like I do. It was her that got me into it, actually.

That's what I am doing right now – trying to gain that sense of self for the first time in almost six days. A morbid sense of worthlessness that can only be banished by the dying is what brings me here, day after day.

I look up at the large brick building, the local hospital, and take a deep breath, wishing I could feel the chilly October air fill my lungs. Shoving my hands into the pockets of the thick, waterproof jacket that I'm perpetually stuck wearing because it was my garment of choice when I died, I step into the building and immediately turn left. I know where I'm heading for today. The oncology department. Rupert Brown is on palliative care and has been clinging to life for the last few days. His time will be up soon, everybody knows it; it's just a matter of when.

The door to the ward is closed as I approach, so I hold my breath and walk directly through it, ignoring the uncomfortable sensation of passing through an inanimate object. It doesn't exactly hurt, it feels more like a squeezing, pinching pressure that starts deep inside and works its way outward.

Once inside the ward, I stop and take a look around. The place is the same as normal; the beds are still full of faces I recognise; the nurses and doctors make their rounds. Morning visits have not long started, so people are saying their greetings to loved ones or talking to nurses about how their relatives were overnight.

Rupert's private room is five doors up to my right. I make my way there, casually looking into the other rooms as I walk past. Sylvia, an elderly lady with stage-four lung cancer, is sitting up in her bed, watching TV and raggedly sucking air through her oxygen mask. I know from listening to doctors that she's been given less than a week to live. She'll probably be my next visitation after Rupert.

As I step into Rupert's room, I see his condition has worsened since my visit yesterday. He looks paler and has a sort of sickly-grey tinge to his skin; his lips are dry and cracked; his cheeks hollowed where the skin clings to his bones. His body is frail and fragile, his muscles long since wasted away now he barely eats or moves. Today, his eyes are closed and he clutches an old photograph to his chest with long bony fingers. As I take a seat at his side, I study the photograph. It shows a younger, healthy version of him and a pretty, brunette lady with a boy of about six or seven attached to her hip. I know this is his family; he spoke about them last week to a nurse while I was here. Rupert is immensely proud of his son, a soldier in the British Army, currently posted overseas. He'd boasted about his boy and how he serves his country, just like Rupert had when he was young and able.

My gaze flicks to his chest, watching the slow, lazy rise and fall of it, and suddenly I find myself talking to him. I talk random nonsense really, about the Formula One race and football matches coming up this weekend, I tell him about the weather outside and how I have a feeling it might rain later, I tell him the joke that Jade told me early this morning before we parted ways and she went to her favourite hangout, the Garden House Hospice. I tell him anything I can think of just because, if I were sitting in the room alone with only a photograph for company, I'd want someone to do the same for me. It's ludicrous really because I know he can't hear me, but I can't stop the useless drivel tumbling from my mouth.

I sit there all morning, talking to a man who can neither see nor hear me. I watch as nurses come and check on him, turning up his oxygen, fiddling with his morphine drip, fussing with the bedcovers as they smile down at him sadly. He wakes for a little while; the nurses sit him up so he can look around, but he's barely able to move anything more than his eyes.

Just before lunchtime, his breathing becomes extremely laboured, and even the oxygen mask isn't helping. His fingers tighten around the edge of the frame, clutching it closer as his eyes squeeze closed. His forehead crinkles as he lets out a little groan of pain. Clearly the morphine isn't enough anymore.

My stomach sinks as I realise that he's at his end. Although I've been waiting for this moment for the last six days, I still hate that he's having to go through this. No man should die alone with only a photograph for company. But because he's not attached to a heart monitor and hasn't pressed the 'call' button, no one is aware that Rupert Brown is about to slip over to the other side at seventy-four years of age.

Involuntarily, my hand reaches out, closing over his, trying to support him even though I know that he'll not feel it. His body spasms a couple of times and his eyes pop open as he desperately gasps for breath.

His eyes widen as he looks at me for the first time, this stranger, standing by his bed, clutching his hand as if we are old friends. The sense of recognition washes over me as his gaze latches on to mine and I see the silent question there – 'who are you?'

I smile kindly, deep-down hating that I'm taking some small measure of satisfaction from this man's death, but I just can't help it. This is what I come here for, day after day.

'Relax. Breathe. Soon it won't hurt anymore,' I promise. 'Everything's OK now, Rupert.' Somehow, despite the pain that he must be in, calm seems to descend over him, and his eyes stay locked to mine until he wheezes in his last breath.

'What happened? Am I … am I dead?'

I turn my head. Rupert is standing at my side in his maroon pyjamas. He looks healthier now as he stares at his body that lies on the bed, unmoving. I nod. 'Yeah, you're dead,' I confirm, finally releasing my grip on his now lifeless fingers.

He gulps and turns his attention to me. 'I don't understand. Who are you? Are you an angel?'

An involuntary chuckle slips out of my lips as I shake my head. I've been asked that a lot. 'No, just someone who's lost.'

Rupert blinks a couple of times, and then squints, turning to look behind him, shielding his eyes as if he's looking at the sun. I take a deep breath, knowing his light has come to collect him. I can't see it, but judging by the wondrous, awed look on his face, I'm sure he can.

'You should go.' I nod in the direction that he's looking in. 'Go, Rupert, trust me, don't stay here.'

'It's beautiful,' he whispers. 'What's beyond there?' He reaches out as if trying to touch the light only he can see and stares, transfixed.

I sigh and drop my head. 'I have no idea, but I know you need to go there.'

He shuffles forward, moving slowly, looking around to his left and right, his lips parted, his hands outstretched. I sigh, looking away and scowling towards the window, knowing that Rupert is the lucky one here because he gets an end, he gets to know what peace feels like, instead of being stuck in purgatory, forever alone, forever wanting.

Moments later, when I turn, I'm alone in the room with Rupert's cadaver, all peaceful-looking in death, photograph still cradled against his chest.

When the nurse comes into the room to do her rounds, I slip out of the door unnoticed.

I need air; I feel a little suffocated and my stomach is twisted in knots. Usually a death doesn't affect me as much as this. I normally enjoy the recognition a lot more, but today all I feel is grief, guilt and jealousy.

Grief because that little old man had to die alone. Guilt because I'd hung out in his room for the last six days waiting for it to happen. And jealousy because he got his peaceful ending, yet I was still here. It was the look on his face, that awed look that did it.

Slumping down in the rain onto the blue-painted metal bench outside the busy hospital, I put my head in my hands and try to breathe through my stress, attempting to focus on the feeling of validation that his acknowledgment had given me. But that fulfilled feeling is today overshadowed by anger and frustration.

I don't know how long I sit there in the rain, scowling at the floor, pondering the meaning of my 'life'. After several buses have pulled up and sped away again, I finally drag my eyes to the ornate clock mounted on the front of the hospital. It's almost four.

Knowing there's nothing here that can drag me out of this depressive, dark state I'm slipping into, I force myself to stand and go to the one place that's bound to lift my mood. Ashleigh Care Home. It isn't the care home per se that I long to see, but someone that frequently visits there.

When another bus pulls up, I hop on, propping myself up on the luggage rack, and look out of the window, ignoring everyone around me and not even bothering to nose about to catch any gossip. Usually on bus rides, I'd read over someone's shoulder, or eavesdrop on their conversations. Today, I have no desire to do either.

Ashleigh Care Home isn't too far away, so I jump off when we approach and make my way up to the grand, old building with my hands firmly stuffed in my pockets. Today is Thursday, so it is one of her days and I know, within an hour, I'll be feeling a lot better.

Making my way in, I look around, examining the familiar elderly people milling around in their house slippers and thick warm cardigans. The lounge of the care home is only half full, but I smile when I spot who I'm looking for.

Doreen Nichols is sitting in the corner, knitting away, with a bright red ball of wool on her lap. Her petite frame is accentuated by the large, old-fashioned armchair she sits in. Her short, curly hair shines silver in the daylight. A smile sits on her face despite her being alone. Even though she's lost in her own little world most of the time, reliving her past while sitting in her present, Doreen is one of the happiest, most lovely people I know. Almost as lovely as the one I've come here to see.

I make my way over to her and take the empty seat at her side. 'Hi, Doreen. How are you today?

Hope you've not been giving the nurses a hard time again,' I say, even though she can't hear me. Doreen is a full-time resident at the care home and has vascular dementia caused by a bleed on the brain – a result of the severe stroke she suffered three months ago. 'Today's Thursday, you know what that means.' I sink back into the chair and look her over, taking her in, making sure she's well, as her knitting needles click relentlessly. On the outside, you wouldn't think there was a single thing wrong with this tiny lady. Trouble is, when she has an *episode*, she can become a little violent – hence her being placed in a home where they know how to care for her properly.

As she shifts her leg, the ball of wool drops to the floor and rolls away. One of the male attendants picks it up and walks over. 'You dropped something, Doreen,' he says, setting it carefully onto her lap.

Her smile widens as she touches the wool. 'Oh, thank you, dear! Wouldn't want to lose that,' she smiles, tucking the wool down the side of her leg and continuing her hypnotic knitting movements with her arthritic hands.

'Your granddaughter is due here any minute. It's after four,' the guy informs her.

My back straightens and some of the tension starts to leave my body at the mere thought of her.

Doreen sighs happily and nods. 'I was hoping to get this row finished before she comes. It's a Christmas present for her; I'm making her a scarf. Do you think you can put this away for me, so she doesn't see it?' She carefully holds up the knitting and needles to the attendant.

'Sure thing, I'll put it in your bottom drawer in your room, how 'bout that?' he offers, wrapping it up more securely.

'You're a good boy. If I were twenty years younger...'

I watch as he laughs and walks off towards the back hallway where the residents' rooms are located. Moments later, as if on cue, the front door opens and closes. Although I can't see her yet because she's around the corner in the reception area, I can hear her talking to one of the nurses and signing in as a visitor. I hold my breath, waiting.

CHAPTER TWO
~ RYDER ~

Maggie Nichols is the very definition of awkward. The dictionary people should probably consider adding her name under the description of shy, demure, clumsy and withdrawn. But, the thing is, that all just adds to her charm and adorability.

Finally, she steps around the corner, shouldering her schoolbag. I smile and watch as she stops, glancing around the room, searching out her grandmother. When she spots her, her lips pull into the most beautiful warm smile that dimples her cheeks. Maggie steps forward and, because she's not paying full attention, or because she's simply the clumsiest person in the world, her foot catches on the leg of an armchair and she stumbles, barely managing to catch herself.

The attendants in the room rush forward to help her, but she rights herself quickly, waving off offers of help as her cheeks turn a cute shade of pink. I grin and sit forward in my seat as she drops her eyes to the floor and lets her hair fall in front of her face as a little embarrassed giggle escapes her lips.

I can't take my eyes off her.

There's just something about this girl. I have no idea what it is, but she captures my full attention as soon as she steps into the room. It's not that she's overly beautiful in the conventional way, it wasn't her looks that first attracted me to her at all, it was her fierce ability to love. She's ridiculously shy, but when it comes to her grandmother, she's like a lioness protecting her cub: tenacious, ferocious, and with a quiet strength. That was what attracted me to her at first, but after that, getting to know her quirky, book-loving self, it was like I was sliding down a cliff, unable to grasp anything, unable to stop the momentum. I was a goner within a couple of weeks, head over heels in love with her. She's beautiful inside and that radiates from every single pore of her retro-shirt-wearing, Freddie Mercury-loving body.

She takes off the bulky, soaking-wet coat that dwarfs her. It's one of those old-fashioned ones with shoulder pads and looks like it came straight from the 1980s. It's obviously a hand-me-down, and I would give anything to be able to ask her why she wears it all the time when it so clearly doesn't fit her.

Everything about Maggie Nichols screams 'frightened and shy' apart from her hair. Rain soaked, untamed curls the colour of burning embers bounce as she walks, with bits falling over her face so she has to do that thing, blowing them away using the corner of her mouth that I find the most adorable trait ever.

'Hi, Nan. How are you today?' She bends and engulfs Doreen's small frame in an affectionate hug. Doreen's eyes flutter closed, and a fond smile tugs at the corners of her pink lips.

'I'm well, sweetheart. It's lovely to see you.' Doreen pats Maggie's back softly, but then pulls away and frowns. 'You're soaking wet.'

Maggie laughs softly and looks down at herself. 'Yeah, it's chucking it down out there and I forgot an umbrella.' She drops her schoolbag at her feet and sets her coat over the back of the chair so it can air as she sits down.

Doreen clicks her tongue. 'You shouldn't have come in such bad weather. I wouldn't have minded.'

Maggie waves her hand dismissively, pushing her damp curls behind her ears as her pale-green eyes lock on her grandmother. '*I* would have minded.' She leans down and reaches into her coat pocket, pulling out a Pez dispenser. I smile. It's Sylvester the Cat today, he's old and the red paint has worn off his nose from overuse. Maggie lifts the head and grins as she takes a sweet and pops it on her tongue, before offering the next one to her grandmother. 'Cherry today.'

A smile twitches at the corner of Doreen's lips as she takes one, popping it into her mouth and then turns her face towards the window. 'This rain is just terrible, isn't it? Some angel up there must be crying up a storm over something.'

Maggie leans and takes Doreen's age-spotted hand. 'So, how have you been? Your cough any better?'

I watch Maggie, letting my eyes sweep over every inch of her face, her flushed cheeks and the little droplet of rain that's itching to fall from her hair any second. How she covers her mouth shyly when she laughs or smiles so that her metal braces are hidden; how her oversized navy-blue school jumper hangs loosely, but how she still fiddles with it, pulling it away from her tummy as if self-conscious. I notice the dimples in her cheeks that my fingers itch to reach out and touch.

Sitting back in my chair, I blow out a big breath and let the day's frustration wash away from me as I listen to her talk. Everything feels better in my world when I'm around Maggie. As a wanderer, time seems to drag. An hour can seem like a day, a day a week, a week a year. It feels like an age since I last saw her but, in reality, it's only been two days.

I've known Maggie for just over three months now. The first time I'd laid eyes on her I'd been at the Norfolk and Norwich University Hospital doing my usual, hanging-out-and-waiting-for-that-validation thing, when Doreen had been rushed in on a gurney. It hadn't looked good for her at all, so, me being me and what I was there for, I'd followed behind her, waiting and watching. Behind Doreen had trailed a distraught-looking Maggie. I'd thought Doreen Nichols was a goner that night, but I was wrong. I hadn't realised how much of a fighter she was.

As usual, Maggie's visit lasts about an hour before the staff begin bustling around, helping the residents out of their chairs and escorting them into the dining room for dinner. Today was a nice visit – unlike the last one. Last time, Doreen had been having an off day. She'd not recognised her granddaughter and had instead thought it was her only daughter, Margaret, Maggie's mother. It was heart-breaking to watch Maggie have to explain to her nan that Margaret had actually died over seven years ago. Doreen had been distraught and incredibly confused at the news. Unfortunately, as with a lot of dementia sufferers, it wasn't the first time I'd witnessed something like

21

that, and it wouldn't be the last either. This visit, though, was a lot brighter. Doreen was on good form, joking and laughing. The two of them were nattering like old men standing by a fence, setting the world to rights.

'I guess it's time for me to go,' Maggie mutters, looking around at the emptying-out room.

'What? Already? You just got here.'

'It's dinner time. You're having shepherd's pie and roasted carrots, I asked on the way in.' She smiles affectionately at her grandmother.

As she stands to leave, Doreen's breath catches and she leans forward, grabbing her granddaughter's hand. 'Don't go. Don't leave me here. I don't like it here. It's so noisy at night, and there are bad people. They come in and steal my clothes while I'm asleep. One of them stole my favourite cardigan! Please, please don't leave me here any longer. Take me home with you?'

Maggie gulps. 'I can't, Nan.'

'I'll be as good as gold, please? I promise I won't be any trouble.'

The heartbreak is clear to see on Maggie's face. Her jaw clenches. 'I wish I could, but I'm not allowed. They say I'm not old enough to be your carer. In less than three years I'll be eighteen, and then...' She trails off, her expression almost pleading as she strokes her thumb on the back of her grandmother's hand. 'Please don't keep asking. I *can't*.'

Doreen's pleading expression turns hard instantly. 'Fine, go then. Leave me here on my own with these people. It's not like you care!' Her tone is venomous as she waves her hand at the elderly residents all seated around the room. 'I shouldn't be in here. I shouldn't have to sit here listening to them all complain about arthritis and how they want their food mushed up without lumps!'

Maggie's eyes close as she takes a deep breath. 'I have to go. I love you; I'll come back at the weekend.' Before Doreen can say anything else, Maggie bends and plants a soft kiss on her cheek before picking up her bag and coat and walking off.

I get up and follow as Maggie pretends she can't hear Doreen pleading again behind us. She barely makes it around the corner and out of the room before her tears come. I long to wrap my arm around her, to soothe her and tell her that everything is going to be all right, but, of course, I can't. Instead, one of the nurses is there in an instant, passing Maggie a tissue with a sympathetic look.

'OK, sweetheart?'

Maggie shakes her head, her curls falling over her

face again. 'No.' She sniffs, using the tissue to wipe her damp cheeks before blowing her nose.

The nurse sets her hand on Maggie's shoulder and smiles kindly. 'I know it's hard, but she doesn't do it on purpose.'

A sad smile graces Maggie's lips as she nods. 'I know; it's just so hard to see her like that. She thinks I want her in here. She doesn't understand that they won't let me live with her anymore because of the stroke. I want to, I want to take her home and look after her, but they won't let me because I'm not old enough. She thinks I don't care.'

The nurse shakes her head adamantly. 'She knows you care, don't ever think that. It's the dementia, it makes people say and do things they would never normally dream of saying or doing. It alters peoples' personalities so dramatically. It's always hardest on those closest to them, but believe me, she knows you love her, and she loves you to death. On a good day, you're all she talks about. She's so proud of you, always know that.'

Reluctantly, Maggie nods. 'Yeah, thanks, Violet. I'll see you in two days.' Without another word, she steps out of the front door and into the rain.

On visiting days, I usually make the thirty-minute walk to Maggie's house with her. It's become part of my routine now, even though it's the complete opposite direction from where Jade and I spend our nights.

I step out of the door behind Maggie, noticing that she's not put on her coat. She doesn't go far. Just a few steps outside the door, she stops and looks straight up into the darkening sky, not caring that the rain continues to pelt down, dampening her hair and wetting her cheeks. She stands like that for a full minute before she lets out a heavy sigh and slips on her coat, reaching into the pocket to grab another Pez sweet as she stomps off down the path. As she walks, she searches in her schoolbag, pulls out her iPhone and clamps her chunky red headphones over her ears.

An instantly recognisable guitar riff fills the air. She has the volume so loud I can hear every angsty word of 'Mr Brightside' blasting through her headphones. I walk at her side, wishing I had words, wishing I could take away her pain. Slowly, oh so slowly, the music seems to calm her and her shoulders lose some of their tension. It's always like this when her grandmother says something that upsets her – she blasts the music so loudly that it's no doubt damaging her eardrums, and it calms her.

Halfway home, the rain stops lashing down and Maggie starts humming a classic Queen song softly to herself. Maggie is tone deaf and is easily the worst singer I have ever heard in my life. She's so bad she should even be banned from singing in the shower, but I can't help smiling. I still love it.

I have it bad.

Completely lost in song, Maggie steps off the kerb into the road, crossing without looking. Instantly, from my right, I hear a screech of tyres on the road and the long, shrill blast of a horn cuts through the air. My whole body tightens as a white transit van speeds towards Maggie. She is completely unaware. White smoke billows from the tyres as it skids on the road, getting closer and closer. Everything seems to be happening in slow motion.

If my heart were beating, it would have stopped in that moment.

The van isn't going to be able to stop, it's going too fast. Maggie is going to die right in front of me and I am powerless to stop it.

CHAPTER THREE
~ RYDER ~

My mouth opens and I scream her name, mingling with the screeching horror of the van's impending approach still roaring from my right. Behind me, comes a loud, shocked gasp.

'Hey! Look out!'

Turning my head to the side, I see a young lad, maybe seventeen or eighteen. His face is pale as he stares with wide eyes in Maggie's direction ... but he's not moving. He's making no moves to save her, to save the girl with the fiery red hair who has stolen my heart so easily. His feet are firmly planted on the ground. He's going to watch her die.

Suddenly a crazy idea hits me. Before I even consciously make the decision to do it, I'm already acting. I don't even know if it's possible, but I have to at least try.

I rush towards him. If I still had a body, we would have collided and crashed to the floor from the force with which I threw myself at him. Instead, that uncomfortable squeezing, pinching sensation takes me over again, the one I always get when passing through an object, but this time my intent is not to pass through.

The boy's body jerks and twitches as I enter it.

I clench my jaw tightly as everything blurs, then fades, and finally turns completely black. All around me – or maybe it's just within my head, I'm not sure – there's a high-pitched whistling, like the sound of an old-fashioned kettle when it boils. As I struggle to take hold, everything closes in around me; the darkness takes over, pushing me from all directions, squeezing the air from my lungs. Just when I think I can't take the pressure any longer and I'm going to have to avert my plan, the pain ends.

All at once, as if the pain and pressure hadn't just happened, everything comes back into focus again.

I see her, still walking across the road, humming her tune. Barely a second must have passed since she stepped out. The van is still hammering towards her, the driver's desperate efforts doing nothing to stop the impending collision.

Finally noticing what's happening, Maggie looks up, her mouth dropping open in shock as her whole body goes rigid with fright. Her hands fly out, as if that will somehow protect her from the ton of metal screeching towards her.

Instinctively, I move my legs, launching myself forward into the road, throwing myself at Maggie. My body smashes into hers with such force that she's instantly knocked from her feet. It's a tackle I'd done a hundred times on the rugby field when I was alive. Both of us are catapulted into the air and across the road. The engine noise gets louder, deafening even and, as we start to fall, I feel a burst of wind on the back of my head where the van narrowly passes us.

I don't have time to properly register her grunt of pain or the air leaving her lungs in one whopping gust as my shoulder slams into her side. I don't have time to wonder if landing on the cold, concrete road will hurt her. I barely notice her belongings cascading to the floor or her headphones flying off. I don't have time to think about any of these things before they're happening.

We crash to the ground, side by side. The loud thump we make echoes inside my head as it strikes the tarmac. My shoulder hits next, and I feel the roughness of the road cutting into my elbow and forearm as we skid, finally coming to a stop just before the kerb.

Pain.

I've not felt it in so long that I don't quite know how to deal with it. It is almost as if every little scratch or bump is magnified tenfold.

Gritting my teeth against the overwhelming sensations, I manage to push myself awkwardly up to a sitting position. Lifting my hand and tentatively touching the throbbing spot on the side of my head is a struggle because my coordination is way off. I'm not used to being in a body again; it's weird and feels so alien. The muscles seem to protest, fighting against me, as if they somehow know I shouldn't be in control of them. I look down, seeing the boy's hands in place of mine, seeing his clothes covering my body. I blink rapidly as my actions finally sink in.

I've taken possession of the boy's body.

I'm unprepared for the emotions that crash over me. Panic, horror, fear, shock, pain and finally, relief, a lot of relief. I don't quite know how to cope with all the emotions again. There are too many feelings. I'd not realised how detached I'd become since I'd died. Simple things like feeling the wind on my face, and how cold the rainwater is as it seeps into my clothes and wets my face. I'd forgotten what it felt like to actually *feel*.

I quickly test my movements, noticing they're clunky and awkward, but nothing screams in agony so I know I've not broken any bones or caused any permanent damage. The boy will ache for a little while, but it was worth it.

I turn to Maggie as she lets out a groan. She's lying face down on the road; her red hair strewn everywhere, hiding her face. Squinting to see her better under the dim haze of the streetlight, I reach out, placing a hand on her back. The feel of her coat's material under my fingertips causes my hand flinch away, again unprepared for the sensation of touch. Air rushes from my lungs. I just touched her. My hand touched her, actually *touched* her! Despite the pain in my head and my arms burning from the numerous grazes that hitting the road has caused, I can't contain the smile that's crept onto my lips. I touched her. Something I'd longed to do for the last three months, something I usually daydreamed about for hours on end.

Off to the side, the van finally skids to a halt, and the silence now seems somehow deafening.

I reach out again, tentatively touching Maggie's shoulder, brushing her hair out of the way so I can see her face. 'Hey, are you all right?' I manage to rasp out through my dry mouth. My voice is alien to me, too; I guess I'd expected my own voice to come from the boy's mouth instead.

She stirs again, finally lifting her head. Her eyes meet mine for the first time since I've known her. The pale-green is mesmerising, and I revel in the fact that she's actually looking at me. Her lips part as her gaze goes from me, down to her barely damaged and very much alive self, and then over to the van that the visibly shaken driver is now climbing out of.

'Oh, God … I … I … You … You …' Maggie sits up, blinking and shaking her head as if trying to clear her thoughts. 'I wasn't looking, I didn't…' She gulps, reaching up and setting her trembling hand over her heart. 'You saved my life.'

The smile tugs at the corner of my mouth as I shrug, trying not to wince as that causes a sharp twinge to radiate up my neck. Her eyes meet mine again, trapping me there as her shallow breathing begins to even out. Silence stretches out between us. I'm not sure what to say. I've wanted to speak to her for so long, I'd had it all planned out, what I would say to her if I ever got the chance, but now that moment has arrived, I am just sitting here dumbfounded and staring back at her like a complete and utter tool.

'Are you guys OK?' The van driver interrupts my awkward, staring silence. 'Jesus, that was so close. I can't believe how close that was!' He turns his attention to me. 'She was lucky you were there, buddy. I wouldn't have been able to stop in time.' He crouches down, looking at us both in turn. His face is still etched with shock; he looks like he's a few heartbeats from vomiting. 'Are you hurt? Shall I call an ambulance?'

'I'm fine,' I answer before turning to Maggie. 'Are you all right? I hit you pretty hard. I'm really sorry about that.' I wince, thinking about how hard my shoulder collided with her side.

She waves her hand dismissively, her expression a little disbelieving. 'Don't apologise! You saved my life; a little bruising and being winded is nothing.'

I smile, watching the cute dimple form in her cheek as she smiles. 'I guess it beats being smashed with a van,' I agree.

Putting my hands on the ground, I push myself up. At the movement, I feel my grip of the guy weakening and I fight with all my strength to keep possession of his aching limbs. I'm not ready to let go yet, I'm not ready for this interaction to end. But it's hard, so hard that I have to clench my teeth and use all of my willpower to stay in control. I don't know how long I can hold it, everything in me is screaming at me to let go, but I want more precious seconds.

Once I'm on my feet, it takes me a moment to get my balance in the new body, I have to actually work to keep my muscles in position and when I reach out a hand towards Maggie, I have to steady myself not to topple over.

Smiling, she slips her hand in mine. The warmth of her skin makes me suck in a ragged breath. It's the first time anyone has touched me in the five years since my death. I marvel over the soft skin of her hand, the weight of her body as I pull her gently to her feet, how she steps so close to me that I can almost feel the heat radiating from her body to mine. It awes me and leaves me reeling.

As a wanderer I've lost most of my senses, of course I can still see and hear, but I haven't touched, tasted or smelt anything for years.

I thought I knew what it was like to be in love with her, but I'd had no idea. Now, borrowing all of those senses from the boy's body, I realise just how much of her I've been missing out on.

The feel of her skin on mine causes a feeling to stir in my stomach, kind of like a clench, a flutter, a squeezing sensation. I long to feel more of her, to reach out and touch that dimple, to run my fingers through her hair. As she smiles up at me, a gust of wind blows her scent across my face. It's something sweet, like vanilla, but I can't make it out exactly, maybe her shampoo? I want nothing more than to step closer to her and bury my face into her red curls, inhaling that scent deeply. Something like longing settles over me and I breathe deeply, memorising the scent, knowing that any second now I will have to leave the boy's body and that I'll never get to smell it again.

Gingerly she removes her hand from mine as a blush settles over her cheeks. 'Um, thanks.' Somewhat awkwardly, she looks down at herself, brushing the dirt and muddy rainwater from her coat, her shoulders hunching. I know she's embarrassed. I've studied her enough over the last couple of months to know her body language.

As she looks up at me again, it suddenly dawns on me that I'm just silently staring at her, mouth agape, just like some kind of mute stalker. No wonder she's embarrassed. I clear my throat and stoop to pick up her fallen possessions and rucksack.

'So, you're both OK then? Definitely don't need an ambulance?' the driver asks, looking between the two of us for confirmation as I bend down and reach for Maggie's headphones.

'No, everything's fine. I'm really sorry I walked out in front of you. I wasn't paying attention; I didn't hear you approaching,' Maggie answers, gnawing on her lip guiltily.

The guy lets out a huge breath and runs his hand through his hair. 'All's well that ends well, I guess. You get home safe, though, all right? No more listening to music while you cross the road,' he instructs, his voice stern.

'Doesn't look like that's going to be a problem anymore,' I mutter, standing up and holding out Maggie's broken iPhone and headphones as evidence. A small, sad smile tugs at the corner of Maggie's mouth as she takes them from my hand and inspects the shattered screen and the left earpiece dangling loosely from the plastic.

'Still, on the upside, this could have been my face,' she replies, shrugging and putting a positive spin on it as she pushes them into her coat pocket.

The guy laughs and heads back to his van, muttering to himself about thanking his lucky stars and needing a stiff drink.

Once we're alone, Maggie's attention turns back to me. The sweet smile on her face instantly brings one to mine, too. Our eyes lock again and, in that moment, something passes between us. Some sort of energy, a connection, something that feels like it's on another level to anything I've felt before. I can't look away.

For a couple of blissful seconds, I forget that she

doesn't actually see *me*, but the boy whose body I've currently borrowed. But then I do remember and it ruins the moment for me completely.

I hold out her school bag.

As she takes it, she smiles gratefully. 'Thanks, Charlie.'

My body stills. *Charlie? The boy's name's Charlie? She knows him? Shit!*

I hadn't thought it through at all. I'd just assumed that I could save her as a stranger would and she would be grateful. If I'd had time to think, I'd have hoped that when I left the poor guy's body, he would just wonder where the scratches and headache came from. But … she knows him? This could be a problem.

I shift on my feet. Again, lost for words.

She smiles, her blush deepening as her eyes fall to the ground. 'You probably don't recognise me. I'm Maggie. We go to the same school. I'm in Year 11.'

I gulp. They go to school together. I don't know how to answer. Do they have classes together? Should he remember her? Should I tell her that I'd seen her around? Or should I fake memory loss from the blow to the head?

She speaks again, though, saving me from making up some lie. 'It's OK that you don't recognise me. You're in Year 13 so why would you even notice me?

It's not like our paths would ever cross or anything. I mean, yeah, I once stood behind you in the food queue in the canteen and you made a joke to me about a turkey drumstick, but…' A frown lines her forehead as she squirms on the spot. 'It's not like we've spoken properly or anything other than that one terrible joke which was about a year ago.' She kicks her toes on the road and rolls her eyes. 'And now I'm rambling. Sorry.'

I grin widely. That is a classic example of Maggie's awkwardness. I love it. I know I should walk away. I know I should leave the boy's body – everything in me is screaming at me to let go of him – but I'm rooted to the spot, watching her. Greedily, I crave more of her time before I give up this connection.

'I like your rambling,' I admit. 'Can I, um, walk you home? To, you know, make sure you don't try to cause any more accidents?' I grin teasingly.

She laughs and nods. 'Sure. I'd like that.'

The walk to Maggie's house only takes a couple of minutes; we'd already broken the back of the journey before the almost-accident.

'So, where were you headed anyway, before you saved me from being smeared over the road?' she inquires, eyeing me curiously.

I shrug. 'Nowhere really. Just out for a walk.'

She looks doubtful but nods absent-mindedly. 'I thought maybe you'd just been coming back from Justine's house. She lives somewhere around here, doesn't she?'

Justine. Another person I should have knowledge of, but don't. I give a non-committal shrug and bob my head. Thankfully, she stops outside her two-storey terraced house so further reply is unnecessary. 'This one's me,' she says, motioning towards the house.

I smile up at the house. 'OK, well, I'm glad you're all right.'

She nods, absentmindedly tucking one of those damp, wild curls behind her ear as her eyes drop to the floor. 'Would you like to come in? I have a first-aid kit; I could clean your cuts for you? It's the least I can do after you saved my life.'

My breath catches. I should say no. I *know* I should, but I don't. I've never been inside Maggie's house before. I'd walked here with her lots of times, but I always departed when she got to her door, not wanting to cross the invisible line that would take me from Ghost-Stalker to Mayor-of-Stalkerville. So, instead of declining, walking away and letting poor Charlie have his damaged body back, I nod, say thank you, and follow behind her up the concrete path towards her house, eager to catch a glimpse at the side of Maggie that I'd never been privy to before.

CHAPTER FOUR
~ RYDER ~

Maggie's house is small, though not cosy-small; it's the complete opposite of what I would deem 'cosy'. In fact, the word 'clinical' would be a better fit. Every wall I can see as I step in through the front door and straight into the living room is painted an off-white, the carpets are beige, the ornamental knick-knacks that are sparingly dotted around are either grey, brown or cream. The house looks like a tin of magnolia threw up all over it. It's immaculately clean and feels like I've stepped into a show house rather than an actual home where people live.

Maggie's smile is shy as she turns to me. 'Um, do you mind taking off your shoes? There's a no shoes on the carpet rule.' Her blush is endearing.

'Sure. No problem.' As I look down at my feet, I'm grateful that Charlie's choice of footwear is a pair of loosely tied Converse. It's not that I can't tie shoes, because of course I can, it's just that it's been years since I tried and I wasn't sure how compliant Charlie's fingers would be; after all, walking had been a Herculean effort so doing something so intricate was probably out of the question. Snagging one heel with the toe of my other foot, I ease it off.

'Thanks. Lorna would probably pitch a fit otherwise.'

'Is that your mum?' I know it's not; her mother died years ago. In fact, up until her stroke, Doreen was Maggie's sole guardian, so now she's in the system. *I* know this … but chances are Charlie wouldn't.

A frown creases Maggie's forehead and her eyes seem to darken. 'No.' She kicks off her own shoes before stooping to pick them up and set them onto the rack beside the front door. 'Lorna is my foster mother.' She's nonchalant as she says this, busying herself taking off her coat and hanging it on the hook on the wall.

'Oh, sorry, I didn't realise.' Another lie. My mother would have warned me about getting a spot on my tongue if she were here, and I wasn't dead…

Maggie shrugs, reaching for the shoes I've shucked, placing them on the rack, too. 'Why would you?' She nods towards a door on the other side of the living room. 'Kitchen's that way, all the medicines and stuff are in there.'

It's clear she doesn't want to talk about her living arrangements, though I can't help but probe. There are so many things I want to ask, to know, finally. I take my own jacket off and hang it next to hers on the rack. 'Do you get on with them?' I ask, turning and heading towards the kitchen. Casting a quick glance back, I see the momentary tightening to her eyes before it's gone and she puts on what seems to be a fake smile.

'They're all right. I've only been here seven weeks, so it doesn't feel like home. They're nice enough people,' she answers, shrugging. There is a sadness to her tone that tugs at my heartstrings. 'I just stay out of their way and get on with things. Chances are I'll be moving on from here soon anyway.'

'Why's that?'

'Because of my age. Foster parents all prefer younger kids that they can bond with; cute babies or toddlers they can cuddle. No one wants to be stuck with a fifteen-year-old girl, do they? They'll move me on to somewhere else once they find someone more suitable to live with the Fishers. It's happened to me twice already. This is my third placement in three months. I've stayed at this one the longest so far, though.' She shrugs again, as if it is no big deal.

I open my mouth to say something, but close it

again as I'm not sure I have the right words. She's probably right, foster parents probably did prefer having younger kids placed with them, fewer issues for them to deal with rather than having a grieving, hormonal teen thrust into their lives.

'Are they not home now?' I ask, even though the answer is clear. Maggie had turned on the living-room light as we stepped in, so it is obvious we're the only ones here.

'No, Chris does shift work so he won't be home until around ten-thirty tonight. And Lorna's out Christmas shopping with one of her friends and then they're going to dinner after.'

'Christmas shopping? It's October!' I exclaim.

Maggie shrugs, nodding in an I-know-she's-crazy type of way. 'Lorna is a bit of a control freak; she likes to do everything as early as possible. It wouldn't surprise me if she was one of those people who start buying their Christmas presents in the January sales!' she replies, shaking her head. 'She said she's almost done with her shopping already.'

'That's mental.' My parents always had more of a rush-around-and-get-everything-the-week-before-Christmas mentality.

We reach the kitchen then, so I step in. Again, it's sparkly clean and minimalistic. The high-gloss cream units are smear free and there's not even a dirty teaspoon in the sink.

'You can sit down.' Maggie motions towards one of the leather-effect stools at the breakfast bar. I sit, and she heads over to the sink, washing her hands before rifling through the corner cupboard and pulling out a clear lunchbox that looks to be full to bursting with all kinds of medical supplies. Satisfied with the box, she gets a ceramic bowl from another cupboard and fills it with water. Medicine box in one hand and a small bowl of water in the other, she walks over to me with a small, embarrassed smile.

A thought occurs to me then as she pries open the box and lifts out cotton-wool balls. Maggie is going to touch me again. For the second time, I am about to feel her skin against mine. Almost instantly, Charlie's heart starts to beat slightly faster, his palms seem to grow slick with sweat, and I can't manage to stop his feet from twitching on the footrest of the stool I'm perched on. When a faint whiff of the cherry Pez she was eating blows across my face, it's like a jolt of longing hits me so hard I'm grateful I'm already sitting down. It's too much. Too overwhelming. Too many feelings and sensations I've forgotten all happening at once. I can barely process them all. But I hope they never stop.

Dipping a cotton-wool ball into the water, she turns to assess me. 'These don't look too bad on the outside, are you sure there's no concussion or anything? You hit your head, it looks like.' She reaches out towards my face and I hold my breath, waiting. Warm, soft, wet cotton presses against the first graze on my temple. It's nice, though it makes the cut burn again.

'I'm fine, honestly. No concussion,' I reply, focusing on the way her hand moves, the softness of her touch, how careful she's being, and how she presses her lips together tightly in concentration while she works deftly to clean my grazes. I memorise it all, breathing deeply, and again, filling my lungs with that vanilla shampoo and cherry Pez scent that makes my insides clench with a deep longing to get closer to it.

'I'm not exactly a nurse so I'm not sure what I should be doing. I guess just cleaning the dirt out of them and filling them with cream, that sound about right to you?' she asks, dipping a fresh cotton-wool ball into the water before heading to my elbow this time.

'Yeah, it's clear you're no Florence Nightingale, but you'll do,' I joke.

This makes her smile and those dimples make an appearance.

'Are you sure *you're* all right?' I question.

She nods, waving her hand dismissively. 'I'm all good. Probably have some bruises but it's nothing at all.' Her eyes flick up and meet mine. 'I don't know how I can thank you, Charlie. You saved my life.' She's looking at me in awe, her gaze so grateful that it's almost piercing.

'Don't mention it.' *Period. Don't ever mention it, ever, because hopefully Charlie will have no recollection that this ever happened!* I gulp and search desperately for a change of subject, the wrong thing drops out of my mouth. 'Guess this will make a pretty interesting story to tell your nan next time you go visit,' I muse, shrugging and inspecting the freshly cleaned graze on my forearm.

Maggie's hand, which is on the way to pick up the tube of cream, stills. Her forehead creases and her eyes flick up to meet mine. 'How do you know I was visiting my nan?'

Crap and double crap. I shouldn't know that. Charlie doesn't know anything about Maggie.

Thinking quickly, I smile. 'You told me, remember? On the way back to your house.'

Her frown deepens. 'Did I?'

'Yeah,' I confirm, nodding. 'Are you sure you didn't bang your head?' I tease, trying to keep my voice steady so she won't catch me out in my lie.

Her shoulders loosen then and she laughs, picking up the cream she was reaching for earlier. 'Guess I'm just forgetful. My nan always said I'd forget my head if it weren't screwed on.'

The pale pink cream she squeezes out onto her finger and then wipes into my wounds smells disgusting, but thankfully doesn't sting like I was expecting. Once she's done fixing me up, she stands and starts packing everything away.

'Do you want me to do the same for yours?' I offer, looking down at her grazed hands.

She shakes her head. 'Nah, I already washed them, I'll put some cream on them later but they're fine.'

I nod, knowing it is time for me to leave. I have no more excuses. I shouldn't have agreed to come into her house in the first place, so I can't linger any longer. I stand, my heart sinking at the realisation that my time with Maggie is up.

'I should get going. It was really nice talking with you, and thank you for taking care of me.'

Her eyes widen fractionally as she looks up at me. 'Oh. Um, no problem. It was nice talking with you, too.' Her cheeks turn a cute shade of pink as she smiles.

Turning on my heel, I force myself to walk back into the living room and to the front door where my shoes and jacket are. Luckily for me, there is only one pair of red Converse on the rack so I know they must be Charlie's. Picking them up, I slip my feet inside and stand again, snagging my jacket but not putting it on. As I glance up, I catch sight of myself in the mirror hanging on the wall. The stranger staring back at me makes my muscles bunch. I swallow a lump in my throat as I realise I can't remember exactly how I looked anymore. It's been too long; the details of my face are too faded in my memory. But seeing Charlie in his blond-haired, blue-eyed glory, I know he's practically my opposite. My hair was never tamed, always a shaggy dark-brown mess and that matched my eyes. Our builds, I notice, are very similar though – both lithe, athletic and toned. I would guess we were around the same height, maybe just an inch or two either way.

I reach up and touch my cheek, feeling the tickling brush of my fingers against my skin. It is so unnerving to look into a mirror and see someone else staring back, it sends a shiver down my spine so I drop my hand and force my gaze away.

Maggie is leaning against the wall watching me, gnawing on her bottom lip. Once I'm ready to go, I look down at her and smile sadly, memorising, one final time, what it is like to actually be this close to her in person.

'Bye then,' I mutter.

She nods, reaching out and catching the door handle, pulling it open. 'Bye, Charlie. I'll see you at school.'

I nod, wishing that I really would see her at school. 'Yeah. Night, Maggie.' Stepping out of her front door takes a lot of effort on my part.

Once I'm on my way down the garden path, I turn and offer Maggie a little wave. She waves back, smiles shyly, and then closes the door behind me. I carry on walking to the end of the garden but then stop, knowing it's time for this charade to end.

Squeezing my eyes shut and clenching my hands into fists, I concentrate on trying to leave Charlie's body. It's difficult. I have no idea how I'm actually supposed to let go once I've taken possession, but I just try to focus on recognising where my 'body' ends and where Charlie's begins. It's easy to differentiate between my body and his; while I have possession of him, I have to work to tense his muscles, to lift his feet, to move his arms. The way I would describe it later to Jade was that I felt like a puppeteer who has to move someone around – but without the strings. It was kind of like his muscles were wrapped around mine but were still utterly separate.

Suddenly, while I'm concentrating on letting go,

the squeezing, tightening, pinching sensation begins again. First in my fingers, then spreading up my arms to my chest and finally all over my body. I'm being compressed from the inside out and the sensation is very disorientating. The high-pitched whistling sound is back, and I clench my fists tighter, wincing as the shrillness of it batters my eardrums.

All at once, as if it had never been, it stops. My chest heaves from the effort as I stagger back a couple of steps. Exhaustion overcomes me, my knees buckle and I sink to the floor. I feel like I've just run the London Marathon. Every single muscle in my body feels weak, not painful, because I don't feel pain, just like there is no substance to them anymore. I feel like I've been turned to jelly and I can do nothing other than sit on the floor and take deep breaths.

When I look up, I see Charlie standing before me. I can see from his bemused expression that he's completely unaware of what's happened in the last hour, or that he's a hero who saved a girl from dying tonight. He's still on his feet, clearly not feeling this exhaustion I'm feeling. He's frowning, looking around the dimly lit street, clearly disorientated and confused. Wincing, he suddenly reaches up and touches the side of his head, his fingers dipping into the smelly cream that Maggie had applied rather generously.

His frown deepens as he rubs the cream between his thumb and forefinger.

'What the hell?' he mutters, shaking his head. 'Ouch, shit!' he grumbles, touching his head again. 'Son of a...' He trails off and stands there for a good thirty seconds, staring down at his grazed and sore-looking hands. Obviously, he's trying to work out why he's injured and standing in a street that he has no recollection of coming to.

A wave of guilt washes over me because he actually looks kind of freaked out and scared.

Suddenly, he shakes his head and stomps off up the street, presumably in the direction of his house. I'm left sitting there alone, trying to gain some semblance of sense of myself so I can stand.

Upstairs in Maggie's house, a light flicks on. I turn my head weakly, seeing Maggie there. She's watching Charlie walk away. A small smile resides on her lips as she rests her chin on her hand. She looks contented. Something settles in the base of my stomach, something ugly and unwelcome. It's a pang of jealousy. Deep down I know I've started something that is going to eat me up inside, but I hadn't had a choice. I couldn't let her die, and Charlie was the only one around. My only hope now was that this wasn't going to come back and bite me on the arse.

CHAPTER FIVE
~ RYDER ~

Once I have enough strength, which takes a good couple of minutes, I push myself to my feet and begin the half-hour walk back to the place that Jade and I spend our nights.

I'm unsteady. I liken it to when you're really hungry and thirsty and your body feels a little weak and lifeless – though that's just my best guess; I can't actually remember what it feels like to be hungry anymore, it's been far too long. As I walk the dark streets on my wobbly legs, I start to wish that the stuff I'd read as a kid was actually true – that ghosts could simply close their eyes, think about where they wanted to go, and just evaporate or teleport to their desired destination. Wouldn't that be grand? But the sad truth of it is that I have to walk to places the same as I did when I was alive. Now, though, I get to jump on a bus and ride for free whenever I want. Just my luck though, there are no buses along this route.

By the time I get to the Fox and Hound pub where Jade and I usually spend a good proportion of our evenings, it's pushing eight o'clock. The car park is dotted with a few of the regulars' cars, but being a Thursday, it's not that busy. As I hold my breath and pass through the heavy wooden door and into the pub, the noise grows as people shout at the roll-down projector screen that covers one wall. The Fox and Hound is normally a quiet, quaint place complete with old-fashioned, patterned carpets, dark wood panelling and beer tankards as decorations, but when a football match is screened the place comes alive and even the grey-haired, usually reserved old boys get involved while sipping their pints of ale.

Without paying much attention, I turn left and walk to the back corner, knowing without looking that Jade will be sat at 'our' table. It's the best seat in the house, the one with the unrestricted view of the television and furthest away from the bar so no patrons actually use it.

I'm right. She's sat at the table, her bright blue eyes glued to the screen, her full pink lips parted into an O as she watches the Champions League game play out. She lets out a heavy breath at a near-miss goal and shakes her head, making her super-tight, perfectly bound blonde bun at the back of her head shake. Her long legs are folded under her body as she sits on the faded and ripped cushion that covers the bench running under the window.

'Hey,' I mutter, stopping at her side and glancing at the screen just long enough to check the score.

'Where have you been? You're usually back by now. You missed the start of the match.' Jade shuffles up so I can sit next to her. She's barely taken her eyes from the TV to acknowledge me.

Instead of sitting on the bench, I perch on the stool and lean my elbows on the small round table, still feeling the after-effects of what I'd done tonight. I hadn't realised it was going to last this long and I silently wondered if I'd ever feel right again. 'I was with Maggie,' I reply.

'You were following her around like a love-sick puppy again, weren't you?' Her tone is teasing and light.

I nod unashamedly.

'What is it you see in her anyway? She's so, so...' Jade waves her hand, searching for the correct word. 'Ordinary,' she finally finishes. To Jade, a beautiful, once-had-everything-going-for-her, future Olympic gymnast, everyone is ordinary. She has seen Maggie only once. After growing sick of listening to me jabber on about a girl she had never met, she followed me to the nursing home one night wanting to see what all the fuss was about. Needless to say, she wasn't impressed.

'She's not ordinary,' I protest. Maggie is far from it.

'Yes, she is. She's a ginger-haired, freckle-covered, a little on the dumpy side, shy moose. Plus, when I saw her, she was wearing a T-shirt with Elvis on it, and not even hot, heartthrob, in-his-prime Elvis, but fat Elvis! There's nothing appealing about her in the slightest. And another thing, she barely speaks. I think I heard her say, like, four words when I saw her. She's not exactly the kind of girl you would have ever gone for in the real world. She's weird.'

Real world. I frown at that, feeling my temper rise. 'You just don't know her, that's all. She's not weird, she's just a little … quirky. But I like it. She's different and not like every other teenage girl. Yes, she's shy but that's just because she has low self-confidence. And anyway, what's wrong with ginger hair and freckles? I happen to love her hair.'

Jade rolls her eyes. 'Of course you do, you're smitten.' When I frown, she continues speaking as she turns her attention back to the TV again. 'All I'm saying is, if you were still alive you wouldn't give her the time of day. You'd never have hung around with a girl like that. You would have been in completely opposite circles. I bet you wouldn't have even known her name.'

'Yeah, well, I'm not alive, though, am I?' I snap. I don't mean to lose my temper with her, Jade is all I have left in the world, but sometimes her immaturity really shows through. Sometimes I forget that, mentally, she is only fourteen years old, perpetually stuck in her younger body even though she's been wandering for over ten years.

She shrugs, not bothered by my outburst. 'Yeah well, it's not like you're ever going to talk to her or anything is it, so give it up and stop torturing yourself!'

'Actually, about that…' I trail off, unsure how to word tonight's actions and explain to Jade without her calling me a pathetic love-sick puppy again.

Jade half turns her attention from the game. 'Huh?'

I take a deep breath before launching into my tale of what happened, how Maggie had her headphones on and wasn't paying attention and how she stepped in front of the van. When Jade's eyes widen, I hold up a hand. 'She's fine. I, um, intervened.' I smile proudly, thinking about the situation again.

Her eyebrows knit together in confusion. 'Intervened? Intervened, how?'

I shrug, grinning now. 'Possessed someone and pushed her out of the way.'

She doesn't react how I thought she would; she

doesn't grin and congratulate me for being a hero. Instead, she shoots to her feet, accidentally catching her hip on the table, causing it to fall over and crash to the floor. Her eyes are wide, fearful even. 'What? You did what? How? What the hell! Ryder, you can't do that!'

I frown, more than a little taken aback by her reaction and how she'd had such an emotional response to it that she'd even managed to knock an inanimate object over by accident.

'I think I already did,' I reply sarcastically, glancing around to see that a few shocked patrons are looking in our direction, not seeing or hearing us, but wondering how the little round table managed to randomly fall over.

Jade recoils, shaking her head. 'You possessed someone else's body? Like, went inside them? How? Explain!'

I shrug and look down at my hands. 'Honestly, I don't even really know.' That was the truth. I had just done it; I hadn't thought it through properly; I didn't know the *hows* of it.

Jade swallows and shakes her head again. 'But you saved her? She was going to be hit by a car? You shouldn't have interfered, Ryder. If it was her time to go then it was her time. You can't just go around saving people, that's not how it works!' Her voice is manic, almost a shout. I can hear the tremor in it.

I scoff, rolling my eyes at her over-dramatic outburst. 'And how do you know how it works? Were you given some sort of magic wanderer rules and a list of dos and don'ts? Just sit down and calm down. You keep knocking things over and you'll give Jim a sleepless night thinking there's a poltergeist or something.' I nod towards Jim, the landlord, who is now standing less than two feet from me, picking up the table and setting it back in place, wobbling it slightly to see if the legs are loose.

Jade doesn't sit; instead, she turns gracefully on her heel and marches out of the pub. I frown, not really knowing what I've done to upset her so much.

Jumping up, I notice my body is finally regaining some of its strength. I run after her, holding my breath as I pass through the heavy pub door. Jade is nowhere to be seen, but I know where she'll be. Stuffing my hands into my jacket pockets, I turn to my right and start to walk.

After a couple of minutes, I see her. She's sitting on our bench by the side of the river. Around her on the damp grass, ducks and swans are all curled up, fast asleep. Moonlight filters down through the sparse trees, twinkling on the river. A green tugboat lazily knocks against the concreted side of the river in time with the slow but steady tide. This is where Jade and I sit when we're bored of walking around the city or watching TV in the pub – days and nights can be hard to fill when you have all the time in the world and no real way to spend it. This place is peaceful and quiet, and one of my favourite places on Earth.

Clearing my throat to announce my arrival, I sit beside Jade, playfully bumping her shoulder with mine. 'What's got into you? You practically bit my head off,' I ask, still confused as to what had caused her reaction.

She turns to me, her tear-filled eyes glistening in the soft light of the moon. 'Sorry, I didn't mean to snap. I just…' She looks down at her hands. 'I just know. Trust me. It was her time and you shouldn't have interfered.' Her tone is deeply sad but I don't know why.

Confused by her words but knowing she needs support, I put my hand over hers, stopping her from picking at her nails like she always does when she's agitated or upset. 'It was fine, I saved her. It's nothing to worry about. No one saw me do it and the guy that I jumped into doesn't even know what happened.' I squirm inwardly – he didn't know *yet*, but I was pretty sure Maggie would mention it when she saw him next.

Jade lets out a strangled noise that sounds like a sob. 'I never told you what happened with my mum, did I?'

I nod, squeezing her hand. 'Yeah, you did. She had a massive heart attack.'

She shakes her head. 'No, I meant what happened before that.'

'No?' I mutter, now watching her intently, confused at the sudden and weird change in direction that this conversation has taken.

Jade takes a deep, shaky breath, pulling her hand from mine and smoothing back her bun – not that it looked anything other than perfect before. Her eyes glisten with tears.

'When I died, I couldn't bear to leave my mum. I stayed there with her for a year or so. She was really depressed after I died. It had only ever been the two of us, so she took it really hard. She stopped caring about herself and barely got out of bed most days. She lost her job and couldn't pay the rent on the flat. When the bailiffs started knocking on her door and repossessing half her stuff, she obviously decided enough was enough.

One night I sat and watched her write a suicide note. She wrote that she couldn't live anymore and that she had nothing left to fight for. She pinned it to her raggedy, dirty cardigan and then she found a long piece of blue rope from the understairs cupboard. She took it into the garage and then tied one end to the rafters there, climbed onto the workbench, and looped the other end around her neck.' Her voice cracks with emotion.

My stomach clenches, imagining the scene as it played out, and Jade having to watch it all. My heart aches for her.

Jade sniffs and reaches up to swipe at a tear as it slides down her cheek. 'I was screaming at her not to, but she couldn't hear me.' She finally turns towards me, her arms wrapped around her midriff, hugging herself tightly. Tears make tracks down her face as her eyes meet mine. 'I saved her,' she whispers.

'What? How?'

'When she stepped off the side and was hanging from the rope, suffocating, I picked up a pair of shears and I cut the rope. I don't even know how I did it, it must have been all the emotion made my essence stronger or something. I don't know how.' She looks down at her hands and I notice they're shaking. 'Anyway, my mum fell to the floor, she was winded and gasping, but she was alive.' Jade smiles wistfully. 'She knew it was me too. She started crying and wailing my name and thanking Jesus for sending me to watch over her.'

I smile weakly. 'I bet that brought her a lot of comfort, knowing her daughter was there.'

Jade doesn't smile though as she continues her morbid story. 'For a while, things were better. My mum would talk to me as if she knew I was there with her. She started picking herself up and taking care of herself, she started living again. I guess she saw it as a second chance.'

'That's good.'

Jade shrugs. 'Thing is, she started to live her life again. She went to the doctors and began therapy, talking about everything. Then, just like that, she was gone.'

'Gone?' I repeat, gulping at the finality of the word.

Her head bobs sadly. 'She was walking home from a job interview. She'd been offered a part-time job in a florist, she was smiling, and she stopped to buy herself a celebratory bottle of the wine that she liked.' She takes a deep breath. 'A blood clot detached from her leg, a varicose vein she'd never got around to getting looked at. It went straight to her heart. She was dead before she hit the floor, lying in a pool of the cheap wine she'd bought to toast moving on in life. So you see, you shouldn't interfere, you shouldn't give people false hope. You can't prevent the inevitable.'

I shake my head. 'You can't really believe that. The idea of fate is crap,' I say before I can stop myself. As I make the quip, I can see real pain in her eyes. I immediately feel guilty for dismissing her sad story so quickly. I'm being insensitive. 'Look, Jade, I'm sorry about your mum, I really am, that must have been awful to watch all of that, and I can understand why you would feel like that, but it's just a coincidence,' I assure her firmly, trying to banish the theory from her head. 'Your mum was just sick and didn't know it. It's just a coincidence, that's all,' I repeat, reaching out to add a supportive squeeze on her shoulder.

Jade looks sceptical. 'I don't know, Ryder; I just don't think you can mess with stuff like that. After all, we're not even *supposed* to be here, are we?'

I smile kindly. 'Jade, trust me, it's nothing like that. You've been dead how long?'

'Eleven years.'

I nod. 'And in that time have you ever seen the Grim Reaper following anyone around, waiting for their time to be up?'

'No.'

'No. Exactly. Accidents happen, people die, medical conditions happen. That's it. There's no rhyme or reason to existence.' I truly believe that. Human life is fragile, here one minute and gone the next, there is no plan. I don't believe in fate.

Jade sighs and nods, as if accepting my words even though I can see she's still picking furiously at her nails. 'I guess you're right. I'm just being silly.'

I stand and smile down at her. 'Yep, you are. And you've also missed the end of the match...' I nod back over my shoulder towards the pub off in the distance.

Jade groans and unfolds her long legs, pushing herself to her feet. 'Come on, let's go see who won.' She kicks at the dirt and damp leaves with her immaculately white trainers. 'Hopefully nothing will happen to Molly.'

'Maggie,' I correct.

She grins then and finally meets my eye. 'I know, I just get a great deal of pleasure winding you up.'

Laughing, I roll my eyes and we walk back to the pub in silence. In the back of my mind, Jade's words are rolling around, nagging at me. *Had I done wrong by saving her? Was it just Maggie's time?* I dismiss the thought with a shake of my head. She was wrong; it was just a coincidence with Jade's mother. What happened with Maggie was a near-miss accident, nothing more, nothing less.

CHAPTER SIX
~ MAGGIE ~

'Maggie! Are you awake or not?'

I groan and turn my face into the pillows, wincing as moving hurts my ribs. Memories of last night's events rush at me all at once. The usual stuff: Nan being mean to me … again, me crying … again. And then the unusual stuff: almost being hit by the van, Charlie saving me, him walking me home, talking to me, actually noticing my existence for once, and then me falling asleep wondering if maybe, just maybe, today at school would be different from every other mundane day.

'Maggie! Hurry up or you'll be late!' My foster mother's voice sounds louder now, maybe just at the bottom of the stairs.

I turn my head and shout back, my throat croaky and dry, 'I'm almost ready; I'll be down in five.'

Leaning up on one elbow, I rub at my stinging, still tired eyes. I spent way too many hours last night obsessing over my exchange with Charlie. Today is going to be a long day! As I climb out of bed, I test my muscles, rolling my shoulders and neck, checking for stiffness caused from the fall last night. Thankfully there isn't much.

I wash my face and brush my teeth before changing quickly out of my pyjamas and into my ugly navy-blue and maroon school uniform, inspecting myself for injuries as I do so. I have bruises on my shoulder and upper arm and there are scratches on my knees and hands, but they're not too bad. My side definitely looks the worst and is shades of blue and black where Charlie's shoulder connected with my ribs. I'm lucky nothing is broken.

Once dressed, I look in the mirror just long enough to confirm there isn't a massive zit I need to sort out and not a second longer. Unlike most girls that attend my school, I don't bother trying to flout the school no make-up rule, I never have done. In my opinion, there'll be plenty of time to act like a grown-up. I'm happy being able to get away with being fresh-faced for as long as possible.

When I'm ready, I stop at my desk and check on my ruined phone. I'd put it on charge last night and discovered, thankfully, that it still worked despite the smashed screen. It was only the headphones that were beyond repair. Thank goodness too, because I couldn't survive without my music. I'd just have to use it on loudspeaker for now, and be careful not to slice a finger off every time I used it. But hey, a girl's gotta have her tunes! I decide to leave it charging for the day, to really give it time to recover.

Before leaving my room, I tug open the drawer of my desk and run my finger along the line of my Pez dispensers, pursing my lips, contemplating each one, my gaze lingering on my favourite one, my first one. It used to be my mum's. I was five. We'd been having a clear-out of old boxes in the loft, looking for stuff we could sell at a car boot sale, when I'd found it. Mickey Mouse, immortalised in plastic. I'd been fascinated by it, and once Mum explained about sweets going inside, I'd fallen in love and we'd set off to the shops on a mission to find some refills, the car boot stuff long forgotten. Ever since then, I've collected them. The sickly, chalky sweets reminded me of nicer times, plus, you know, sugar. Who could say no?

I finally decide on my Minions dispenser and shove it, and a pack of sweets, to load it with, into my school bag and head downstairs. My foster mother, Lorna, is on me before I even take the last step.

'Why do you cut it so close all the time? Every

morning is like this. For once I'd like to do something other than rush you out of the door with a piece of cold toast in your hand.' Her tone is disapproving as she holds out a plate of Nutella-smothered toast.

'Thanks.' I smile weakly and take the two halves of the toast, folding one on top of the other to make a sandwich before taking a bite of the chocolatey goodness.

She rolls her eyes and flicks her long, perfectly straightened, brown hair over one shoulder as she holds out a piece of kitchen roll to me so I can catch my crumbs. Lorna is a meticulous clean freak. I take the proffered towelette and turn for the door, wanting to leave before she draws me into a conversation and makes me late.

'You have money for lunch on your account, right?' she calls to my hastily retreating back. Her concern is obvious and my stomach clenches. Lorna is an extremely nice lady, and seems to genuinely care about my welfare instead of just the money she's paid to foster me – unlike the last placement I was at. The last place was more of a dosshouse, crammed to the rafters full of kids that the adults barely even spoke to, who they just took in so they could collect their cheque each month. Even surrounded by other kids night and day, with no space even to breathe on your own for five minutes, I'd never felt lonelier than when I was there. I never said anything to anyone, but I was glad when they moved me the second time.

I try not to let Lorna's concern affect me, I don't want to start liking this woman, form a bond with her, and then leave when some other unfortunate waif comes along and needs to take my room. I made that mistake with my first placement. After being told by a social worker I could no longer live with Nan following her stroke, I was placed with a lovely homely lady who baked cookies of a weekend and gave great hugs. I stupidly got too close to her, and then it hurt to be ripped from the place I'd started to call home, only to be dumped into another house full of strangers. I won't do it again. I've learned my lesson.

I nod, shouldering my heavy bag. 'Yep.' Lorna checks this every day. Each week she gives me money on Monday to load my school account with enough credits for five dinners and snacks, too, yet she still worries I've run out. Every. Single. Day. 'I'll see you later.' I step out onto the street and begin to close the door behind me but she catches it and pulls it open again.

'Don't forget your appointment with Nicola after school.' Her plum lipstick-coated lips pull into a warm smile. 'Come straight home, she'll already be here by the time you get back.'

I nod. Of course she would already be here; Nicola, my social worker, would want to speak to Lorna alone to see if there are any issues with me that she needed to address during our appointment.

'I remember.' She looks like she wants to say something else, so I quickly wave and walk off before she has the chance, calling a goodbye over my shoulder.

Fresh, chilly air stings my cheeks as I head down my quiet street. I pull my mother's coat around me tightly, hunching my shoulders to stop the morning drizzle from finding its way down my neck. My mind turns to Charlie again. I wonder if he'll talk to me or mention last night. No doubt he'd have told everyone what happened, acting the hero, lapping up the worship from his friends.

By the time I get to school, I'm sopping wet and wishing I'd thought to find an umbrella before leaving the house. As I use my damp sleeve to wipe the drizzle from my face, I can't keep my mind from travelling to Charlie yet again.

Will I see him today? Will he even look in my direction?

My eyes scan the packed hallway, searching amongst the students who are dumping their bags and collecting their belongings from their lockers before making their way to their respective classrooms … and just like that, my question is answered.

Charlie is leaning against his locker, all chiselled cheekbones, Luke Hemmings-blue eyes, and stylishly overgrown blond hair. He's ridiculously good-looking, tall, well proportioned, just an all-round exquisite specimen. And his smile: it could melt ice it's so hot. He's talking to a group of his friends, laughing at something I don't hear. Suddenly his eyes flick in my direction and I see recognition wash over his face as his body straightens and a smile tugs at one corner of his mouth.

I smile back awkwardly and offer a small wave in greeting. When his hand rises in response, my heart leaps and my throat tightens. He acknowledged me! For me, just a smile and a wave means everything. I usually go all day without other students doing that, and Charlie, one of the most popular and lusted-after boys in school, just bloody waved at me. I'm not really sure how to deal with it. Heat blooms in my cheeks and I hold my breath, that small wave meaning everything.

All is right in my world for exactly two and a half seconds before someone breezes past me from outside, unceremoniously bumping my shoulder, bringing me out of my own little world and flicking rain water from their bubblegum-pink umbrella all over me in the process.

Justine saunters past, her eyes firmly latched on the object of her affection for the last month – or, more correctly, the object of her *obsession*. Charlie offers her a million-pound smile that makes her hips sway a little more prominently as she sashays her way over to him.

I stand there, unable to look away as his head dips and their lips touch for a few seconds before he pulls back and offers her a lazy smile that makes her sag against him. As his arm drapes over her shoulder and he continues talking to his friend, I swallow and wonder if I should just leave them to it and go about my day as usual. I'd thanked him last night, I didn't really need to go over to the popular group of sixth formers and start a conversation, did I? As I was just about to decide to skip the gratitude fest, Charlie raises a hand and scratches behind his ear – and that's when I see the grazes and little cuts on the side of his hand disappearing down the sleeve of his jacket. My feet carry me across the hall and over to them before I've even thought through what I intend to say.

Charlie's friend George is the first to see me as I

stop next to their group. A look of curiosity pulls George's eyebrows together as he cocks his head to the side. 'Help you with something?' he asks, his tone both mildly amused and annoyed in equal measure.

All eyes turn on me and I squirm on the spot wishing I'd waited until Charlie was on his own before approaching him. Charlie looks at me questioningly and I feel my palms grow slick with sweat. His eyes hold no recognition as he looks at me; his face is blank, expressionless, as if he genuinely has never seen me before in his life and has no clue why I've rocked up next to him and interrupted his conversation. The silent question in his eyes makes my mouth dry. The whole of his group are regarding me as if I've lost my mind.

Before I get a chance to say anything, Justine barks out a vicious laugh. 'Did the Salvation Army not have a coat in your size?' she teases, and I feel her gaze rake over me.

My cheeks flame with embarrassment as I pull my mum's old coat tighter around me, trying to ignore her comment. I've had worse comments about my mum's coat before, kids often remarked about it and its complete lack of style, but it was one of the only things I had left of her. I like to wear it because it feels like I am wearing a part of her every day.

I keep my eyes locked on Charlie's, pretending that the small twitch at the corner of his mouth as he fights to keep his amused smile in check doesn't make my heart take a nosedive.

It's when Justine stands up straighter and sets her hands on her hips that I realise I've made a monumental mistake. I shouldn't have approached him in front of his friends, I should have waited and done this in private. Charlie is probably thinking the same thing, because he's just staring at me, his face impassive, as if I'm some kind of nuisance.

Why did I do this? Why didn't I think it through? Why, why, why? Ugh! What an idiot!

But I press on, despite the fact that my face feels like it's on fire and I can feel sweat prickling on my upper lip. 'Um … hi…' I squeak.

'Hi?' Charlie answers automatically, though it sounds more like a question. Our gazes lock, my stomach clenches and I wait for him to continue, to maybe ask me how I am today or tell his friends that I was the girl he saved last night. He doesn't do any of those things, though. His eyes remain nonchalant, cool and aloof as he raises one eyebrow in expectation. 'So, what do you want?' he asks, his tone almost bored.

And with those five words it feels like he just

rugby tackled me in the chest all over again. I flinch and then shake my head quickly. Understanding washes over me. Of course he wouldn't want to talk to me today. Had I seriously expected that last night would have changed anything? He saved my life; he didn't owe me anything else. Why would he want to talk to a nobody like me in front of his friends? My earlier thoughts were right; I should have done this in private instead of drawing attention to it when he clearly didn't want it.

I shake my head again and adjust the strap of my bag. 'Nothing, sorry.' I force a smile as I turn on my heel and scurry away up the hallway as fast as the crowd allows. I grind my teeth and scowl at the floor when I hear Justine say incredulously behind me, 'Was she hitting on you, for reals? Like, was that what just happened?'

The group laugh at my retreating back and I duck my head, staring at my feet as I rush towards my locker, chastising myself for being so thoughtless.

CHAPTER SEVEN
~ MAGGIE ~

During the rest of the day I keep my head down and get on with working hard, the same as usual. My classes are relatively easy, they've never been a stretch. I guess if I must be pigeonholed, I would sit firmly in the 'nerd' category – but not one of those preppy nerds that society seems to deem cool lately. No, I'm most definitely not one of those cool people. I'm distinctly average in every way: the girl that always hands her homework in on time; the one that can be relied upon to answer the question in class if called upon; the girl with the carrot-top hair and no parents; that one that reads a little too much; and likes old music instead of the mainstream, popular stuff. I'm unremarkable, unmemorable and forgettable in every way. But that's OK, I knew how I fitted in the school hierarchy, I knew my place and, other than that one uber-awkward moment this morning with Charlie and his friends, I'd never tried to step out of the pigeonhole.

School work has always come easy to me, it's the socialising aspect of school that I find particularly challenging. It isn't that I don't want friends, I just seem to lack that gene that allows me to chat freely with strangers or build relationships. Whenever I try to talk to new people, my face goes a shade of beet and I seem to fumble over my words or ramble. I've embarrassed myself enough over the years to know that socialising isn't part of my skill set, so I've all but given up trying.

The day seems to pass incredibly slowly, classes blurring into each other while I scribble notes that might help me in a few months with the remainder of my GCSE exams. At lunchtime, I buy a sandwich from the canteen and huddle alone under the bike shed to eat it, hunkering down away from the drizzly rain with my book. By the time it gets to last period – a free study period – I excuse myself to my most favourite place of all. The library.

As I step in, I let out a big sigh as my muscles loosen and the tension seems to leave my shoulders. The library is where I come to when I need to clear my head and ground my feet. When everything seems too overwhelming, I know that I can come here and lose myself and my problems, even if only for a little while. Music, books and the library have been my one constant in an otherwise turbulent few years. When my mother died, books helped me through, took me away from my grief for a couple of hours while reading. When Nan was in hospital and I was placed into foster care, music and books were the things that kept me from breaking down; they helped me cope when I was moved from one place to another. Books never abandoned me or gave up on me – and they smelled pretty damn good, too.

The school librarian, Mrs Rice, looks up as I walk in and offers me a warm smile. 'Hi, Maggie. Got a free period?'

I nod, reaching into my bag and pulling out the *Dorothy Must Die* book I'd finished at lunchtime. 'Yep. I came to return this.' I hold it up and smile. 'And order in the sequel, please.'

She smiles widely. 'Oh, I just knew you'd like that one. It's very creative, isn't it?'

'Yeah, it was great,' I agree, walking to the returns shelf and setting it down. 'Got anything new in?' I ask, eyeing the box of books that sit on the floor behind her desk.

Mrs Rice steps to my side, a glint in her eye as she lifts the box onto her desk and opens the lid so I can see the spines. She reaches in and plucks out two books, a knowing smile on her face. 'I just knew you'd want the *Dorothy Must Die* sequel, so…' She winks as she pushes the sequel across the desk to me.

I squeal excitedly, throwing her a grateful smile. Usually I have to order in books that I want, which takes a few days. I'd prepared for the fact that I wouldn't find out what happened to Amy Gumm until the following week. Now my Saturday reading was sorted thanks to Mrs Rice's thoughtfulness. 'Thanks!'

She nods proudly. 'And I've heard rave reviews about this one.' She holds up a beautiful hardback copy of *Caraval*. 'It's right up your street: magic, romance, a feisty heroine and rich scenery. Maybe you can let me know what you think of it. It's supposed to be beautiful.'

I take the book gratefully, already bursting to read it. 'Oh, I'll start it this weekend and let you know.' I run my fingers over the beautiful cover. 'But first I need to find out what the Wizard is up to and if Amy kills Dorothy!'

She laughs and rolls her eyes, busying herself picking up a stack of returned books as I head over to the comfy chairs at the back of the library, being careful of my bruised and aching side as I lower myself into the cushion.

I lose myself in the book, too wrapped up in the

heroine's problems to even think about any of mine, until the last bell rings, signalling the end of the school day. Instead of jumping up and rushing out like every other student in the school I finish the chapter I'm reading, getting to a convenient stopping point, before setting a bookmark in to mark my place.

I frown as I push the book into my bag when I remember that I have an appointment with my social worker when I get home. Since moving to this placement, I meet with her every week so she can check how I'm getting on. I hate these appointments, they're so fake. She always tries so hard to be my friend, all the while scribbling secret notes about me in her little folder. Don't get me wrong, Nicola is nice enough, but I just hate all the forced friendliness and fake caring, and the probing questions into my life. I wish they'd just let me get on with it my own way and not keep offering me counselling or trying to get me to open up more. She always spouts the same old rubbish, the same old lies about how I can settle in this placement and be happy with Lorna and Chris. But I won't allow myself to fall for that crap again; she'd said the same the last two times I was placed with foster parents ... only to move me on again within a few weeks. No point in getting settled or attached; I wouldn't allow myself to be let down again like that. Who needs that kind of disappointment in their lives? Certainly not me. I have enough to deal with.

I trudge slowly towards the exit, throwing Mrs Rice a little wave as I let the door swing closed behind me. The normally busy corridor is deserted, and I glance down at my watch seeing that school ended over twenty minutes ago. Instinctively, I pull my bag open and start rifling through, looking for my phone and headphones. But just as I remember that I don't have them because they both broke last night, I walk smack into something hard and unforgiving. Pain courses through my already bruised side, and I look up quickly to see I've come to the end of the hallway and have just walked into the closed front door. I stumble backwards, my bag falling from my grip and hitting the floor, sending my books and pencil case scattering everywhere. I reach up and wince as I rub at the top of my head where it struck the wood.

I grind my teeth thinking about how stuff like this is always happening to me. I'm so clumsy that if there's something that *can* go wrong for me, it *will*. Sod's law: I'm a prime example of it.

'Hey, you OK?' a guy asks behind me, the amusement in his tone is barely disguised.

My face fills with heat and I don't look up at the

person as I mumble I'm fine and then stoop to start gathering up my possessions.

'You're supposed to open the door before you walk through it,' he teases, bending and picking up my English book.

'Oh, really? All this time I thought you just face-planted into them,' I mutter sarcastically under my breath.

He chuckles and pushes the book into my open bag before retrieving my pencil case from the corner where it skidded when I dropped it.

Once I have everything else gathered, I stand and finally look up into the face of the guy. My breathing catches when I see that it's Charlie.

Oh, crapola, it's him! How frigging embarrassing.

Charlie holds out my pencil case, a cocky, amused half-smile on his face, and I immediately get a flashback of him doing the exact same thing last night before he offered to walk me home. My cheeks flame with heat. 'Thanks,' I mumble, ducking my head and mentally chastising myself for being sarcastic to him a few seconds before.

'Welcome,' he replies, half turning and pulling open the door in one smooth movement, before gesturing for me to go through. 'See, it opens,' he says smartly.

Despite his teasing, I laugh and roll my eyes, stepping over the threshold. 'You learn something every day, huh?' My eyes dart around, seeing that the outside of the school is practically deserted too, just a few stragglers waiting on the kerb to be picked up.

Charlie steps to my side and silently we walk towards the gates of the school. I don't think he'd specifically meant to walk with me, it was more like we were just two people walking in the same direction. But I secretly revelled in it. He was so handsome, and while I'd always appreciated his good looks from afar (as had practically every girl in the school) I'd never really had the chance to be up close and personal with him. Other than last night and the one time I was behind him in the lunch queue, this was the closest I'd been to him.

'So, how's your head?' I ask nervously.

His forehead creases with a frown as he looks over at me, not breaking stride. 'Shouldn't I be asking you that? You're the one that just headbutted a door.'

I smile awkwardly, fresh heat colouring my cheeks. 'No, I meant from where you banged it last night.'

He stops suddenly, so suddenly that I take another two steps before I even realise he's no longer next to me. When I turn back to look at him, he's frowning in confusion, his hand touching the spot on the side of his head that struck the road last night. 'How'd you know I banged my head?'

His question is so unexpected that I recoil, seeing the blatant confusion in his eyes. I study him, checking to see if this is some sort of test or joke that I'm not aware of, but he looks genuinely confused as he stares at me, his fingers still touching the spot on his head.

I swallow nervously. 'Seriously?' I grip the strap of my bag and hold it tightly as my eyes take in his every move.

'Seriously.' His head tilts to one side, his lips parted as he nods, waiting.

'You … you banged it last night. You know, when you saved me from being roadkill,' I say, watching for signs of recognition, but I see nothing. One of his eyebrows rises in a silent question, so I continue. 'You pushed me out of the way of that van … last night … remember?' His lips part in what look like shock and I start to get a little uneasy. I swallow the lump that's rapidly forming in my throat. 'Is this a joke? Because if it is, I don't get it.' I fold my arms across my chest, assuming he's playing some sort of trick on me. But doubt still lingers in my mind. He genuinely looks like I've just gave him a piece of a puzzle that he's been trying to solve.

'I did what?' He steps closer to me, dipping his head so he can look directly into my eyes.

Fear grips my insides and tightens, and my heart begins to speed up. He doesn't remember? 'Charlie, seriously?' This has to be a joke.

He reaches out and takes hold of the tops of my arms, his grip a little too tight to be comfortable. 'Yes, seriously! What do you know about me banging my head? I … something weird happened last night and I … I don't know.' He shakes his head, the traces of humour in his voice from earlier are long gone, and I sense the urgency in his question as his hands tighten on my arms.

I gulp, looking into his eyes as I answer. 'Last night I was on my way home and stepped into the road without looking. There was a van coming straight for me. You saw and you tackled me out of the way. You saved me. I definitely would have been dead if you weren't there. You hit your head on the road when we hit the ground,' I say all in one breath, watching confusion cloud his eyes as he took in my words. 'You really don't remember?'

He shakes his head slowly, letting go of me as he steps back and runs a hand through his hair. 'No. All I remember from last night was being at Justine's and then … there's maybe something there about a van but I don't know what … and then everything is kind of fuzzy, like when you're trying to tune in a TV and the signal isn't quite there, there's bits of things I don't understand, flashes of things but they're so quick I can't make them out. And then I just remember being on a darkly lit street and my head hurting and cuts on my arms.'

A wave of guilt hits me like a punch in the gut. This is all my fault. He has some sort of concussion or something from the blow to the head, and it's all my fault. 'You really don't remember any of it? Oh God, maybe you have concussion or brain damage or something,' I blurt, panic setting in.

He snorts at that. 'Brain damage? Cheers.'

I step forward, setting my hand on his arm. 'I'm serious, Charlie. You should maybe go to hospital or something and get checked out.'

He's quiet for maybe a full minute, his eyebrows pinched together as he frowns down at his feet, and eventually he shakes his head. 'Nah, I'm fine. I don't need a hospital. If it was concussion then I'd be feeling sick and tired. I've had it before from last year when I hit my head, I know what that feels like and this isn't concussion. I feel fine. If you hadn't mentioned about my head, I probably would have forgotten all about it in a couple of days.'

'You really don't remember any of it?' We'd spent a bit of time together after, we'd talked a lot, he'd seemed lucid and with-it then, he hadn't seemed like a guy with concussion.

He shrugs and shakes his head. 'Not a damn thing. It's so weird.'

'It is weird,' I agree. 'Has anything like that ever happened to you before?'

'A blackout, you mean?' he asks. I nod in confirmation and he shakes his head. 'No, not that I remember.' He snorts a laugh. 'Hey, at least I got hurt playing superhero though, rather than just tripping on a kerb and banging my head like I'd figured I'd done! A superhero blackout is much better than what I'd been assuming.'

I grin and drop my gaze to my feet, digging the toe of my shoe into the damp grass. 'You really should go see someone about it, though,' I encourage again, worried in case there was some permanent damage done on my behalf.

His nose scrunches up in disagreement. 'I'm fine, don't worry. If it happens again I'll go see someone.' He glances down at his watch and then sucks in a breath noisily through his teeth. 'I should go, I'm supposed to meet Justine down Riverside in, like, ten minutes. My class ran over a little so now I'm in a rush. I really need to go. She'll bitch for hours about it if I'm late.' He's already stepped around me and started to walk quickly down the road.

'Charlie?' I call to his retreating back. He stops, turning to look at me. 'Thanks again for what you did last night, if you don't remember me thanking you last night then I guess I should say it again now the superhero blackout has passed.'

He grins and raises his chin proudly. 'No problem. Have a good weekend … er…' I can practically see the cogs of his brain turning, searching for my name.

'Maggie,' I call, smiling awkwardly.

'Maggie, right. Well, see ya.' He waves then turns and jogs away from me and I just stand there on the pavement watching him until he's out of sight, my mind whirling at a mile a minute.

CHAPTER EIGHT

~ RYDER ~

I watch Maggie and Charlie's exchange at the end of school through gritted teeth and with jealousy burning in my veins. The way she looks at him with that light in her eye and the small, shy smile playing at the corner of her mouth makes my chest ache. She clearly likes him. Her blush and the way she doesn't really seem to know what to do with her hands while they talk show that. When he plays off the event last night as some kind of 'superhero blackout' I scoff loudly and shake my head in annoyance.

'Superhero, my arse! You were going to watch her die. You did nothing,' I blurt, knowing neither of them can hear me.

But she grins and looks at her feet. I groan in frustration, wishing their conversation was over, that he'd walk away and never talk to her again. I want him as far away from her as possible.

I hate that I've facilitated this, that I've fuelled

this attraction she so clearly has for him. By using this boy that she knows to save her life, I've now made him some kind of hero to her, someone to worship. I hate that. Because he definitely doesn't deserve it. Why couldn't he have been a random passer-by instead of someone she knew? Karma sucks.

I'd come to their school today to see what was said about events last night, to see if Charlie was suspicious about the time he lost when I took over his body or if he remembered anything and, most important of all, if Maggie was going to talk to him about last night. But other than their brief encounter at the beginning of the day, they'd not spoken again until just now.

I'd followed Charlie around all morning, just in case. I'd wasted all morning listening to his conversations with friends and with that airhead Justine who had been hanging on him at every available opportunity. I'd observed him while he paid zero attention in class and played games on his phone under his desk instead. I'd witnessed the so-called locker-room banter that he had with his friends about girls and his bragging about far he'd managed to get with his current squeeze, Justine, and when he expected to score with her.

My observations of the guy led to one conclusion:

he is a first-class prick. I don't want him anywhere near Maggie.

Thankfully, their conversation now seems to be winding up. When he steps around her and starts to walk off, I feel my body sag with relief that their interaction is over. He's too self-centred and arrogant to interact with her again, so I'm off the hook.

But just as he starts to walk off, she calls after him, thanking him again. His chest puffs out proudly and I struggle to rein in my anger as he answers, 'No problem. Have a good weekend … er…'

'You don't even know her name? What a twat,' I rant angrily.

I look at Maggie, hoping to see annoyance that he doesn't know her name, but she's smiling and not even seeming a little bit bothered as she casually tells him.

'Maggie, right. Well, see ya,' he replies and starts to jog down the road.

My frown deepens. The soft, almost yearning way she is looking after him is like a punch in the gut. All I had wanted since I met her was for her to look at me like that – screw that, just to look at me *at all* would have made my year – and yet this guy isn't even paying attention to the amazing girl he has in front of him.

Still annoyed, I look after Charlie again, seeing the distance increase between us. I'm torn. Part of me desperately wants to stay with Maggie and walk home with her, to let her know she's not alone somehow. The other part of me knows I should follow Charlie and make sure he's not calling anyone or telling anyone about what happened last night. It's a toss-up, but responsibility finally wins and I take one last look at Maggie before sprinting after Charlie.

'So, how did it go?' Jade asks as I flop onto the bench next to her, looking out across the river as the heavy breeze blows the tall grass in this direction and then that. 'Any problems?'

'No problems at all. It was fine.' I run a hand over my face, trying to wake myself up a bit. The last few hours had been boring as hell. I needn't have bothered keeping up with the surveillance, to be honest. There wasn't much talking during Charlie and Justine's 'date', it was basically the two of them sucking face in the back row of the cinema while he tried fruitlessly to get his hand under her skirt or inside her bra. After that they went to McDonald's and he hadn't even offered to pay for her. I hadn't realised how much had changed since I was alive. After watching Charlie all night, witnessing him not open doors for his girlfriend or offer her his jacket when she shivered, I was pretty sure chivalry was dead in dating now.

'The guy didn't even seem to know about what had happened. He and Maggie talked at the end of school but before that he didn't even know what he'd done,' I continue.

Jade chews on her nails, tucking her long legs up under her as she turns to face me. 'Are you sure? Did you follow him all day?'

I blow out a breath and nod. 'Most of the day, yeah.'

'Most of the day? What does that mean?'

I shrug casually. 'I followed him all morning, but then it was apparent nothing was being said, so…'

She groans and slaps her palm against her thigh, her eyes flashing with annoyance. 'So you followed *her* around instead,' she guesses. I smile sheepishly in admission and watch as she rolls her eyes. 'Ryder!' Her tone is exasperated. 'We agreed, you'd follow *him*.'

'I did,' I counter, 'but I was losing my mind listening to the prat all day so I decided I should check Maggie out for a bit.'

'Check her out being the optimum phrase,' she deadpans, and then we both laugh.

'I checked her out a bit,' I admit, sitting back against the wooden slats of the bench and sighing wistfully. My day had revealed a lot about Maggie that I hadn't known before. I'd soaked up all the details and committed them all to memory.

Giving up the pretence of following Charlie, I'd watched her all afternoon, noticing how she kept herself to herself, ate alone in the bike shed, and didn't even try to interact with other students. It was pretty clear to me how unhappy she was. She had no one: her grandmother was in a nursing home; she was living with strangers and didn't even seem to have a friend to offload any of her problems to. It had made my heart ache. I understood perfectly. I was lonely too. I missed my family, friends and home, but at least I had Jade to keep me sane.

When she'd had a free period at the end of the day, she hadn't sloped off early like some of the other students, disappearing in loud, chatty packs and walking out of the school gates, turning left towards the shops. No, instead she had opted to go to the library and read.

Jade settles back again, leaning her head on my shoulder. 'You should just stay away from her now. Let the dust settle. You shouldn't keep getting involved in her life, it's just not right.'

Tipping my head back, I scowl at the sky, hating the injustice of it all. When I was alive and could have actually had a girlfriend, I never met one I liked. Maggie is the first and only girl I've had feelings for, and I can't even tell her!

'Ryder, do you hear me? I said–'

'I heard what you said,' I snap, interrupting her. Instantly, I hate myself for taking my issues out on Jade again. 'Sorry. It's just that … I … don't want to stay away from her. I like being near her. I like watching her; she makes me feel alive.'

Jade sighs loudly and stands, looking down at me with sorrowful eyes as she shoves her hands deep into the pockets of her tracksuit top. 'But Ryder, you're *not* alive.'

'No shit, Sherlock,' I grumble, forcing myself to stand too.

She tilts her head to the side, regarding me sympathetically. 'All I'm saying is, you shouldn't let yourself keep obsessing over this girl. It's not right and it's certainly not healthy.' We start walking towards the park where we hang out sometimes. 'Nothing good will come of it and you'll just end up making yourself depressed that you can't speak to her again. You're dead, she's not. What exactly do you want to happen?'

Everything.

Anything.

I scowl down at my feet, not wanting to admit she was right. 'I don't know,' I finally admit.

She loops her arm through mine as we begin to walk slowly down the road. 'Ryder, nothing *can* happen. Ever. You need to stop this now. The longer you let it go on, the harder it will be to stop it. You should just leave it, not see her again, go cold turkey. Cut her out of your life completely, her and her grandmother. It'll be better for you in the long run to make a clean break, like ripping off a plaster; it'll be painful for a little while but then you'll wonder what all the fuss was about.'

The thought of not seeing Maggie again is like a punch to the gut, but deep down I know Jade is right. Maggie is becoming a bit of an obsession. I'm already in a routine where I plan my days around seeing her at her grandmother's nursing home. For someone like me, there is never going to be a happy ending, and hanging out just so I could see her is just prolonging the inevitable and reminding me that she is everything I can never have.

'You're right,' I say grudgingly, nodding agreement. 'I'll stay away from her.' The words hurt to say, but I know it is for the best. Hopefully a clean break is what I need. I can focus on something else for a while and maybe I'll forget all about the girl with the red hair and cutest smile I've ever seen.

CHAPTER NINE
~ RYDER ~

After a reckless and rather out-there couple of days, my weekend returns to business as usual. Although we split up a lot during the week and do our own thing, Saturdays are a day Jade and I always spend together. During the football season there's one place we can be guaranteed to attend in the afternoon – a home game at Norwich City Football Club. Jade has a thing for football, she always has done. Being a local girl when she was alive, she was brought up by her footie-mad mother and dragged along to every home game from the age of six until she learned to love it, too. Even dead, she never misses a chance to support the Canaries.

'Ready?' Jade asks excitedly, getting up from the vigil we've been keeping on the swings at the park, dragging my mind from all places Maggie. I'd been trying not to think about her, as per my agreement with Jade, but I just couldn't help it. I wondered what she was doing today, if she was thinking about Charlie, if she was reading that book…

I nod and stand, forcing thoughts of Maggie away. What Jade had said had been right, it just wasn't healthy for me to be obsessing over someone I could never be with. I was dead. I needed to let go. 'Yep, let's go.' *Keeping busy will help*, I tell myself.

As per our usual routine, we follow the crowd towards the stadium. Jade and I both automatically quicken our pace and offer a curt nod to Malcolm, another football-mad wanderer who attends the games. We don't stop to talk, we never do anymore. Malcolm, a grouchy, dead man in his late seventies, likes to moan and grumble about everything and anything, and my God it can be depressing being stuck listening to that for half an hour! We had, unfortunately, learned that the hard way, so now we avoided him as much as possible.

When we get to the stadium gates, we pass through the ticket barriers as if they're smoke. Jade grins over her shoulder at me and automatically makes her way towards the Upper Barclay Stand – apparently, it's the place she had her season ticket with her mother – and stops off to one side, waiting for the seats to fill up so we can choose two empty ones next to each other. The crowd chatter happily around us, sipping their beer from plastic cups and munching on sausage rolls and Delia's pies.

Finally finding two unoccupied seats together, we sit and wait for the match to start while Jade chats animatedly about the game, the players and her prediction of a 2-1 score. I smile politely and join in when necessary, but going to the match is definitely more about Jade than me. It's not that I hate football or anything – and when I was alive geography made Norwich my home team, too – it's just that I'm more of a rugby fan. The football players' tendency to overdramatise the smallest touch from another player drives me nuts. You never see a rugby player dramatically fall over clutching their head or leg after barely a tap. But I couldn't exactly complain about the free live sport entertainment, and if we weren't here every Saturday, I'd only spend my day like every other mundane day of my non-life. So at least this was a break from the bleak.

I spend the next one hundred or so minutes immersed in the match, shouting at the team and bitching about their performance at half time, the same as everyone else. All in all though, the match is a disappointment; the effort dismal, even for Norwich. They lose one nil, which isn't great just three months into the season. They're hanging out mid-table, something that Jade will gripe about all afternoon, no doubt.

When the final whistle blows, we hang back to let the crowd disperse. Passing through a human body isn't the most pleasant of feelings, so we usually try to avoid the jostling crowd. It isn't like we're in any rush to go anywhere, after all; wanderers have no time commitments.

Once everyone else has left, we head down to Riverside and into the Odeon cinema. The latest Marvel movie is showing, and Jade and I have been waiting months for it: we've been planning this day for weeks. I don't tell Jade that I watched it the other night when I was surveying Charlie and Justine on their date.

Jade and I spend a lot of our free time at the cinema or the theatre. At least three times a week we'll sneak in of an evening and binge watch movies one after the other – another perk of being dead. It started out great when I was a fresh-faced wanderer; seeing all the movies for free and sitting in the plush gallery seats at the back of the cinema was an exciting experience. Unfortunately, the novelty wears off when you've seen every movie at least five times, and coming to the cinema becomes more about killing a few hours and having somewhere comfortable to sit rather than hanging out on a bench in the rain. Twenty-four hours a day is a long time to kill; breaking it up in any way possible makes the time seem to pass faster.

A new movie, especially an epic Marvel one, is something of an event for us and I find myself grinning like a fool as we bypass the queue of people and pass through the foyer into the right screen, plopping down into the sofa-like seats in the back row. We're a little early so the cleaners are still in, sweeping up popcorn and collecting rubbish before the next crowd are allowed in.

'After this we should hang around out front for a while, we haven't done that in ages. After watching all this Marvel action, I'll definitely be in the mood to watch a real punch-up,' Jade says, wriggling to get more comfortable in her seat.

I nod and shrug. 'Whatever you want.' Hanging out on Riverside on a Saturday night was a show in itself. Riverside, known for its pubs and clubs, was the place to be if you liked a drink and, boy, did people like a drink around here. An evening at Riverside for us was taking bets on who was going to puke on their shoes, who would fall over, and who would start a fight over a late-night cheeky Nando's (this one almost always goes to a pack of drunken girls cat-calling at each other which turns nasty). It was a favourite pastime of ours and never failed to entertain.

When the people are finally let into the screen, Jade watches them file in with a scowl on her face. She doesn't like it when anyone sits near her, or when people chat during a film: she prefers an empty cinema. I hide my smile as a teenage couple, clearly on a date, start walking towards us, shyly smiling at each other as they shimmy down the row and take the two seats directly in front of us.

'Oh, hell no. Move! Go sit somewhere else, the rest of the cinema is empty. Bloody hell,' Jade mutters. Her forehead creases with concentration as she aims a swift kick at the seat in front, causing it to judder slightly from the impact. If she focuses all of her energy and tries hard enough, Jade has a particular talent for being able to move small inanimate objects. I don't know how she does it, but she says she's always been able to, even from the beginning. The kick makes the boy shift in his seat. She does it again which makes him look around, confusion clouding his face when he sees our seats empty. When the kicks don't make him change seats, Jade huffs out a groan and stands up, reaching over to knock an almost-full drink out of the boy's hand. She laughs wickedly as some of it slops on the girl's leg and her faux designer handbag. The girl lets out a breathy squeal and jumps up as her date swears and apologises quickly, his eyes widening in horror.

Yep, first date, I think. *Poor guy!*

They have a harshly whispered conversation before they both get up and leave – which makes Jade clap her hands in triumph.

'You're so extra.' I roll my eyes.

She settles back into her seat, a smile now covering her face. 'Oh, come on. Her jeans will dry and if they're in the gallery seats then he'll get a free refill anyway.' She shrugs nonchalantly. 'Least the seat in front is wet now, which means I get to watch men in spandex suits without having to look around some tall bloke's head.'

I sigh and sit back too, closing my eyes and waiting for the film to start, my mind travelling to Maggie. As the idea of not seeing her again washes over me, my chest tightens uncomfortably with the loss.

The next day is Sunday and Jade goes off to visit the care home she likes to stalk. Usually my Sunday afternoon is filled with Maggie and her nan, but as I've vowed not to do that anymore, I plump for going to the hospital instead. I need to move on, and Sylvia, the cancer patient I'd scoped out while visiting Rupert, will help me do just that.

The hospital is a hive of activity when I get to her ward; it's right in the middle of visiting time and the nurses seem a little frazzled and hectic as they make their rounds. There's a more sombre mood hanging in the air than normal – and as I go into Sylvia's room I realise why. Her family have been summoned, as has the hospital pastor. They all stand around Sylvia's bed with sad faces and slumped shoulders while an unconscious and sickly pale Sylvia raggedly wheezes in shallow breaths through an oxygen mask. Her IV slowly drips morphine into her system, easing her pain enough to allow sleep.

I swallow my guilt at why I'm there and silently walk to the side, standing by the head of her bed out of the family's way. Over the next hour or two, their conversation is stilted and quiet, as if they're trying not to disturb Sylvia's medically induced slumber. The nurse comes in to apologise but tells them visiting hours are over. The pastor says a prayer, making the sign of the cross over Sylvia's body, and then quietly excuses himself to wait outside to console and offer kind words. One by one the family make their watery goodbyes and leave – all apart from Sylvia's daughter who has obviously been granted some sort of extension due to the circumstances. The daughter bids farewell to her family, promising to call with updates then sits quietly at her mother's side. Her eyes shine with sorrow, but her tears have dried up. It's obviously been a long and heartrending day for her. She waits, her lips pressed into a thin, anxious line.

After another half an hour or so my anticipation builds; it's like the air has changed somehow. Become thicker, heavier. I'm not sure if Sylvia's daughter can feel it, too. She doesn't acknowledge it, so maybe it's a wanderer thing to know when death approaches, but either way my heart picks up a gear as the overwhelming sensation of anticipation seeps into my skin, making the hairs on my arms prickle. I gulp. This is what I came here for, the validation, for someone to acknowledge my existence, for someone to show me that I'm still here – even though I'm not. Not really.

Sylvia's eyes crack open, she stares at the ceiling, blinking, and a tear slides down the side of her face and soaks into the pillow. Her chest wheezes and crackles. Her daughter makes a strangled sob and sits forward quickly. 'Mum?' The pain in her voice makes my heart ache. I lean forward too.

Sylvia slowly turns her head, as if it pains her to

do so. 'Rosemary?' Her voice is paper thin and almost a whisper. A small smile of recognition twitches at the corner of her mouth.

Rosemary nods, absent-mindedly rubbing her mum's arm gently. 'Yeah, hi, Mum.'

Sylvia coughs, wincing as she does so and her daughter fusses, trying to help but unable to. When the coughing fit subsides, Sylvia's watery and dull eyes flick to my chair and back to her daughter again. 'Who's that?' she rasps, her voice distorted slightly through the mask.

She sees me, I think. A tingling begins in my stomach and my whole body tightens as Rosemary frowns and leans forward, closer to her mother. 'Who's who, Mum? It's just me ... Rose.'

Sylvia's face tightens, her hands clenching into fists as pain takes over. Her eyes flick to me again as her raggedy breaths turn into a strangled groan, and then the light in her eyes finally blinks out. Rosemary's crying gets louder.

I gulp and quickly look around the room for her, but Sylvia hasn't stayed behind. Not everyone lingers after death, most just close their eyes and move straight on to whatever waits for them after. From what I've seen over the years, I've concluded it's the people that die a sudden death that stay behind the most. Or sometimes the person simply isn't quite ready to let go, so they stay until their light comes to collect them. But it appears Sylvia was ready and has already gone.

After taking a deep breath, I stand and quietly exit the room.

I lean against the wall, seeing the nurses rushing around me, bustling into the room, hearing Rosemary's hysterical crying for her lost mother and one of them consoling her. I realise in that moment that I feel nothing.

Of course, I feel sorry for Rosemary's loss.

And I feel the guilt that I intruded in such a private moment and went there just to watch Sylvia die.

But the validation and sense of *being* that I usually get after someone sees me is so infinitesimally small that it's barely recognisable. I feel empty. She saw me, she looked right at me, usually I would take something pleasurable from that, but today, nothing.

I swallow, my mind whirling. This was my thing, this was what I did to make myself feel something, this was what made me feel alive, the *only* thing that made me feel alive … and yet, I feel nothing.

Suddenly it dawns on me why this just wasn't enough to register: Maggie.

Maggie made me feel alive, too. Maggie looking

at me on Thursday night after the van incident, Maggie touching my skin, talking to me – after that, nothing was going to compare. That was *everything*, nothing would ever come close to that feeling. Maybe it never would. Maybe I would be doomed now, not even to have the one bit of pleasure I usually had.

I groan and rake my hands through my hair, staring at the floor.

Now that my mind is on Maggie again, I can't move it. Over the last couple of days I've tried my hardest not to think of her, but now the loss of not being able to see her is unbearable. Today is a day I'd usually see her and her nan. I miss her; I miss them both if I'm honest. I've been stalking her visits so much over the last three months that I almost feel like Doreen is my family, too. I miss her smile and her cheeky personality. I miss watching their interactions and seeing how she is. The disappointment and sadness settle in my stomach like a lead weight.

I huff out a frustrated breath and kick at the wall behind me.

But why? Why do I have to deny myself, though? Yes, Jade doesn't like it; yes, she has a point about it not being healthy for me. It *isn't* healthy, I know that, but does that mean I have to give up what little I have left? I love the time I spend watching Maggie;

knowing I would see her soon is what keeps me going every day. I couldn't go through forever never feeling anything again, wandering through life with nothing to hold on to. That isn't healthy either.

I decide then. Screw what Jade had said. I don't need to go cold turkey. I don't need to give up Maggie at all. I'm not hurting anyone other than myself by seeing her. She isn't aware of it, and if I take some small measure of life from it then what harm am I doing anyone else? None.

But at the same time as I am convincing myself there is nothing wrong in it, I decide not to tell Jade. I neither want nor need her earache on the subject. It really is none of her business.

Glancing at the clock on the wall in the nurses' station I see it's after nine. It's too late to see Maggie now, but tomorrow, tomorrow I will go to her school and just watch her for a while. No harm in that. Nope, none at all.

I smile, and for the first time in two days, I feel like I'm able to breathe properly.

CHAPTER TEN
~ RYDER ~

Lying to Jade that morning before we split and go our separate ways makes me feel like a total jerk, but it has to be done. She simply doesn't understand my need for Maggie. For Jade, the validation of the dying is enough, as it used to be for me, but now...

As I lean against the school gates, my eyes are peeled for a glimpse of her. When she steps around the corner, her gaze on the ground, her chin dipped close to her chest and the collar of her coat turned up to block out some of the cold wind, it feels like the knot that has been constricting my insides all weekend finally unties.

Since I first met her three months ago, this weekend was the longest I'd gone without seeing her. She was part of my routine now, and it was surprising how quickly you become used to things and how they became a part of you. That extra day of not seeing her made the whole weekend drag. The thought of never seeing her again was just too much. Here, now, in her presence, I realise how unrealistic it was for me to expect my feelings to turn off just because I'd decided not to see her again. She is an addiction, and like any addict, I need a vast amount of willpower to get that addiction under control. Clearly, I just don't have the grit to quit, no matter how right I know Jade is.

As Maggie walks past me, merging with the crowd of other students entering the school, I follow behind at a slight distance, trying not to get tangled in the throng of bodies. She stops at her locker, swinging her bag around so she can unload some books and swap them for others.

Commotion and laughing at the end of the hallway catches her attention and I watch her eyes widen fractionally as she takes in the scene. Charlie is with a group of his friends walking towards her. The crowd parts to let them through almost as if they're some kind of school royalty and a lot of the younger girls openly gawp as they walk past. When one of the group gives another one a little push into the lockers, another round of laughter erupts from them.

I can't hold in my sneer of contempt as I watch Charlie interacting with his friends. He really is an idiot.

Maggie's back straightens as they draw closer. When they're about five feet ahead of her, she fiddles with her bag strap furiously. 'Um, hi Charlie,' she squeaks.

His eyes flick to her and narrow slightly, as if he's trying to recall where he knows her from, but he seems to lose interest before he can even remember and breezes past her without so much as an incline of the head in acknowledgement. One of his friends also glances over at her questioningly, but she doesn't hold his interest for long either.

I groan in frustration. I don't want him talking to her, but his ignoring her is almost worse. I see the hurt flicker across her face. Her cheeks flush with embarrassment and her eyes drop to the floor again. I see a frown mark her forehead for a couple of seconds, but then she seems to shake herself and lets out a big breath before turning in the other direction and stalking up the hallway to her first class.

I follow behind, still glowering inside that Charlie ignored her, but knowing that's ultimately for the best considering neither of them have a clue about what really happened on Thursday night.

I watch her all morning, noticing how smart she is, how she gets on with her work with minimal fuss, how if she's called upon to answer a question, her teachers smile fondly at her while she speaks. She keeps herself to herself, though, not even trying to join in with class antics or conversations. It makes me sad to see how alone she is.

At lunchtime she buys a sandwich from the canteen and takes it to the deserted bike shed again, sitting cross-legged on the floor with her back against the wooden wall. She eats with one hand and holds her book with the other. When she's finished, she pulls out a Goofy Pez dispenser and begins to reload it with a new packet of tabs, popping a couple in her mouth as she does so. I can't help but smile at the sight. It's been a real eye opener, following Maggie when she's not visiting her grandmother. I've learned things I never knew – like the fact that she almost always has her nose stuck in a book. When I was alive, book nerds weren't really my type, but Maggie makes me think differently. Watching her read is mesmerising.

I sit down on the ground, facing her, stretching out my leg so it rests just against hers even though I can't feel it and neither can she. A sharp wind blows Maggie's amber curls forward, covering her face and she struggles to tuck them back behind her ears as she dips her head against the cool blast, the pages of her book riffling.

My jaw tightens as I remember the wind blowing her scent into my face on Thursday night: that sweet scent of vanilla shampoo and the tang of cherry on her breath. I smile. I can recall the exact fragrance and it makes my skin prickle. But then the realisation hits me that I'll never smell it again and my happiness is doused as if by a bucket of cold water.

I was wrong when I thought simply seeing her again would be enough for me. It isn't. Being this close, after knowing how good it feels to be closer, is like teasing someone with a greasy, delicious-smelling bacon sandwich or slice of chocolate cake when they're on a diet. Bloody cruel.

The desire to be closer is almost overwhelming. I reach out a hand towards her face, trying to touch her hair, but my fingers go straight through and she doesn't even react.

I huff out a breath and scowl angrily. I would give anything for just another ten-minute conversation with her. There are so many things I didn't get a chance to ask her. I long to hold her, to breathe in her scent one more time, to have her smile at me, for her eyes to meet mine, and see that blush creep across her cheeks. After Thursday, I can't stop myself thinking about the sensation of her, the closeness of her. I long for it more than I've ever longed for anything in my life. Now that our relationship has progressed beyond just being one-sided semi-haunting/stalking, I'm greedy for more. Now I've had a taste of what it was like to be seen by her, I need more. This just isn't enough. Not even close.

It feels like such an injustice.

Why did I have to die? Because of that stupid damn accident, I was doomed to be alone and wandering forever. Why couldn't I have met her when I was alive? Maybe then it would have made wandering more bearable because I would have a plethora of Maggie memories to draw upon.

From the corner of my eye I see other students meandering around, chatting amongst themselves, heading to their form rooms, not even glancing in Maggie's direction. A swell of anger flares inside me. These people could interact with her any time they wanted, but choose not to. They have no clue what they are missing out on. I've never resented people for being alive before, but now I can't stop myself.

The realisation that I would never get to talk to her again, would never kiss her, or know what it was like to be loved by her, that hurt the most.

Sitting with her in the quiet solitude of the bike shed, wallowing in my own self-pity, I silently wish I could just have one more opportunity to talk to her, to ask everything I've been longing to ask for the last three months, to be an actual part of her life – even if it was just for a few stolen minutes.

Then a crazy idea formulates, one that Jade would categorically chastise me for, one I knew was wrong, selfish and self-serving.

Maybe … maybe I *could* have more. After all, I got away with it once, who's to say I couldn't make it work again?

I just had to bide my time and look for the perfect opportunity.

As it turned out, the perfect opportunity arose just a couple of hours later, at the end of school, when Charlie was just finishing up with the after-school club he had been teaching and Maggie was just leaving the IT block.

School had finished almost an hour earlier, so the corridor was empty. With no witnesses around, I simply couldn't help myself. All thoughts of this being selfish were gone, all that was left was my aching need to talk to her, just once more.

I was slipping into Charlie's body and taking control of him before I could talk myself out of it.

CHAPTER ELEVEN
~ MAGGIE ~

'Maggie?'

I jump at the sound of my name being called. I hadn't realised anyone else would still be here. I turn and see Charlie stepping out of the boys' changing room; he's wearing a mud-splattered tracksuit and has a whistle dangling around his neck and a pair of muddy football boots tied together at the laces are hanging from one shoulder.

When he smiles and raises a hand, my body stiffens in shock and I blink before quickly checking to my left and right to see if there's another Maggie standing right beside me. Nope. I'm alone in the corridor.

Huh. Maybe that's why he's talking to you now, because you're alone!

The sting of him ignoring me earlier resurfaces but I force myself to forget it – this boy doesn't owe me anything. He saved my life. He is entitled to ignore me in front of his friends all he wants.

'Um … hi,' I mutter. When he closes the door behind him and struts towards me, all lean muscle and long legs, my stomach erupts with butterflies the size of fruit bats. Even splattered with mud he is easily the most handsome boy I've ever seen in real life.

He stops in front of me, shouldering his sports bag and tilting his head to the side as his eyes rake over my face so intently that I feel my blush spread from my neck to my hairline. 'Detention?' he asks, motioning with his chin towards the IT room behind me.

I swallow and shake my head quickly, dropping my eyes to the floor. 'Oh, um, no. I had some research to do for my history coursework and the laptop at home is on the fritz, so…' I trail off, embarrassed and still in slight disbelief that he's talking to me after my earlier attempt at a greeting was such a spectacular fail. 'What about you? Why are you still here, and so … filthy?' I wave my hand at the grime covering his football boots that dangle over his shoulder smearing mud on his jumper. My voice is scratchy, awkward, and I almost die inside when I acknowledge my flirty choice of word.

He looks down at himself then, his mouth popping open for a couple of seconds, seeming unsure what to answer before he regains his composure and looks back at me, shooting a smile that dazzles me. I feel it all the way down to the pit of my stomach. 'I was assisting an after-school club.' He pulls his football boots from his shoulder, holding them by the tied laces before pushing them into a boot bag he has swinging from one finger.

I nod. 'Is it part of your course to do that? You're doing PE or something, right?' My breath catches as I realise my mistake. I've just revealed that I know more about him than I should. I shouldn't know that he's studying an advanced sport course, or that he wants to be a personal trainer. But I do. I do because I've had a crush on him for the last year. He sucked me in with that lame joke about where turkey drummers kept their sticks, and I've been secretly fantasizing about him falling in love with me ever since. The one consolation in my unrequited crush was that I knew I wasn't alone. Everyone crushes on him; he's hot and desirable, even though I've heard he can be a bit of a jerk sometimes.

He doesn't seem to notice my slip-up though as he answers, 'Yeah, I have to coach a certain number of sports clubs as part of my course.'

I nod and suddenly he's leaning in, his arm brushing my side gently as he grips the handle of the door and pulls it open. The scent of him – earthy, rugged, distinctly manly – surrounds me. It's extremely hot. My skin prickles where the accidental touch occurred and suddenly my brain goes into overdrive, imagining him stepping closer, his body pressing against me, his blue eyes meeting mine as his breath blows across my face.

I snap back to reality, heat burning my cheeks at my daydream, my palms sweating profusely. I gulp and discreetly wipe them on the side of my coat as he gestures for me to go through the open door. 'Ladies first.'

I mutter a thanks and walk through, eyes glued to the floor so I don't trip over or make a fool of myself again. It seems that every time I'm in this boy's company I end up on the ground.

As we approach the front door of the school, he speeds up a step and opens the door for me again. When I glance up at him and offer a surprised smile of thanks, being sure to keep my lips closed over my braces, his answering grin makes my heart canter in my chest.

'So, I'm guessing you usually walk home from school, seeing as you don't live that far away?' he asks, stepping into rhythm with me as we cross the car park towards the gates.

'Sometimes. I live in Thorpe, but some days I get the bus to go visit my nan,' I tell him. 'Today is a bus day.'

'Ah cool. I'm getting the bus, too. I'll walk with you.'

I smile happily and look up to find him watching me. It almost doesn't feel real. Charlie, popular, handsome, make-all-the-girls-swoon Charlie, is smiling and walking with me. 'Where do you live?' I ask as we start to walk down the road, pushing my hands into my pockets because I realise I'm fiddling with the button on my coat so much that the thread is beginning to come loose. My fingers close around my Pez dispenser and I fiddle with that discreetly instead.

'Little Plumstead,' he answers casually. As we walk our bodies are so close that his swinging hand accidentally brushes against my hip and sets my tummy fluttering again.

'Ah, OK, that's nice.' I have no idea if it's nice or not, I've only ever driven through it. I gnaw on my bottom lip nervously because I'm not used to talking to boys. 'So, how was your weekend? Any more superhero blackouts?'

He makes a sound that's almost a cross between a laugh and a scoff. 'No, I've hung up my cape now.

Just plain old Charlie from now on. Though I'll always be on the lookout for the next damsel in distress to save.' He nudges my arm playfully.

I smile widely and quickly reach up and put my hand in front of my mouth to cover my braces. I don't even think about it now, it's an automatic gesture. When I look up, I find he's watching me again. His eyes lingering on my face and my hand that covers my mouth with so much intensity that my knees weaken.

As we approach the bus stop, I turn to him, expecting him to bid his farewells, but he doesn't; instead, he steps under the cover and perches on one of the angled bars made for sitting against, his long legs stretching out in front of him as he crosses his ankles and watches me.

I clear my throat before asking, 'Um, so do you usually get the bus? I've never seen you at this stop before.'

His smile falters for a second but one of his shoulders rise in response. 'Yeah, but normally I leave off much earlier than this, we probably miss each other. Just a happy coincidence today.'

I nod. That makes sense. Usually I stay behind later at school, either to use the IT facilities or basically to just hide in the library for a while so I don't have to go home and make polite conversation with Lorna and Chris. Feeling like a stranger invading someone's home isn't a pleasant feeling so I put it off every day as long as possible. I've never seen Charlie after school, but I suppose if he usually left earlier than this then our paths just never crossed. Though his explanation makes sense, I still couldn't shake one thought … wasn't Little Plumstead in the other direction? Wouldn't the bus stop be on the other side of the road? Not wanting to sound stupid, I dismiss the thought.

'So, what did you do this weekend?' he asks, glancing expectantly from me to the seat at his side, one eyebrow raised.

Taking the hint, I self-consciously wrap my coat tighter around myself and sit down next to him. I shrug, trying to appear casual so he doesn't know I'm overanalysing everything, scanning for the punchline of this joke, hoping it isn't somehow me. 'Well … nothing really. Proper quiet one. On Saturdays I usually waitress to help my foster mother at her café, you know, free child labour and all that.' I roll my eyes playfully, even though I actually quite enjoy working there and helping out.

'Your foster mother has a café?'

I nod, tucking a strand of hair behind my ear,

wishing it wasn't as unruly as it was and just for once I would have had a good hair day. 'Yeah, it's in the city, she does everything there from toasties to full dinners. She's recently had it done out inside and there's this new coffee machine that makes amazing hot chocolates, they're even better than Costa.' I laugh uncomfortably, knowing I'm dangerously close to rambling and tell myself to rein it in a bit. My eyes slide over him discreetly for a second, taking in everything about him from his intense blue eyes to the full bottom lip, to the tiny speck of mud on his right cheek. I commit it all to memory. He's watching me again, his eyes intense as he listens to me talk, and I mean *really* listens. Not just the polite conversation, he's turned in his seat, facing me, his attention undivided as if he finds listening to me the most important thing in the world in that moment.

'Sounds nice. What about Sunday? Do anything exciting then? Dive in front of anymore vans?' He grins widely, his eyes twinkling.

I laugh and shake my head. 'No, I save that for weekday nights.' The grumble of an engine draws my attention away from him and I turn to see my bus trundling down the road. 'Oh, this one's me.' I stand and stick out my arm. Behind me, Charlie stands too. I smile over my shoulder, seeing him patting his pockets before pulling his bag off his shoulder and looking inside quickly. He comes out with a bus pass and runs a hand through his messy hair as he steps closer to the kerb next to me just as the bus rolls to a stop and the door creaks open. 'Does this bus even go to Little Plumstead?' I ask, smiling quizzically.

Charlie's mouth pops open and his eyebrows raise in surprise, before he rolls his eyes and nods. 'Right, autopilot, you got up so I figured my bus was here.' He reaches up and playfully knocks the heel of his hand against his forehead. 'Anyway, g'bye Maggie.'

My insides fizz at the sound of my name from his lips and I turn, smiling widely, not even remembering to feel embarrassed about my braces. 'See ya.'

His answering smile almost looks sad as he raises one hand just as the doors slide closed behind me.

As I scan my bus pass at the ticket machine next to the driver, I replay that sad smile over and over, wondering what it could possibly mean. Was it disappointment that I'd seen there? Was he sad our encounter was over? Or was I totally missing the mark? I wasn't sure. Maybe he was just sad he now had to sit on his own and wait for the bus. That was probably more likely. But either way, I decided not to dwell on it, I was just happy that I hadn't made a fool out of myself or fallen on my face this time and that he'd even bothered to talk to me.

Slumping down into a seat, I let out a happy sigh and smile all the way to my grandmother's nursing home.

CHAPTER TWELVE
~ RYDER ~

The next day I still feel like I'm walking on a cloud and riding the high of Maggie's company. I'd got away with it and managed to snatch a few minutes of conversation with her again. It had meant everything to me.

Of course, I haven't told Jade what happened. She still thinks I'm going cold turkey and not seeing Maggie. It's easier to let her think that, that way I don't have to explain my actions, like why I'm currently perched on the wall outside Maggie's school, waiting for her to arrive. I'm definitely addicted to her, but surely it's not a big problem. After all, it's not like she *knows* I'm stalking her and watching every little move she makes, filling my day with her smiles. If she did it would be weird, but as it stands – no harm, no foul. That's a saying I've decided to apply to this situation.

When she finally does arrive and I follow her to her locker, I can't keep the grin from my face. I know

I'll do anything for just another of her smiles. Consequences be damned.

I keep her company as she walks to her classroom for registration, and then I hover around the back as she sits quietly waiting for first period bell to ring. When it finally does, everyone files out and I trudge behind Maggie to wait outside her first class. When whispering starts in response to laughing from the end of the hallway, I see a group of three older students who've stolen the backpack from a younger, smaller student and are tossing it to each other in a game of piggy in the middle. The younger student fake-laughs and tries to catch it goodnaturedly, even though his face is red with embarrassment and his eyes look like they're filling with tears.

Maggie's eyes widen a fraction, her lips parting as she draws in a little breath. Her attention is fixed on the scene intently, and so I look closer and realise that one of the older kids is Charlie. I groan.

Charlie catches the bag, waits for the student to lunge for it then quickly tosses it to one of his friends, a shit-eating grin plastered all over his face the entire time. His chin is up, chest out; he's clearly enjoying the scene they're creating and all eyes being on them.

I scowl over at him. *What a prick.* When I look back at Maggie, I see she's frowning too. I'm not quite sure what she makes of it, but she doesn't exactly look thrilled that Charlie is being an idiot. When the kid finally manages to grab his bag and scrambles off up the hallway, clutching it to his chest, Charlie slaps his friend on the shoulder and they breeze past us without even looking in Maggie's direction.

She dips her head and tilts it discreetly, her eyes watching Charlie from under her hair as he walks off up the hallway.

A pang of jealousy hits me hard in the chest. Clearly him being an arse hasn't quelled her crush.

The rest of my day is filled with all things Maggie. All her days are pretty much the same; she's stuck in a lonely routine that I long to break but can't. Spending all day following her, the longing to talk to her builds inside me again until it's all I can think about. It's driving me insane not being able to ask how she is, or how she's enjoying her book, or how her grandmother was on her visit last night. I missed going because I was too busy recovering from the woozy effect of leaving Charlie's body after I watched her bus trundle down the road.

By the end of school, the need to interact with her is almost painful. Disappointment settles inside me as I realise my day with her here is almost over –

of course I plan on visiting her nan with her, but after that she goes home and I have to say goodbye and go back to my crappy 'existence'.

As the bell rings, signalling the end of school, I watch with a heavy heart as she pulls out her History exercise book and heads towards the IT block again.

I *need* to talk to her. I need to hear her voice directed at me and not just answering a teacher's question.

I sigh, hating my life. But then an idea hits me, one along the lines of yesterday. What if I could find Charlie and use him again, just for a few seconds, just so I could say hi and her eyes would meet mine again?

Before I know what I'm doing, I'm running through the building towards the front of the school, dodging past students as they funnel from their classrooms towards the exit.

I spot Charlie's blond head over to one side. He's standing with three male friends, Justine and another girl standing a few paces away, hips jutted out seductively as they smile over at the boys. Two of the boys Charlie is with turn and call something to the girls as they walk away, hips sashaying. That's when I take my opportunity. Of course, I know it's stupid, doing this in broad daylight while surrounded by people where so much could go wrong – but I need this. So I don't allow myself to consider the consequences for longer than a split second as I move across the car park and slip into Charlie's body.

Everything tightens, pinches, screams, my vision funnels, and then I'm in. With an effort I raise Charlie's hand and look down at my fingers, giving them a little wiggle to check I'm in full motor control. I am. Just. It's still difficult possessing his body, but this is the third time now, and I'm growing used to the level of concentration and effort it requires to retain hold of him.

'Ready or what?' one of Charlie's friends asks, looking over his shoulder at me expectantly.

I gulp and shrug, hoping Charlie hadn't made plans to go anywhere with them now. 'Actually, I just remembered my mum asked me to bring home my kit to wash tonight. I'm gonna go back inside and get it; you lot go on without me.' I wave my hand at the road ahead.

One of them frowns, jangling a set of keys in his hand proudly. 'I thought I was giving you a lift home?'

I inwardly groan. 'Nah, it's fine. You two go. I might try and catch my teacher as well, see if I can get an extension on my coursework.' The lies tumble from my mouth as I will them to leave. I mean, do sports courses even have coursework?

'I don't mind waiting,' the guy protests, though I can tell from the way his gaze flicks to the car park and a beat-up old Fiesta that he's itching to go already.

I smile. 'Nah, honestly, you go on. I might be a while begging. I'll get the bus and see you tomorrow.'

The one without the keys frowns. 'Tomorrow? Are you not online tonight? Thought we were playing Fortnite?'

I have no idea what he's talking about. Obviously Charlie is some sort of gamer. 'Oh, right, yeah. I'll be online later,' I agree, bending to snag Charlie's school bag where it's been dumped onto the grass, taking the moment to let my lie sink in. Clearly it's the correct thing to have said.

'Cool. All right, speak to you in a bit,' he answers.

I raise a hand in a wave and smile as I turn, not waiting for them to answer before I strut back towards the school.

The hallways are empty now as I make my way towards the IT block, my brain whirling with all the things I want to ask Maggie. There are so many that I settle on just seeing her smile. That's my goal for however long this conversation lasts: just to make her smile.

The door to the IT room is open and I stop

outside, taking a deep breath and trying to calm my racing heart. When I look in, I see that Maggie is sitting with her back to me. She's furiously tapping away at the keyboard, and on her screen is what looks like a Google page about some medieval operation.

I glance around the room quickly. There's no one else in there, just her, not even a teacher to supervise. Jackpot.

Taking one more deep breath, I head in and keep my eyes averted as I walk past her, taking a seat at the computer that faces hers. It's a strategically chosen station – it means I can steal glances at her but if someone does come in they can't see my screen and realise I don't have the required access to log on to the laptops.

She looks up as my chair scrapes along the lino floor. As her eyes meet mine, a blush creeps across her cheeks. 'Oh, hey. Fancy seeing you here.' I try for nonchalance, like I had no idea she was in here and it's just a happy coincidence.

'Um, hi,' she replies, reaching up to smooth her unruly hair down with one hand. As the colour on her cheeks deepens, she looks back at her computer, but I note that her fingers have stopped the furious tapping so she's not actually gone back to work.

'Laptop at home still broken then?' I ask, not

looking at her as I prod a few buttons on my own computer, waking up the screen and watching the cursor flash in the UserID section.

'Yeah,' she answers.

I nod, making a show of tapping in some random letters and numbers as if I'm logging on.

'So, how was your day?' *Ugh, so lame! I need better chat. What would a confident, good-looking, alive boy of my age say to a girl?*

'It was good, thanks,' she answers.

I look up and catch her eye, offering a small smile. 'What you working on?'

She rolls her eyes and grimaces at the screen. 'History project about medicine during World War One.'

'I suck at history. Was it Custer that won the Battle of the Alamo or was that Billy the Kid?' I joke.

This garners a laugh from her. It's a soft, tinkling sound that sets the hair on my arms tingling. I grin proudly and tap on a few keys to keep up appearances.

'You off to see your nan again tonight?' I inquire.

She smiles fondly, seeming shocked that I'd remember something she told me, and nods. 'Yeah, I see her as much as I can. Tuesday is always a visit day.'

I know. I also know the only days she doesn't go

there are Wednesdays, Fridays and Saturdays. 'How is she?'

'She's good, thanks.' She rummages through her bag for another textbook and the zip unfastens, tumbling the contents to the floor. I grin. So clumsy. Her face flashes red again as she stoops to pick it up.

'How's the book? It's about some sort of circus, isn't it?' I ask, nodding as she picks up *Caraval*. I've read the blurb from the back of the book which she's been reading at every opportunity today.

Her head tilts to the side. 'It's good, actually. Have you read it?'

I snort and shake my head. 'No. My sister has it.'

'I didn't know you had a sister.'

Oh shit. Has Charlie got a sister? Dammit. 'Mmm,' I reply, tapping away at my keyboard and frowning at my screen as if I'm doing important work. She looks away and goes back to her own screen.

Silence descends over us and I can feel the awkward tension filling the air as neither of us know what to say or how to behave. 'If you were stuck on a desert island and could only take one book, what would it be?' I blurt out one of the many, stupid, questions I've wanted to ask her.

She laughs that tinkling laugh again. 'How random. Is this part of your course or something?'

'No, the question just popped into my head.'

'Um, I guess it would be *Lord of the Rings*. My nan used to read the series to me.' Her eyes soften as she says it, clearly lost in the memories.

'Good choice.' I nod in approval.

'What about you?'

'*Frankenstein.*'

'Mary Shelley?'

I nod.

'Huh, didn't think you'd be a fan of the classics.'

'There's a lot you don't know about me. Appearances can be deceptive, you know.' I take a deep breath and have an idea about how to keep the conversation going. 'Like, for example, I like green apples but not red; I like swimming but only in a cool pool not a warm one; I can't wear socks to bed; I'm pretty great at drawing; when I was younger I always wanted to be a cartoonist. You know, one of those guys that hangs out at the seafront and draws those passive-aggressive caricatures that highlight people's flaws? That was my dream.' I grin at the memory.

Her head cocks to one side, her eyes regarding me curiously. I have her full attention now. 'What changed?'

'Huh?'

She pushes a curl behind her ear and leans

forward. 'You said you *wanted* to be a cartoonist when you were younger, which implies you don't want to now, so what changed?'

I swallow awkwardly. Nothing changed, that would have been my chosen career, along with comic-book illustrator, if I'd not died, but I need an answer that appeases her vision of Charlie. 'I got into sports and realised I could make a better living from it. Who wants to be a struggling artist, anyway?'

She smiles and it goes quiet so I carry on with my random thoughts. 'I'm also pretty beast on a skateboard. Oh, and I can burp the alphabet … backwards.'

She bursts out laughing, her hand covering her mouth as she does so, her eyes twinkling. 'That's impressive.'

'Tell me some stuff about you that barely anyone knows.' I hold my breath, waiting, ready to take it all in and absorb it.

She thinks for a second or two. 'I'm allergic to cats, but I love them. I can't catch, like, at all. You wouldn't want me on your team, ever.'

I would actually, I think.

'I can eat a whole doughnut without licking my lips.'

I wave a dismissive hand. 'Too easy, everyone can do that.'

'Ah, but I can do it in about three seconds. Two bites and it's gone,' she adds proudly.

I raise one eyebrow. 'Impressive.'

'Obviously not as impressive as being able to burp the alphabet backwards.'

I grin and puff out of my chest in mock pride. 'Obviously.'

She grins, looking back at her screen. Typing for a few seconds, so I do the same. A minute later the printer whirls to life in the corner of the room which makes me jump.

She smiles apologetically. 'Sorry. I just need to print off a few bits, then I'm outta here and you can have some peace to work on whatever it is you're doing.' She stands and walks to the printer, collecting the sheets as they slowly come out. When she's collated them, she folds them in half and walks back to her station, leaning down to type a few commands before stuffing the papers in her bag and shrugging on her coat which has been hanging over the back of her chair.

'You get everything done already?' I ask, trying not to let the disappointment show in my voice.

She nods, shouldering her bag. 'Yep. And if I run, I can make the three-fifty bus to get to my nan's.' She eyes the clock behind me on the wall. 'Well, bye,

Charlie.' She smiles shyly and my stomach bubbles with happiness.

'Bye, Maggie.' I grin, my eyes never leaving her as she shoulders her bag and walks out of the room, not looking back. I give her a few minutes before I stand and exit the room too.

As soon as I step out of the IT room door and verify that there's no one around to witness it, I leave Charlie's body.

The sensation feels like falling, but never hitting the ground. It's like losing your balance, losing yourself even; it's so strong that it makes my stomach lurch. I slump back against the wall, my legs no longer supporting me as my own body slides jelly-like to the floor. I heave in large breaths, trying to slow the spinning in my head and the screeching that still permeates my ears.

Through the fog of exhaustion that I'm overcome with, I look up to see Charlie's confusion. He's frowning down at his hands, his lips pressed into a thin line as he glances this way and that up the empty hallway. The tight bunching of the muscles in his arms tell me he's alert and anxious.

'Oh shit,' I mumble. I didn't think this through at all.

He stands there for a few seconds, his straight

white teeth clamped down on his bottom lip, before he shakes his head and gives a disbelieving snort and walks off up the hallway, dragging a hand through his hair roughly.

I breathe a sigh of relief that he didn't question it further and, using my elbows as leverage, I push against the wall, attempting to get to my feet. My body sways drunkenly, my knees wobbling precariously before I give in, sliding back down to sitting position. I need more time to recover.

I think back over everything that just happened.

However, witnessing Charlie's confusion and then quick dismissal of finding himself back in the school makes me realise I've made a mistake. I don't mean using his body – seeing Maggie's smile and the twinkling in her eyes, no that was definitely not a mistake – it was the way I ended it that was wrong. Maybe I should have taken him back to his house, laid him down on his bed, or opened TikTok on his phone so he thought he'd been watching in a daydream or something. Suddenly leaving his body in a random place was not my smartest move, but I hadn't thought it through at all. I vow to be shrewder next time.

Wow. Next time.

I snort an exhausted laugh. I'm already planning my next stolen moments with Maggie, already looking forward to it. Charlie's confusion isn't even a consideration. I just needed to be smarter next time, plan it more and figure out how I can get around the lost time he'd experience. It would all work out, it had to.

CHAPTER THIRTEEN
~ MAGGIE ~

You know those times when you're not quite sure if you're awake or asleep? As I step out of the main entrance of the school at the end of the day on Wednesday, I have one of those moments.

The school is deserted, as usual. I'd stayed behind when the bell rang to avoid the crowds, heading instead to the library to return my book and borrow another. I'd been drawn into conversation with Mrs Rice and had spent a while writing a list of books she would try to order in for me from the central library. By the time I leave, there are only a few students remaining, and those that are here are busy either preparing to leave or running off to after-school clubs.

My feet falter on the threshold, my eyes landing on him immediately. He's casually leaning against the brick wall, one leg crossed over the other at the ankle, arms folded across his broad chest, hair messily falling over one eye, tanned skin glowing against the darkening afternoon. He's the picture of ease.

Charlie.

I gulp, and that's when I wonder if this is a dream. I've had this exact dream before. Granted in my fantasy he was wearing a short sleeve T-shirt instead of a jacket so I could see the toned muscles of his arms, and in that dream he was waiting to whisk me away in his Elvis-replica pink Cadillac and shower me with affection, but still, it was pretty similar.

I feel my face warm as my eyes widen. *Is he going to talk to me again?* I've not seen him all day, but maybe after our chat yesterday in the IT block he will actually acknowledge me. He knows my name after all.

Then something occurs to me. *Is he actually waiting for me? Was he waiting to talk to me?*

The thought is so irrational that a little manic chuckle slips out of my lips and I immediately shake my head at myself.

He hears and his head turns and, to my delight, a warm smile appears at the corners of his mouth as his eyes meet mine. I watch in fascination as he pushes himself away from the wall, hands dropping down to his sides, his head flicking as he moves his hair from his eyes.

His smile is a grin now; it hits me with the force of a sledgehammer, right to the heart.

My insides are aflame as I feel my own matching smile blossom.

'Hi, Maggie. I thought I saw you heading out of the library. I figured I'd wait for you,' he says, shrugging casually, as if this is no big deal.

He was *waiting for me!*

My breath catches. 'Oh, hi, Charlie,' I answer, willing my voice not to betray my excitement.

He turns to the side, and I think he's about to walk off, but instead I realise he's just stepped aside to give me more room next to him. I glance down at the four or five steps I have to navigate down to him and silently pray I don't fall in front of this boy *again*. His smell assaults me when I step to his side. His hair is damp, he's clearly recently showered, the smell of his woody deodorant mixed with his skin makes my pulse speed.

'So, how's your day been?' he asks as we walk together towards the gate.

'Um…' *How was my day? Quiet, boring, lonesome, same as usual.* I don't say that though, instead I say, 'It was OK. Yours?'

He shrugs, 'Same. Pretty boring to be honest.'

We're out of the school now and I can feel my shyness and awkwardness wrapping around me like a cloak. I drag my eyes up from the pavement and gaze at him, immediately averting my eyes when I see he's looking directly at me, a beautiful grin stretched across his face, his straight white teeth on full show. This immediately makes me feel more self-conscious so I bring one hand up to cover my braces as I smile back and let out a little embarrassed snort.

'Getting the bus today?' he asks, motioning towards the bus stop that we're fast approaching.

My disappointment hits me as I realise he's stopping here and we're going our separate ways after only exchanging the barest of words. But I have to admit, my disappointment is also tinged with a little bit of relief. I *want* to talk to him, but I feel so out of my depth and nervous that maybe it would be best to put an end to this whole embarrassing charade before I do something that'll make me look stupid … again.

'Oh, no actually, I'm not.' I stop next to the bus stop and drag my eyes up to meet his. 'Tomorrow I'll get the bus, but today isn't a nan-visit day, so I'm walking home.' I kick at the ground with one foot and frown.

His head tilts to one side as he regards me. 'I could walk you home, if you like?'

I almost choke on air. *Walk me home? Why?*

'Um…' I don't know what to say. Thankfully he saves me.

'I'm heading to a friend's house in Thorpe anyway, so we could walk together I meant,' he clarifies, one shoulder lifting in a no-big-deal gesture.

'Oh right, well, sure then, if you're going that way. Saves me walking on my own. Not that I don't like walking on my own, I mean, it's not that it's dark or anything. Not that I don't like the dark either, because I don't mind it, but you know…' I blink a couple of times, gulping down more word vomit that threatens to come up. *Oh God, I'm babbling again. Stop it, Maggie!*

'You ramble when you're nervous.' It's a statement, not a question. Charlie looks at me, his eyes showing their amusement at my outburst, then he laughs, actually laughs and the sound sends my heart into a frenzy. My whole face burns from the base of my neck to the top of my hairline. 'Don't be embarrassed. It's quite endearing actually,' he adds.

Endearing? My mouth pops open and I force it closed again, not allowing myself to say anything in return as he simply turns and starts to walk before stopping a couple of steps away and waiting for me to catch up. I laugh and rush to his side, my fingers twisting and fiddling with the button on my coat nervously.

The silence isn't too deafening as we walk to the end of the road. The word endearing is still ringing in my ears but I make a mental note to try and douse my rambling from now on.

'Are you heading to Justine's?' I ask.

He glances sideways at me. 'What makes you ask that?'

'She lives a couple of streets away from me. You said you were going to a friend's.'

He shakes his head, reaching up to run a hand through his hair. 'Oh, nope. I'm not.' When he doesn't expand, I hide my unreasonable grin that he's not going to see his girlfriend by ducking my chin into the collar of my coat, rubbing the wool gently against my lips.

'So, I saw you coming out of the library with another book. I don't think I've ever met anyone that reads as much as you do. What sort of stuff do you like to read? You have a favourite genre?' His hand accidentally brushes against mine as we walk and I revel in that smallest of contact, knowing I'll be playing that glorious skin-on-skin accident over in my head again and again later.

'I read all sorts of stuff. I'm actually a blogger. Well, I have a blog page on WordPress and I review books, not sure I could actually call myself a blogger really, I suppose there are certain things you have to do to call yourself a blogger – social media is one of them. I guess I just read a lot and I review it on the blog page I've set up. My favourite genre is probably young adult fantasy. I like an epic series I can get my teeth into, and if it has magic in, I'm there.' *Rambling again. Seriously, stop it, you're showing yourself up.*

He nods along, listening to me with a small satisfied smile on his face.

Endearing.

His word from earlier hits me again and my insides squirm with pleasure.

'I've never been much of a reader. I guess I liked Jules Verne and *Frankenstein*, but really, I only read when I was made to,' he admits. 'I like a lot of movie adaptions, though I suppose as a book enthusiast you're gonna tell me the books are always better?'

'Of course they are!' I scoff at his suggestion playfully and roll my eyes. 'Unless you're talking about *The Maze Runner*. In that case, I actually liked the movies better than the books.'

'I love *The Maze Runner* films. I've probably seen them at least ten times each.'

'Ten times? So they're, like, one of your favourite series?' I ask. I didn't think I'd seen *any* movie ten times.

His smile falters; a frown lines his forehead. 'Not really. I just watch a lot of movies, it's a hobby of mine.'

'Watching movies isn't a hobby,' I quip, scrunching my nose up.

'Course it is! That and people watching are the two things I do most in the world. Hobbies,' he states, nodding.

The sternness of his face makes me laugh and shake my head. 'People watching?'

'Don't tell me you've never sat somewhere and just watched all the people pass you by. It's like a free movie, so much drama, so much hidden meaning. I like making up little stories that I think go with the scenario, where they're going or have been, why they're angry with their partner, who wants to sleep with who. It's humanity at its finest … and worst.' We stop walking and talking as we reach the wall at the end of my garden. The trip has passed way too quickly for my liking.

'I guess, I've never really thought about it too much,' I admit, leaning back on my heels and clicking the toes of my shoes together absentmindedly, waiting for him to rush off and make excuses to stop talking to me. Instead, he leans on the pillar at the edge of my gate and looks at me curiously.

I bite my lip. I don't want him to leave, there's so much more to him that I'm only now finding out. I like it, I feel like we're sharing secrets, like he doesn't show this silly side of him to anyone else. I'd certainly never seen this side of him at school.

He doesn't seem to be making any moves to leave. He'd said he was going to a friend's house, but he's just leaning against the wall, gazing at me, his eyes so probing and curious that it makes my breathing shallow. His hesitation encourages me, daring me to do something against my better judgement.

'Do you um…' *Oh no, I can't do this.* 'Oh, never mind,' I chicken out at the last second, my face flaming as I silently curse myself for even opening my mouth.

'Do I what?' he questions.

I take a deep breath. 'Do you want to come in, for a drink or something?' I almost whisper.

He grins and nods. 'Sure.' That one-word answer sets my heart galloping in my chest as my whole body tingles with pleasure.

'OK, great.' I turn to the gate, unlatching it and pushing it open. 'Great,' I repeat for good measure, laughing quietly, sticking my hand into my bag, digging out my keys.

'Hey, did you get your phone fixed in the end?' he

asks as I push open the door, kicking off my shoes and removing my coat, hearing him do the same behind me. His being in my house again, all glorious and gorgeous, is weird.

How is this happening? I muse, grinning from ear to ear.

'Not really. It actually still works. The screen is a goner but other than that it's OK.' I smile and watch him hang his jacket on the hook, before I motion for him to step into the living room. 'What do you want to drink? We have some fizzy stuff, you like Pepsi? Or I think we have some orange juice in the fridge,' I offer, but then I stop dead in my tracks, just as he does.

Lorna is sitting on the sofa, cup of tea in one hand, pen in the other, a stack of her work papers balanced precariously on her knee.

'Oh! I–I–' I stutter, 'Sorry. I didn't realise you were home already. I thought you'd be working.' My face is burning. I can only imagine the shade of my cheeks and the more I stress about it the more embarrassed I become.

Lorna's mouth stretches into a wide, welcoming smile, her eyes landing on Charlie before flicking back to me. 'Maggie! It's OK, you can come in. You're not interrupting anything. I'm just catching up on some paperwork for the shop. I need to do a big order, make sure we're well stocked with all the Christmas essentials, plus I'm coming up with some new specials for the holiday season.' She places her cup down on the side table, then shuffles all the papers into a pile and puts them onto the sofa as she gets up. 'Who's this?' she asks, looking behind me to Charlie. There's a twinkle to her eye that tells me she's happy I finally brought someone home. She's been telling me since I arrived that I could invite friends over any time.

Oh God, kill me now!

I look at Charlie, mortified. She's just being polite. I know she's not doing anything wrong, but could this be any more awkward?

'This, er, this is Charlie.' I have no other explanations.

Charlie seems to be in full control, though. He doesn't even look bothered by the fact that he's just walked headlong into an ambush. No one likes to meet parents; they're embarrassing and awkward. Do-gooder, try-hard foster parents are surely even worse.

He sticks out his hand in a very grown-up gesture. 'Nice to meet you. I'm a friend of Maggie's from school.'

Friend of Maggie's from school. The words send a shiver of excitement down my spine that I fight not to show.

Lorna seems charmed as she takes his hand and shakes it. 'I'm Lorna. I'm so glad to meet you, Charlie. I've not met any of Maggie's friends before, she likes to keep us hidden.' She nudges me with her elbow, sending me a little wink.

I groan inwardly but force a smile.

Charlie laughs politely then turns to me. 'I should probably get going anyway. Maybe another time for that drink, huh?' he says, and I'm part relieved this is over and part devastated. I nod in agreement, not trusting my voice to speak. He nods too and smiles at Lorna again. 'It was nice to meet you.' He turns on his heel and goes back to the hallway.

He's just slipping on his trainers as I follow him, wincing apologetically. 'Sorry. She's usually at work at this time,' I whisper.

He waves a dismissive hand and reaches for his jacket. 'No problem. I should get going anyway, I've been too long already,' he says. I nod, silently wondering what I was holding him up from. Was he meeting Justine, or was he really heading to someone else's house? 'I'll see you tomorrow, Maggie.'

'Bye,' I reply, holding the door open for him and

closing it as he walks up the path. I sigh and lean against it, grinning from ear to ear, my insides squirming with happiness.

What the hell just happened?

My happy bubble is burst when Lorna leans her head around the doorframe, grinning at me conspiratorially, a playful glint to her eye. 'Well, he was certainly good looking,' she says triumphantly.

I laugh and drop my eyes to the floor, shaking my head, before pushing away from the door and picking up my school bag. 'I have homework to do; I'll be in my room. If you need me to help with dinner or anything, give me a shout.'

She groans loudly. 'Oh come on, I get no gossip? No details at all? First time you've ever brought a friend home, and he looks like that, and I don't even get the tea?' she calls playfully to my back as I walk up the stairs unable to hide my smile.

CHAPTER FOURTEEN
~ MAGGIE ~

'Oh hey!'

I jump at the voice and turn from my workstation in the IT block to see Charlie. He stops at the door, casually leaning against the doorframe, one long leg crossed over the other at the ankle, a smile on his face.

'You're here again, huh? Do they charge you rent?' he jokes.

I laugh quietly. 'They probably should.'

His answering smile is dazzling. 'I just got finished for the day. Are you almost done? I'm heading to the bus stop if you want to keep me company? I can wait if you're not going to be long,' he offers, shouldering his bag and motioning his head towards the hallway.

Inwardly, I groan. I'm not almost done. I still have half an essay to type up ... but ... 'Actually, yeah, I'm finished now,' I lie, swivelling in my chair and saving my document before logging off the computer and pocketing my USB with my history project on it. I desperately don't want to pass up on an opportunity to talk to him again. I'll just have to finish this essay in my lunchbreak tomorrow, no big deal.

'Great timing then,' he says. 'Today is one of your grandmother visit days, right? I remember you mentioning it yesterday.'

'It is,' I confirm, standing and picking up my bag, watching as he waves his hand for me to go first in a very gentlemanly gesture that makes me sigh with delight. When he reaches to open the door for me again I smile, not daring to let my eyes meet his. 'Thanks,' I mutter.

'Your foster mother seemed nice.'

I wince, thinking about the whole uncomfortable interaction yesterday – then wince again when I think about Lorna asking me again over dinner for the 'tea' on Charlie. To be honest I was surprised she even knew what that meant and used it in the correct context. 'Yeah, she's OK,' I reply, embarrassed. 'I'm sorry again about that. She's usually never home at that time.'

He shrugs as if it's nothing and flashes me another of those million-pound smiles. 'Honestly, it didn't bother me.' He runs a hand through his hair, pushing it away from his face and I can't help but steal a look as he does so. 'Anyway, let's play a game of this or that,' he suggests as we walk towards the bus stop.

'This or that?'

He nods eagerly, grinning. 'Yeah, like, I say two things and you have to choose this or that as quick as you can without thinking about it. For example, Pepsi or Coke?'

'Pepsi,' I answer without missing a beat.

He grins and nudges my arm with his. 'See, you've got it.'

'Not much to it really,' I joke, rolling my eyes playfully as we stop at the bus stop. There's already an elderly couple waiting there, taking up the seats, so we stop at the side and I lean against the frame. Charlie sidles up next to me, leaning in way too close, making my pulse quicken. His body is turned towards me, his eyes locked on mine as if he's trying to see into their depths. 'Ready? Quick fire round, no hesitation, just answer,' he says, grinning. I nod and wait, preparing myself for the barrage of questions.

Music or movies: Music.

Pizza or burgers: pizza, obviously.

The movie or the book: Books, always.

Coffee or tea: Tea.

YouTube or Netflix: Netflix.

Cats or dogs: dogs because I'm allergic to cats.

Chocolate or crisps: chocolate.

Beach or pool: pool, I don't like sandy toes.

Waffles or pancakes: both.

At that, he laughs. 'You can't choose both, that's the point of the game.'

I shrug. 'Any game that makes me choose between two equally amazing food stuffs is not a game I want to play.'

His eyes crinkle at the edges as he looks down at me and I can see he's enjoying himself and is legitimately interested in my answers.

I hold my breath, my heart racing. Charlie makes me feel incredibly special. The attention he is showering me with lately, the way he listens, really listens to what I'm saying, and the way his eyes probe mine when waiting for an answer to a question, like I'm the most interesting thing in the world ... it makes me feel like I'm a hundred feet tall. The power of his presence, it's transcendent. Is this how Justine feels when she's around him? Does he pay her the same amount of attention and make her feel like she's the only girl in the world? I think about it, *really* think. Actually, I'd rarely seen them talk, just the two of them. They're either usually with a crowd of friends or snogging. I guess I couldn't really judge their dates, though, maybe he treated her like a queen then.

I sigh and jealousy swirls in my stomach. Not that I should let it. It's not like I have any claim on him, and I've barely known him a week – because, really, being at the same school and thinking someone is hot can't really be classed as knowing them. We've had just a handful of snatched conversations. I have no right to be jealous of his *actual* girlfriend. But that doesn't make it stop; instead, at the word girlfriend my stomach constricts some more.

Before we have the chance to say anything else, my bus ambles down the road. The elderly couple stand and stick out an arm and I smile sadly as my heart sinks. I wasn't done talking to him. I push away from the bus stop and swallow my disappointment. 'Well, this one's me, hopefully yours won't be too long.'

He runs a hand through his hair and looks up the road. 'It'll be along soon. I guess I'll see you tomorrow then.'

The bus stops at the kerb, hissing as it lowers and the doors swing open. The elderly couple board first and I fumble in my pocket for my pass. I step on, smiling politely at the driver and beep my pass before turning and throwing Charlie a little wave. 'Bye.'

He stands quickly, his eyes locked on mine. 'Maybe tomorrow we could grab a hot chocolate or something after school?' He steps forward, putting his hands on the doors, pushing them back open as they begin to close.

Did he just ask me out? No. No way. 'Um…' I'm so taken aback, I can't find the right words so an awkward silence falls over us. An irritated and deliberate cough from the driver makes me wince but Charlie's blue eyes don't leave mine. He's not going anywhere, or letting the doors close until I've answered. 'OK. Sure, that'd be great,' I reply, nodding and feeling my face warm with happiness.

He smiles, that adorable smile, and nods, finally letting go of the doors.

The driver immediately closes them and Charlie raises a hand on the other side in a wave as the bus pulls off quickly, the driver obviously in a rush. As I turn and take the first free seat on the bus, I can't keep the happy smile from my face.

The whole way there I think about him and what just happened, my excitement growing by the second. It wasn't a date, of that I was sure of because he was seeing Justine, but maybe, just maybe, I'd found a friend. A very hot friend.

When I arrive at my nan's nursing home, it appears my good luck is about to continue. As I walk in the door a huge smile crosses her face and she shuffles out of her chair to stand, her arms open wide for a hug.

I grin. She's herself today. These days happen so sparingly that it lights my heart with joy. She gives me a squeeze, and sighs happily when I finally break the embrace and step back.

'Hello, my sweet girl,' she says, reaching up and cupping my cheek.

'Hi.' Happy tears prickle in my eyes. I haven't seen her this clear and lucid for a few weeks. Her cough seemed to have knocked her for six and zapped all of her remaining energy; there had been more bad visits than good lately, some of them so upsetting I'd cried myself to sleep, so this one is like a shock to the heart – in a good way for a change.

'So tell me, how's all things Maggie?' she asks as she sits back down, patting the space on the old floral sofa for me to sit next to her. 'I want to hear it all. I haven't seen you in such a long time.'

I wince inwardly at the 'long time' comment, in reality it was only Tuesday, two days ago, that I came to see her but she's obviously forgotten that visit. I slip off my coat, throwing it over the back of the wooden chair to my left and take a seat next to her on the sofa, preparing myself to tell her everything about my life all over again – from where I was living, to what I had for breakfast, she'd ask it all.

Half an hour later, Nan's waffling about some shove ha'penny tournament the housemates had this morning and my mind, unintentionally, wanders to Charlie and the offer of hot chocolate tomorrow. Was he serious? Would he remember it tomorrow or was it just a casual, throw-away suggestion? But the way he'd leaned in and held the bus doors open told me it was anything but casual.

'You're thinking awful hard about something,' Nan says, bringing me out of my reverie.

I shake myself and laugh gently. 'Sorry, Nan. I was just thinking about…' I stop, it feels awkward to say it out loud.

'About what, dear?' she prompts.

I hesitate for a few seconds, but then it all comes out, all of it in one big flood of word vomit. I tell her all about my crush on Charlie: how he's the most popular boy in school, how everyone hangs off his every word, how good looking he is, how we had a conversation last week and then how he's walked me to the bus stop and home a couple of times. I tell her how he listens to me, really listens, and how it makes my heart thunder in my chest like a jackhammer. Of course, I leave out Charlie saving me from the road accident, I don't want a lecture on road safety or to have her worry about me taking care of myself. She has enough to worry about all the time.

Her smile is huge, and probably matches my own. 'Is he your boyfriend, this Charlie?'

I feel the blush creep up my cheeks as I duck my chin. 'Not really. I mean, we've just talked a few times. I mean, it's not even really a thing. I just want it to be.'

'But you think he wants to be a thing too?' she questions, her gaze penetrating. I can see her desperate need for details and it makes me chuckle.

I shrug. 'I honestly don't know. It's difficult because we don't actually speak at school. It's only ever after, so we've only had a few short conversations. He walked me home the other day and he waited for me so we could walk to the bus stop together today. But at school, we don't really interact.'

Her forehead creases with a frown. 'Oh, why is that?'

I shrug again, staring down at my hands, picking at a loose thread on my jumper. 'I don't know, Nan. I think he's just busy with his friends. I don't often see him around school.' The lie drops from my lips. 'He's older than me so we have different friends, I guess.'

She shifts in her chair and has a bit of a coughing fit. I wince, passing her the glass of water that's on the side, watching as she slowly gets her cough under

164

control and takes a sip. When she's righted herself, she looks up at me with a firm glint in her eye. 'Well, he should be proud to show you off and talk to you. I mean look at you, you're beautiful, smart and funny, you take care of your old nan, plus, you're going somewhere in life, you have goals. What boy could resist that?' She reaches out and pats my hand, a fond smile on her lips.

'Well, you're only *slightly* biased.' I roll my eyes playfully.

'I'm not biased. You're a lovely girl and anyone would be lucky to have you on their arm,' she says, giving my hand a squeeze. 'I just worry, though,' she continues.

'About what?'

She clicks her tongue and shakes her head slightly. 'Well, it's just, he's a bit of a Jack the lad, is he?'

I can't help but laugh. 'A Jack the lad?'

She nods. 'Yes, you know, someone who plays up for attention in front of people, bit brass, bit up himself. The good-looking, popular ones usually are. We had them in my day, too, you know. The gorgeous, popular boy who was a bit rude, a bit of a show-off, but was always allowed to get away with it because of who he was. He also wasn't shy of a bit of female attention, and boy did he know it and play off it.'

I open my mouth to defend Charlie but then

think better of it. Because, actually, sometimes that's exactly who he is. At school, when he's surrounded by his friends, he likes to be the centre of attention and does things I don't approve of, like knocking people's books out of their hands and laughing, or the other day when he was tormenting that first year with his school bag. But other times, when we're alone and he opens up, he's like a completely different person. Now that I've come to think about it, he definitely could be a bit of a jerk at school. But outside of it, when we've spoken and he's revealed more of his personality, he's actually a really nice guy. It's almost like there are two personas, the Jack the lad, as my nan calls him, who cares what people think of him and belittles people, and the burping-the-alphabet people watcher who thought my rambling was endearing. It's hard to reconcile the person who asks about my nan and remembers things I've previously said, with the Charlie who blatantly ignores me at school and who once shoved a kid into a locker for looking at him the wrong way.

'I don't know, Nan. Maybe. Anyway, it's nothing serious, we're just talking,' I say, wishing I'd never brought it up. I had thought it would be something we could gossip over, that we could analyse things he'd said or done. I don't want to have her worry –

and in turn worry me – that he was somehow deliberately ignoring me at school because of his reputation. That suggestion somehow took the shine off our interactions a little.

'Well, you just have your wits about you. Don't let him walk all over you. You don't want to be just a number to that boy if that's all he's after, if you know what I mean. Talking leads to other things you know.' Her eyebrows raise into her hairline as her mouth presses into a firm, worried line.

I can't help the embarrassed giggle that slips out of my mouth when I clock what she's referring to. 'I'll keep my wits about me, don't worry,' I confirm, still laughing. Then, wanting to change the subject, I nod at the big bay window. 'It's fairly nice outside for a change today. Let's do something fun before visiting time finishes. Shall we go for a little walk in the gardens? Get some fresh air?' It's beginning to get dark, but there's still enough light to do a lap of the gardens and look at the flowers before dinner – something my nan loves to do on her few-and-far-between lucid days.

And just like that, her face lights up, and so does my heart.

CHAPTER FIFTEEN
~ MAGGIE ~

Is this happening? Is this truly happening? Discreetly, I pinch my leg and yelp, the sharp pain confirms this really is reality.

Charlie walks over, a deep frown of concentration lining his forehead as he carries a tray laden with two hot chocolates, complete with whipped cream and marshmallows, to the table I'm sat at in my foster mother's café. I grin ecstatically and drop my gaze to the table as he sits opposite me, sliding my drink off the tray and setting it in front of me.

'Thanks,' I mutter, pushing a rogue curl behind my ear, gritting my teeth when it pings straight back out again.

'It's nice in here. Your foster mother did a great job renovating the place. I've never been in.' He glances around the busy coffee shop, taking in all the personal knick-knacks she has scattered around the place. The splashes of colour on the walls commissioned from local artists, the plush leather sofas and low-level tables she's arranged in one corner for more intimate coffee meetings and gatherings. It's warm and welcoming, so different from her house.

I nod and wrap my hands around my drink, wanting to keep them still because I keep fiddling when I'm nervous.

Much to my delight, Charlie was waiting for me at the end of school again, flashing me that grin, showing off his pearly whites in all their glory as he asked if I was still up for getting that drink. I'd not been entirely convinced it would happen, especially after I'd smiled and said hi to him after assembly in the morning and he'd not even given a spark of recognition, instead almost looking annoyed that I'd spoken to him.

'She took it over about a year ago apparently and did it all up. The business has been growing pretty rapidly ever since. The cakes are great here so that keeps people coming back. Lorna's a star baker,' I joke, attempting to take a mouthful of my drink but, to my horror, just ending up getting cream and a mini marshmallow on my lip. I groan internally, wishing I hadn't asked for the toppings now. I wipe it off quickly, hoping Charlie hasn't noticed. But when I look up at him he's grinning at me, his eyes twinkling with mirth and I can't help but let out an embarrassed giggle.

'I like it. You can tell she's worked hard on it and loves this place. I can see you working here too, bet you'd look cute in one of those incredibly stylish little apron things,' he jokes, nodding at one of the waitresses as she walks past with her pink apron tied around her waist. They're not exactly on trend, she's from the back kitchen, that's not waiting staff uniform, but I don't tell him that.

I grin, feeling my face flush at the word cute. 'It pays the bills, what ya gonna do,' I reply, shrugging. 'Plus, free drinks are always a winner.'

He picks up his drink and looks at it. 'Time to test if this really is better than Costa like you bragged…'

I throw a confident smirk and watch his face as he first swirls it gently before smelling it like it's a fancy wine, then finally taking a taste. I burst out laughing when he comes away with cream on his lip. He doesn't bother to wipe it away as he says, 'It's not bad.' His eyes crinkle at the edges with laughter in such a way that it makes the hair on my scalp prickle. He picks up a napkin, swiping at his mouth, laughing along with me. 'Hey, did you give people-watching a try? Changed your mind about it yet?'

I pick up my spoon, deciding it would be safer to

eat some of the cream and stir the rest in so I don't have another mishap. 'No, and I told you, it's not a hobby.'

He rolls his eyes and, without warning, shifts over to the seat next to his, before motioning for me to move next to him. 'Seriously, you'll love it if you try. Come and sit here and I'll show you the joys.' He pats the chair gently, his eyebrows waggling in challenge. I look around quickly. My seat faces the wall, I can't really see anyone without it being obvious.

I gulp, my stomach dancing because of the flirty grin he's shooting me. When I push my drink across to the new seat and stand up, his grin widens and he turns in his seat slightly, his arm draping across the back of the empty chair.

As I sink down into the chair, his leg brushes against mine and he's close, oh so close, that I can barely stand it. From the corner of my eye I catch sight of Lorna, she's serving and grinning in my direction with barely concealed excitement. As our eyes meet she winks at me, giving me a discreet thumbs-up. My whole face burns and I drag my eyes away, focusing just on my drink and nothing else. Definitely not the fact that Charlie's arm is across the back of my chair still and there's a slight pressure and warmth of it across my shoulders. No, I absolutely do not allow myself to think about that.

Charlie leans in close, so close I can smell the sweet hot chocolate on his breath as he whispers conspiratorially. 'So, what do you think they're talking about?' He motions with his chin towards a couple a few tables away. They're in their mid-forties, the woman's shoulders are hunched, her arms folded tightly across her chest, there's a deep frown on her forehead and the guy is leaning in close as he talks, waving his hands a lot. Neither of them are paying any attention to their coffees or cake.

'I thought you were supposed to be giving me a lesson,' I tease.

He laughs, the sound of it rumbling gently in his chest makes me catch my breath. 'He's just broken off their affair, she's his wife's best friend. He thought he should break it to her in a public place so she wouldn't make a scene. He's also hoping to bribe her not to tell his wife by buying her a slice of cake. She's having none of it.'

I snort a laugh as the man reaches for the woman's hand and she snatches it away as if confirming Charlie's guess. 'Well, I tell you something for nothing, she's extremely peeved so I don't think the cake is going to help.'

We both laugh at that and he moves on, pointing the end of his spoon at another table. This one has a girl in her twenties and an older guy with grey hair. 'Your turn, what about them. What's their story?'

I tilt my head, considering as I look them over. The girl has a large messenger-style bag hanging over the back of her seat, the corner of a book sticks out – it's a philosophy book. I decide then that she's a student, and her clothes and shoes would go along with my observation. The two are engaged in some intense conversation, the girl fiddles with the top button of her shirt. 'She's a philosophy student who's got behind on her paper, he's her professor. She's offering sexual favours in exchange for an extension,' I guess.

Charlie pulls away, his eyebrows raised as he nods his head at me, clearly impressed. 'Not bad for a first try.'

The whole time we've been talking, Charlie hasn't moved his arm from the back of my chair, filling my body with anticipation and pleasure. If I were brave enough, I would lean back into it and it would almost be like he has his arm around me. But of course, I'm not brave enough.

'OK, I admit, people watching is more fun than I thought it would be. So this is how you spend all your time, is it? Or do you have anything else that you're into?'

He purses his lips and thinks about it for a couple of seconds. 'I like to walk my dog. His name's Sampson. I used to take him to the woods a lot at the weekends. I haven't done it for a long time, though, I miss it.'

He seems almost sad when he says it and now my interest is piqued. 'Why don't you go anymore?'

His breath catches and he blinks a couple of times, seeming like he's said something wrong and is now backtracking. 'I just haven't had time, that's all.' He coughs, moving his arm from my chair and picking up his drink. I immediately think I've said something wrong. Had I misread what he'd said, did he say he *has* a dog or *had* a dog? Had I misread the tense he spoke in and upset him? I open my mouth to apologise, just in case, but he gets there first. 'Say, if you have any free time this weekend, maybe we could go together? Maybe Sunday morning before you go visit your nan?'

It's my turn to blink now, my mouth opens and closes as I struggle for something to say.

His head tilts to one side, a playful smirk on his face. 'Or are you worried me and Sampson might mug and murder you if you're alone in the woods with us?'

That breaks the tension and I laugh, dropping my eyes to the table as I nod. 'I think I could take you; I'd be fine.'

He laughs, a loud barking laugh that sends tingles down my spine. 'Nothing surprises me about you, so you probably could. So, Sunday then?'

I smile and nod, just once. 'Yes.' *Absolutely yes.*

CHAPTER SIXTEEN
~ RYDER ~

Sunday morning I'm camped outside Charlie's house, I've been here almost all night just making sure he doesn't go anywhere. If he does, I don't know what I'll do because I can't exactly change his plans. But no one arranges something for Sunday morning, people sleep in and that's all, surely? I know that's what always happened for me and my brothers. Lazy Sundays. We never used to even dress until my mum called us down for the traditional roast dinner. At the thought of them I get a pang of longing so powerful it makes my insides ache. I miss my family and friends so much; it's been so long since I've visited them and checked to make sure they're OK.

General rule of thumb, I try to stay away mostly; it's too hard to be around them, seeing them getting on with their lives without me – or not as the case actually is.

Truth was, sometimes death brings people closer,

sometimes it rips them apart. My family went for the second option. My parents blindly resented each other, each blaming the other for their part in my death: 'you booked the trip'; 'you wanted to sit the kids at the back of the boat'; 'you chose the route'. Their screaming matches lasted for about a year. After that they barely even spoke or looked at each other for almost another year before they finally called it quits and divorced. Trouble was, the damage was done. My brothers, caught in the middle of all that hate and grief, changed irrevocably. My older brother sank into depression, flunked out of university and currently smokes weed by the bucketload. My younger brother couldn't stand to live in such a toxic environment any longer and left home when he was eighteen. Last I heard, he was working in a bar in Bangkok. My death destroyed them all, one way or another. That was why I couldn't stand seeing them. They were different people from the ones I remembered, their easy smiles and happy laughter replaced by blame, sorrow and anger. The guilt of that was crushing, and I couldn't stand seeing it. So I moved on. It was the right decision for me, for my already fragile and broken mind. Not long after that I met Jade, so things brightened a little for me. I check in on them every once a while, but I never stay too long. It's too painful.

I shake my head and push thoughts of my family away. It's 8am. I push off the wall I've been sitting on and make my way up the path to Charlie's house, holding my breath as I breeze through the UPVC door and take a look around. In the kitchen I can hear his parents chatting and sounds of a kettle boiling. As I stand there, their black Labrador comes sauntering lazily out of the kitchen. He stops abruptly, his ears pricking and his tail no longer wagging as he looks in my direction, sensing but not seeing me. I can feel his unease, so I quickly make my way up the stairs leaving the dog staring at the place I just vacated, his posture still stiff.

I know where Charlie's room is. I've been in this house a couple of times now. After I vowed to be better at where I left his body so he didn't get suspicious of the time loss, I brought him home a few times and laid him on his bed so when he came to he'd just assume he'd been asleep. It worked for the most part, at least he didn't look as suspicious when I left his body as he did that time in the school corridor.

I don't even bother waking him, instead I silently slip into his body, scrunching my eyes shut until the sensation is over. When I finally open them, my heavy body is tired and even more uncoordinated than usual. I struggle to put on some clothes and styling Charlie's thick, long hair into something resembling his usual style is near on impossible so I just do my best and hope that the wind will cover it up.

Heading downstairs, the dog is still in the hallway but now he's lying on the doormat half asleep. As I reach the bottom step I smile and reach out a hand to him. At first his tail wags enthusiastically and he rolls onto his back so I can scratch his belly but, as my hand gets closer he suddenly flips back over, shrinking away from me, a little whine coming from his throat.

'It's OK, boy,' I say in Charlie's voice.

The dog is wary of me and tentatively sniffs the hand I hold out, his ears plastered to his head, and the little whine comes again. He knows something is wrong with his master, but he doesn't know what. I had never realised dogs were so intuitive.

'It's OK,' I say again. I allow him to sniff my knee and my arm, and then he sits up and sniffs my face, finally looking more at ease. He's still wary, but less frightened now. Like he's just telling himself that he's imagining the change in his friend. I let out a happy sigh as my fingers rake through his fur, marvelling over how soft and warm he is. His dog breath makes me chuckle as he lands a couple of well-placed licks on my cheek and jaw. I'm instantly reminded of my old dog, Sampson – he was a licker too. When I was alive, my best friend Ben and I used to walk my dog all the time, I didn't realise how much I missed it until now. Another bout of longing and homesickness washes over me, so I quickly push the thoughts away and focus on today's task.

I stand, looking around for a lead hanging in the hallway, but there's nothing. Gritting my teeth, I know I need to bite the bullet and ask for it. *I hope Charlie's parents aren't as intuitive as their dog is!*

'Wow, good morning. Has hell frozen over?' his mum asks, grinning over the rim of her coffee cup as I walk into the kitchen.

'Huh?' I reply, faking a yawn so I don't have to look at her.

She grins. 'I don't think I've seen you up this early on a weekend since you were about six.'

Charlie's dad looks up from his newspaper. 'Did you crap the bed or something?' he jokes, which makes his wife laugh and nudge his arm playfully.

I shrug, shoving my hands in my pockets. 'I couldn't sleep, I figured I'd take…' *Oh man, I don't even know the dog's name!* I scramble for a word that will suffice, '…dog face for a long walk.' I nod towards the Labrador who followed me in to the kitchen. 'I've just called and arranged to meet Justine. We're going to go walk him in the woods.'

Charlie's dad snorts. 'Justine is going to walk in the woods? What about all the dirt and leaves, won't it mess up her pretty shoes?' He chuckles at his own joke and this earns him another nudge from his wife, this one a little less playful and a little more 'shut up'.

'Oh, that'll be nice,' Charlie's mum says. 'Much better than sitting in your room playing your video games all day. And Bruno could certainly use the exercise, the vet told me he needs to lose some weight.' She turns and catches Charlie's dad as he slips the dog a small toast crust. 'Oi! That's exactly why he's overweight. Stop giving him human food!' she scolds.

I force a lazy smile, leaning on the edge of the kitchen worktop. 'Can you pass me his lead, please?' I ask casually. I can't exactly go hunting for it and I'm sure Charlie knows his way around his own kitchen.

A frown lines his mother's forehead. 'Pass it to you? It's in the cupboard right next to you!'

'Ah, sorry, I'm still half asleep, I think,' I lie. Taking a hopeful guess, I open the wall cupboard that is the closest to me and bingo! I pull out dog lead and poo bags.

She rolls her eyes and shakes her head, going to the kettle and flicking the switch again. 'Do you want breakfast before you go? Coffee to wake you up?'

'No thanks. I'm supposed to meet Justine soon.'

She tsks and, like all mothers do, fusses. 'Well, at least take some toast. You'll be starving otherwise.' She pushes her own freshly made, buttered toast towards me. 'Oh, and I don't know how long you'll be gone, but remember Dad and I are going to be out most of the day, then we have that show tonight at the theatre, so you probably won't see us. Make sure you take your key, all right?'

I nod, grateful that I'll be able to bring Charlie back here and put him back to bed once Maggie and I go our separate ways later.

'OK. Have a great time.' I pick up the toast, taking a big bite as I wave and leave the kitchen. The taste of it assaults me. Taste. It's incredible. This is the second thing I've tasted in five years – the first being the hot chocolate on Friday – and it's unbelievable. I miss eating and drinking; I miss flavours and warmth and touch; I miss the wind blowing in my face and the smells of coffee and wet leaves. I miss everything, but mostly I miss interacting with my parents the way I just interacted with Charlie's. Something so insignificant, you just take it for granted. It almost floors me.

The dog sidles up next to me, seeing his lead, his tail wagging in that lazy way Labs have about them.

I clip on his lead, then slip on Charlie's shoes and coat that'd I've seen him wearing before, patting the pockets and hearing the satisfying jingle of keys in the pocket before Bruno and I head out.

Before I close the door I call out, 'Bye.'

And the chorus of 'Bye!' called back from the kitchen makes my heart ache all over again.

Bruno is great on the short bus trip, but now as we stand at the entrance to the woods, he's getting a little restless. We're early. I'd agreed to meet Maggie at 9.30 and it's only quarter past. Bruno's obviously keen to explore because he hasn't stopped sniffing.

Then suddenly, she's walking up the hill towards us, bundled up in her too-large coat, her hands stuffed in her pockets as she walks with her head down. When she looks up and sees me her frown turns into a smile and my insides clench. I'll never get used to the fact that she's smiling at me. Me. Ryder Edmonds, the dead guy who's been fawning over her in secret for well over three months now.

'Hi,' we say in unison as she gets to us.

'Jinx,' she says, then we both laugh before she leans down and reaches out a hand to the dog. He gives her a cursory sniff to check she's not dangerous, then his tail wags as he licks her fingers. Grinning, she squats down so she can give him a real stroke as he attempts to lick her face.

'I thought you said his same was Sampson?'

My eyes widen as I see her looking at his name tag hanging from his collar. *Shit. Think fast.* 'Well, his real name is Sampson. We rescued him when he was just a couple of years old, he'd been abused, and my mum wanted to give him a fresh start, so we renamed him Bruno.'

Her eyebrows knit together and her lips purse as she talks to the dog, 'Aww, poor baby. I think Bruno suits you much better. Frank Bruno was a fighter, and I think you are too, aren't you?' She gives him a scratch behind the ears. Just like that, he's putty in her hands.

I breathe a sigh of relief. This whole thing had been a slip of the tongue on my part on Friday. Sampson had been *my* dog, and we *did* used to go for walks in the woods at the weekends, that wasn't a lie. It was only by chance that I remembered Charlie had a dog, too, so could suggest this semi-date.

She stands and we automatically step onto the trail that leads into the woods, Bruno at the end of his lead, nose to the ground, tail wagging lazily from side to side. I grin, feeling the early-morning sunshine on my face and the cool chill of the October wind against my cheeks. For a moment, I forget everything: forget I'm dead, forget I've stolen this teenage boy's body, forget the last five years passed in a blur of hospital visits and endless nights by the river with Jade. I'm transported back to being myself again, a dog lead in my hand, birds chirping in the trees, leaves crunching underfoot. It's my idea of paradise.

Maggie clears her throat and I blink a couple of times, coming back to myself as I look over at her. 'I must admit, I wasn't sure if you were going to be here,' she says suddenly.

'Why's that?'

She shrugs one shoulder, fiddling with the button of her coat like she does when she's nervous. 'I guess you just blow hot and cold a bit. I wasn't sure if you were going to turn up or not.' She looks at the floor as she says it, and her cheeks are red as she deliberately kicks her feet in the dry leaves as we walk. 'Like, at school you don't even look at me, but then when no one's around you talk to me and arrange to walk in the woods.'

I gulp. Hating that she'd noticed the differences between Charlie and me. But how could she not, I guess. I've been there when she'd tried to interact with Charlie on several occasions and he's rudely and flat out ignored her. He seems to lack the basic empathy and people skills even to return a cursory smile. I knew she would be thinking about it. I'd recovered enough from possessing Charlie on Thursday to get to the nursing home to catch the end of her visit with her nan. I knew they'd been talking about Charlie and her nan had, quite rightly, pointed out the obvious that Maggie was clearly trying to ignore.

'It's just that it's hard at school, you know?' I wince, wishing I could just explain, that I could tell her the real, ugly truth and make her understand and not freak out or think I've escaped from the funny farm, as my mum used to say. 'I'm older than you are, it's like an unwritten rule that sixth formers don't interact with the younger students. People would get weird about it.'

She nods, chewing on her lip and I know I need to say something else.

'Besides,' I add truthfully, 'I like getting to know you without any interference or judgement from anyone else, it means we can be ourselves. I don't get to do that with many people. I like the fact that we have a secret.'

This hits the spot and I see a small smile and the tenseness in her shoulders loosens. She looks up and catches my eye, and I have to fight with all my might to resist reaching out and touching the loose curl that brushes against her cheek.

'I like that we have a secret too,' she admits.

Our eyes lock and I feel an almost desperate need to lean in and press my lips against hers, just once, so I could savour the feel of it for all of eternity.

Just then Bruno barks at a bird bringing us both back to the moment. I smile and we carry on walking, talking easily, enjoying the morning before we have to part ways.

CHAPTER SEVENTEEN
~ RYDER ~

Today is Halloween. Jade's favourite night of the year. As per our annual tradition, we're out on the streets, watching the little kids trick or treat, dressed to the nines in their scary outfits, completely unaware that two real 'ghosts' are watching their every move.

We judge costumes, heckling the bad ones that haven't bothered to put in an effort (usually older teens who decided to try their luck one last time and get some free chocolate!) We check out who's giving the best sweets, who's made the best display outside their house, who's closed their curtains and turned off the lights because they can't be bothered to keep getting up to answer the door.

Above all else, we cause a little havoc – well, Jade does anyway, I just sidekick along giving her moral support and laughing at the shocked reactions of passers-by.

Jade is much more proficient at being a wanderer

than I am. She's been doing it longer and has managed to master the art of being a poltergeist. If she really tries hard enough, she can move things, break things, push things over. It's the perfect pastime for a spooky Halloween night for two kids that have nothing better to go with their time.

We're wandering around the dimly lit streets. Jade is making people jump occasionally by skittering a rock across the road or making the trees rattle as they pass.

We're following behind two pre-teen boys. They'd caught Jade's eye because one of them is dressed as Owen Grady from *Jurassic World*, complete with leather waistcoat and homemade cardboard knife, and the other is in an inflatable dinosaur outfit. They look pretty epic. *Jurassic Park* happens to be Jade's favourite.

As the two boys knock on another door, I hear a loud screech and then group laughter from down the road. I frown into the darkness, and just as they pass under a streetlight, I realise it's Justine making all the noise. She's with three other girls, Charlie, and his two goon friends from school. They're walking around, a bottle of nasty-looking wine in their hands, laughing, bumping each other and generally being louder than necessary.

Jade comes to stand next to me. 'Oh, watch out, the morons are about,' she says, rolling her eyes. 'Why do girls get so loud when they drink, anyway? One bottle between the lot of them? She's faking it for attention.' She makes a scoffing sound and shakes her head in disapproval.

I nod along in agreement, watching Charlie watch her with that glint in his eye that says he's enjoying the show as she saunters off ahead in her Harley Quinn tiny short-shorts. He's dressed as The Joker, obviously.

'Remember I told you I possessed a guy to save Maggie?' I ask, watching as Jade nods a yes. 'That's him, blond dude, Joker face paint.' I motion to the group with my chin.

'Ah, the douchebag. I remember you said he was a bit of a twat, now I see what you mean.' We watch as Charlie shoves one of his friends into a bush, and finds it hilarious when it obviously hurts him. 'Let me guess, Harley is his girlfriend, am I right?'

'Bingo.'

Just then Justine looks over at us before a devilish grin crosses her face and she pulls a package from her bag. Her group is grinning and whooping now, and then shushing each other noisily as they laugh hysterically. Jade and I both frown, trying to see

190

what's in her hands. But then, too late, we see. It's a box of eggs.

In an instant, I know what's going to happen. I look back at the *Jurassic* pair, my eyes widening, they're putting away their latest spoils as the door closes behind them. But we don't even have time to work out a way of warning them before the eggs fly over, four of them, one after the other. The first misses target, smashing at the dinosaur's feet, he looks down at it, confused, before another whizzes over and smacks him in the shoulder. As they figure out what's happening and turn to hide their faces, their backs are spattered with another eggy missile, ruining their epic outfits and sending their sweets all over the floor.

My fists clench and I glare at the group – it's Justine that's thrown the eggs, but the others are complicit, catcalling, cheering her on, clutching their stomachs laughing as she causes the destruction.

'Son of a…' I shout. At the same time Jade screams, 'You stupid idiots!'

Behind us the young boys are crying now, big fat tears rolling down their faces.

Justine and her group turn tail and run, their laughter echoing into the night like a pack of hyenas. Jade doesn't hesitate, she's running after them in an instant. I turn just long enough to make sure the boys are OK before hightailing it after her. They've only run into the next street, they're walking again now, slapping each other on the back in congratulations.

I fall in step next to Jade. I can feel the anger roiling off her in waves. 'What are we doing?' I ask, knowing there's physically nothing we can do about this.

She shrugs. 'Not sure yet. Payback.'

I raise one eyebrow but don't say anything. When Jade has made up her mind there's no changing it, so I don't even bother trying.

Finally, the group stops at the park. It's abandoned because of the time of night, so they have the place to themselves. Justine and her girlfriends perch on the swings. They're still laughing over the egging – and it turns out the boys weren't their first victims. Charlie and his friends are off to one side, talking in whispers.

Jade and I watch, and then her face brightens as she notices the girls have dumped their bags at the edge of the park. After checking no one is looking in her direction, Jade discreetly pulls open the bag and begins to rummage through it, grinning up at me as she finds her prize.

The egg box.

It's a box of twelve and I pump the air in

celebration as she lifts the lid to reveal there's three eggs left. Jade is full on laughing now; it's an evil chuckle that makes me laugh too.

Instead of just throwing them like I had predicted, Jade walks over to the group of boys, setting the now empty egg box down near Charlie's feet before she looks over at me and winks.

Her first throw hits like a pro darts player aiming for treble twenty. It smacks Justine square in the chest, splattering up her neck and into her hair. She barely has time to react before the next one is hitting her on her bare leg, the egg running down in a gooey, gloopy mess. Instead of throwing the third, Jade puts it back into the box quickly and then steps back, folding her arms over her chest, watching the rest of the scene unfold like a proud parent at a school play.

The other girls have jumped up, attempting to stem their laughter as they rally around Justine, showing support. The boys, though, they've lost it. One of them is bent double he's laughing so hard.

Justine wipes a handful of the gloop off, flicking it onto the grass, shaking her head in disbelief as she looks down at herself, and then in the direction the eggs came from – the boys' direction.

And then she goes absolutely crazy, screaming abuse. She's already put two and two together and come up with twenty-one because she's storming over to Charlie who is laughing but who also looks a bit bemused as she marches over with untamed fury evident on her face.

She slams her hands on his chest, shoving him backwards. 'What the hell did you do that for?'

'Me?' Charlie blurts, recoiling.

Before anyone sees it coming, Justine stoops, picks up the last egg and slaps it on the side of Charlie's head and then wipes her hand on his shoulder, leaving behind a slime trail and yolk dripping from the ends of his hair. 'How do you like it, huh? What an arsehole! Do you know how long it took me to get ready tonight? Ugh, you're so annoying, Charlie! I hate you! We're over!' she screams, then turns on her heel and leaves everyone standing there in shock, before more laughter erupts, most of it coming from Jade and me.

That's when we decide to call it a night. Payback is duly served, and neither of us can stop laughing and re-enacting the moment as we walk away and leave them to it.

Back in our usual evening hang-out, ten minutes later, Jade flops onto the bench by the river and lets out a huge sigh. 'What I wouldn't give to be taking home a big bag of sweets and tucking into them right now,' she muses, closing her eyes and sucking on her lips. 'Just one square of chocolate. I'd let it melt on my tongue and savour every second of it. Heaven.'

'Oh God, yeah. I couldn't believe the sweetness of that hot chocolate the other day, I couldn't even finish the whole thing. And the cream, oh my God, it was just too much,' I answer, thinking back to what I class as my first date with Maggie. 'I swear everything tastes even better after all this time, unless I've just forgotten how good food and drink was.'

Jade turns to me, her eyes narrowing. 'What?'

I gulp, realising what I've said and instantly knowing I've messed up.

Shit.

My mouth closes with an audible pop and her head tilts to one side, her eyes probing mine with such an intensity I feel as though I'm under interrogation.

When I don't speak, she frowns, unfolding her legs and straightening her back. 'What do you mean by "the other day"?'

I weigh my options, wondering if I could talk my way out of this. Dismiss it as a simple slip of the tongue, perhaps. Because I know she's not going to approve, hell, even *I* don't really approve deep down, but I don't want her to tell me the truth: that it's wrong, that it needs to stop, that I'm being selfish, that I'm messing with people's lives and that this is utterly ridiculous, this fantasy life I'm creating for myself using someone else's body.

But, looking into her eyes, the closest person I have to family, I know I can't lie to her any longer.

So instead I lay out the whole story. The whole sorry truth of my depravity laid bare. How, for well over two weeks now, I've been stealing someone's body almost daily, masquerading as them, carving out a relationship with the girl I've fallen for under false pretences.

As I speak, I see her body stiffen and her eyes harden, I see the disapproval and horror in her eyes.

I hold up a hand to placate her and halt the protests I can see are about to tumble from her lips. 'I've not been caught. I'm being so careful, I swear. I only ever take possession if he's alone. I'm not interrupting his school or any of his life plans. It's time he won't miss! He doesn't even know about it. I mean, sometimes it's only for like five minutes while I walk Maggie to the bus stop or chat to her at the end of school, so I just quickly take him back to where I found him and he's none the wiser. Or if it's a longer one I'll take him home and open his phone or lay him in bed or something. He doesn't even know anything happened. Stop looking at me like that!' I wince at her thunderous expression.

A storm is brewing in her eyes and I'm scared to be on the receiving end of it. 'Are you fucking kidding me right now?' She's put so much force behind the words that the ducks that are casually sleeping on the grass near our bench somehow sense it and jump up, waddling or flying off quickly as if they've sensed a predator nearby. 'Tell me this is a joke. Tell me you're not actually that bloody stupid, Ryder!'

My mouth opens and closes again, nothing coming out.

'This is insanity. This is sheer bloody insanity!' She stands and begins to pace in front of me.

'I love her,' I say, simply, as if that will explain away everything, make everything OK. 'I love the way she makes me feel alive. I love the way she talks to me and the way she smiles at me, I love the sound of her laugh. No one else even takes the time to make her laugh! What kind of life has she got, if it doesn't contain laughter?'

'I don't care that you love her! You're dead, Ryder. DEAD!' She rounds on me, poking her finger angrily into my chest on the last word. 'You don't get a second chance. You had yours and you died! You don't get your happily ever after with this girl. This,' she spits, waving her arms around us, 'is all you get. This is your ever after, and it may not be happy but that's tough shit, you have to make the best of it.'

'Well, maybe this isn't enough for me!' I snap, angry now too. *What about my feelings, what about what I want? Why can't she just be on my side for once?* 'Maybe I need something else, someone else.'

She recoils like I've slapped her. 'Someone else? As in, anyone but me?'

'Oh, stop it, you're behaving like a jealous girlfriend. It's not a good look.' As soon as I say it, I regret it. I know this isn't coming from jealousy, Jade is just telling me what's right and wrong, but I just don't – or can't – hear it.

She shakes her head, her eyes flashing with both hurt and anger. 'Maggie deserves her happily ever after, and this guy, regardless of whether he's a prat, deserves his. And you're messing with both of them for your own gain and no one else's. All this "no one makes her laugh" nonsense is bullshit! So she's going through a tough time, so bloody what? People go through stuff all the time but that doesn't mean you get to step in and be the one who sorts it out. Have you even thought this through? What if she falls in love with you, too? What then, idiot? She's gonna live her life being in love with someone she can never have. You're going to break her heart. And where does this all leave the pretty blond dude? He's an absolute arsehole, but he doesn't deserve this. What about him losing whole chunks of his life for this. You think that's OK?'

I shake my head, trying not let her words enter the fortress of denial I've built around this whole situation. 'It's not ideal,' I reply.

She almost chokes on her scorn as she recoils. 'Not ideal?' she repeats incredulously. 'This is so wrong, Ryder. I can't believe you can't see this. I can't believe you're trying to make this sound normal. What you're doing is beyond madness. I honestly never knew you could be so selfish. I've known you for years and I've never once seen this irresponsible, selfish side of you. I don't like it at all.' She shakes her head, her shoulders slumping. She's past her anger now, and what's left behind is even worse. It's disappointment. And it cuts me like a knife to the heart.

'Maybe you don't know me at all then,' I force out, my voice cracking with emotion.

She sniffs, reaching up to swipe at her face, at tears that I put there. 'You're right, maybe I don't.' Her voice is almost a whisper as she turns on her heel

and marches off into the night, leaving me staring at
her back, my heart aching in my chest.

CHAPTER EIGHTEEN
~ RYDER ~

'Two hot dogs, please. One with onions, one without,' I order, smiling politely at the pop-up stall holder, pulling out Charlie's wallet, grateful that he always seems to have an endless supply of money in there, handing over a five-pound note.

Maggie shifts on her feet beside me, leaning over to pick up some extra napkins from the dispenser. 'So are you a ketchup or a mustard kind of a guy?' she asks, regarding me seriously.

'Ketchup. I can't stand mustard. I even have to ask for it to be taken out of my McDonalds,' I reply, scrunching my nose. 'You?'

'Ketchup.' She nods, reaching for her hotdog as the guy holds out the one with no onions. 'Thank you.'

I smile and take mine and we turn and begin walking down the road, back in the direction of her house. Today was a non-Nan-visit day so we'd walked around for a bit just talking, when I smelled the food. It was calling to me and I was unable to resist. Food, the temptation of tasting it, was too strong to resist.

I groan in pleasure as I take the first bite, revelling in the fatty, ketchuppy, oniony, sausagy goodness.

As I chew, my mind flips back to Jade. I hadn't seen hide nor hair of her since she talked about chocolate and I opened my big fat mouth and ruined everything. I hate that we argued. Jade is like family to me, and the thought of her out there now, annoyed with me and alone, feels like being punched in the gut repeatedly. I was out of order. I said some truly horrible things to her. I made her cry. It was her disappointment and tears that hurt me the most. My mind constantly spins back to it, replaying the argument in my head as I agonise over everything I'd said.

For the last three days I'd spent every spare moment I had searching for Jade, checking all the places I knew she liked to go to when we went our separate ways, but I hadn't been able to find her. I missed her more than I even knew possible. Of course, it hadn't stopped me from stealing Charlie's body again and interacting with Maggie. In fact, being so lonely without Jade made these little stolen moments with Maggie even more valuable to me. It was like Catch 22. Jade was right, I knew she was right. I shouldn't keep doing this: it isn't fair on Charlie, and it isn't fair on Maggie who is being swept along in this deception, too. The trouble is, being near Maggie is the only good thing I have going for me in my pathetic half-life/non-existence. Nothing else comes close. My desire to be near her trumps everything – even my moral compass. Jade was right, it *did* have to stop, and one way or another it would. But not yet. I couldn't lose Maggie yet. I wasn't ready.

As we walk past a shop with a sign announcing a three-for-two offer on fireworks, Maggie smiles. 'Guy Fawkes night soon. Do you like fireworks?' she asks, snapping me out of my sombre thoughts of my best friend.

I shrug, taking another bite. 'I do now, but when I was younger I was scared of them.'

One of her eyebrows rise at that. 'Really? Why's that? The noise?'

'I think it has something to do with my dad. He loved them, so every year he used to go totally overboard, buying loads of fireworks, and then he'd do his own mini display at the end of our garden. My brothers and I used to hide in the house, behind the patio doors and watch as he lit one at the end of the garden then ran away from it. I guess seeing my dad run from something taught me to be afraid. Then, one time, when I was about six, my older brother thought it would be funny to open the door when the Catherine wheel was going off and shove me outside. I was nowhere near it, our garden back then was big, but it frightened the crap out of me. I hated my brother that day. When I got back inside, I punched him so hard in the arm he had a fist-sized bruise for days.' I smile as a wave of nostalgia hits me. What I wouldn't give to go back to that moment again, that easy time when we all were happy. I swallow my emotion, noting Maggie watching me carefully. 'For years after that I wouldn't even hold sparklers. I guess I was a bit of a wimp. I like them now though.'

Maggie nods along, chewing more daintily on her hotdog. 'You've moved since then?'

'Huh?' I mumble, trying to swallow my last too-large bite and wipe the grease off my fingers with the napkin.

'You said you had a big garden back then, meaning you don't now.'

Oops, another slip of the tongue. I smile at how perceptive she is, how much she really listens to everything I say. It's adorable.

Suddenly I have the crazy idea I want to tell her

the truth. Talking about my real life, my real childhood, gives me the urge to blurt it all out, reveal everything about what I'd been doing with her for the last couple of weeks and see what happened. Would she believe me? How do you even start something like that? Would that also satisfy Jade and her 'you're not being fair to her' mentality?

I gulp, swallowing my stupid idea. It was ridiculous: there was no way to start, same as there was no way to explain. 'Yeah, we've moved since,' I lie. 'What about you, do you like fireworks?'

She smiles, but somehow I can sense there some sadness behind it. 'I love them. They remind me of my mum. When I was a kid, me and my mum would go to a big display every year, we'd get toffee apples and sparklers. It's one of the clearest memories I have of her.' She sighs wistfully and it makes my heart ache.

'What happened to your mum?' It's something I've always wanted to know. Her head jumps up, her eyes widen and I immediately realise I'm butting my nose in where it doesn't belong. 'Sorry, that was insensitive of me. I shouldn't have asked.'

Her mouth pulls into a tight smile as her shoulders slump a bit. 'No, no, it's OK. I just haven't spoken about her for ages. It was a long time ago now. She died of cervical cancer when I was eight. The disease progressed pretty rapidly so she wasn't suffering too long, thankfully. I was young when she was diagnosed so I don't have too many sharp memories of her now, just foggy ones. But she loved fireworks night, I definitely remember that.' I can hear the pain in her words. 'After that I went to live with my nan.' A frown lines her forehead as she starts picking at bits of her hotdog, scattering breadcrumbs on the floor like she's afraid she's going to get lost.

'That's rough, I'm sorry.' I hate that she's been through so much loss, I can't imagine how hard that had been on her, and after all that now she's in foster care. No wonder she's so shy and lonely, she has no one.

She lets out a small laugh. 'It's not your fault,' she jokes, playfully.

I smile down at the floor and as we pass a bin she tosses the rest of her food. 'No dad around then?' I query, pushing my luck, hoping she'll answer. Another of my burning questions ticked off the list.

She shakes her head. 'Nope. He was never around. I saw a picture of him once, though. He was a ginger, too.'

I smile and nod. Silence falls over us as we both contemplate what she'd said. I want to comfort her, but I don't know how. Suddenly it springs to mind.

'Spend bonfire night with me.'

She looks up, shooting me a puzzled look. 'Huh?'

I nod, my idea growing in my head along with my excitement as I think about the banner I'd walked past near her school. She said she loved fireworks night and it reminded her of her mum. Well, that I could help with! 'There's a display in Fitzmaurice Park, on the 5th, gates open at 5pm, they have some fairground rides and food. We could go?' That was two days away. Another semi-date.

Her answering smile dazzles me and pierces my heart. 'Sure.' She's flipped a one eighty and gone from sad to incredibly happy. 'I'd love to.'

I nod, extremely pleased with myself. Our eyes meet and the air seems to thicken as something passes between us that makes my insides fizz. I'm suddenly very aware of how close she is to me, how the material of her coat scratches against the back of my hand at my side as we walk. It's not close enough. I long to be closer. My eyes drop down to her lips, wishing I could close the distance, feel her mouth pressed against mine even for the briefest of seconds. Her teeth sink into her bottom lip and she looks away, embarrassed.

Suddenly she gasps and grips my upper arm tightly. 'Look out!'

But it's too late. I'm not watching where I'm going and I step in a huge pile of dog poo someone hasn't cleaned up on the pavement. I groan and jump back as Maggie bursts out laughing, her eyes twinkling and crinkling at the edges.

The nice moment has passed, all romantic and kissing thoughts evaporate in the matter of a split second.

Her nose scrunches as she reaches up to cover her mouth with one hand. 'Eww, it's usually me doing stuff like that,' she tells me, giggling as I step onto the grass and begin wiping my shoe roughly, glad they're not my shoes to clean later. Her laughing is infectious and before we know it, we're both snickering as we walk along, her bumping my shoulder playfully, her cheeks flushed from laughing so hard.

And I realise, even stepping in shit is worth it to see her so happy. I have it so bad.

CHAPTER NINETEEN
~ RYDER ~

As I approach the river, I see Jade's outline on our bench and I breathe a sigh of relief. It's now been five days since I've seen her. I knew I'd missed her, but I didn't realise how much I until I see her sitting there. The sight of her on the bench, illuminated in the glow of the streetlight, is enough to make my shoulders loosen.

Stuffing my hands into my pockets, I head over. 'Hi,' I say cautiously, still bracing for another fight, but hoping that her being here means she's ready to call a truce.

'Hey.' She doesn't look at me as she speaks, but she does scoot over, allowing enough room for me to sit next to her.

I smile and take the proffered seat gratefully. 'How've you been? Long time, no see.' I bump her shoulder with mine and stare out over the river, hoping the last of the tension will defuse between us. I hate it when we fight.

She shrugs, her eyes trained on a swan asleep a few feet away. 'OK. Old Mr Bennington died,' she answers.

So she's not going to mention the fight. Maybe I shouldn't either… 'Oh really? How was that?' I turn to look at her.

She nods, a small sad smile playing on the corner of her lips. 'It was good. He saw me and was still fully conscious for about thirty seconds before he passed over.' Her face brightens as she speaks, and she finally meets my eyes. I can see how much that acknowledgment from a living person means to her. I don't think it ever meant as much to me, but Jade thrives on it. I now live for Maggie, as Jade lives for someone, anyone, to notice and acknowledge her.

'Nice,' I say, smiling back. 'Is that where you've been? I've missed you.'

'I missed you too.' She frowns and starts picking at her nails again. 'Yeah, I was hanging there and a few other places. I um … thought we could just use a break for a bit. I don't like arguing with you and I knew we'd just carry on fighting if we didn't have a break. Plus, I couldn't stand another of those "I love her" outbursts. You're no fun when you act like a lovesick puppy.'

Guilt and shame burn in my chest. I decide then

it's time we cleared the air. Jade was the only person who really knew me, so I couldn't lose her. 'Listen, I'm sorry. I didn't mean half the things I said. It was just spur of the moment.'

Her teeth sink into her bottom lip and there's silence for a couple of beats before she nods. 'I'm sorry, too. I was pushy and didn't think about how it made you feel. I shouldn't have been so blunt about it.'

'I should be used to it, you've always been blunt,' I mutter, frowning down at my plimsoles.

She shrugs again, turning in her seat to face me. 'So, have you finally seen sense? Are you stopping now? You realise yet how bonkers this whole situation is?'

Swallowing, I try to keep my frown in check. 'It's not bonkers. Well, it doesn't feel it to me.'

One of her eyebrows raise as she looks at me incredulously. 'It's totally batshit crazy and you know it. Have you been using this Charlie's body again the last few days?' She leans back and waits for my answer, her tongue sucking over her teeth.

I gulp and raise one shoulder. 'A few times, yeah.' Admitting it and seeing the disapproval in Jade's eyes makes my guilt at the whole situation rise again. When I'm with Maggie I can justify my actions, but when she isn't there and I really sit and think about it I realise how absurd it is. I'm a ghost, I possess another guy's body so I can talk to the girl I'm in love with, but she has no idea I'm not who she thinks I am. Yep, definitely batshit when you think about it – that was why I didn't allow myself to dwell on it.

'A few times,' Jade repeats. 'How much time has this poor guy lost, Ryder?' Her tone is scathing and I flinch. When I don't answer, she continues, 'You know this needs to stop, right? Deep down, you know.' Her words are softer now, and she places a hand on my arm, squeezing gently.

I sigh and close my eyes. I know she's right, of course she's right. This can't go on forever. What did I hope to achieve from this in the long run? It couldn't be a permanent thing; I was just stringing out the inevitable. And the longer it went on, the more everyone would end up hurt. Including Maggie.

'I know,' I grumble, pained, as I fist my hands into my hair. I know Maggie is growing increasingly frustrated with Charlie blowing hot one minute and then ignoring her the next like he doesn't even know who she is. There has to be something else I can do, some other way around this rather than it ending completely, though. Can I even go back to the existence I had before this? It was never going to be enough now. I would always feel like I'd lost a part of my soul again. It would be like learning how to live as a wanderer all over again, starting from scratch.

'Maybe I could tell her the truth, tell her what I've been doing?' I offer, looking up at Jade hopefully. I haven't been able to dismiss the crazy idea I had a few days ago.

Jade scoffs in disbelief and eyes me like I've just suggested we push old people down the stairs for fun. 'Are you kidding? She'll think you ... no wait ... She'll think *Charlie* is insane! You can't tell her. People just don't believe in stuff like ghosts. You couldn't even begin to explain this to her; she would laugh right in your face and then suggest you see a psychiatrist.'

'But what other choice do I have?' I ask, willing her to come up with a better solution because the alternative – abandoning Maggie – is unbearable and unthinkable.

'Stop seeing her. Cold turkey, I told you before.' Jade says it flippantly, as if it's really that easy. She doesn't understand just how much it means to me seeing Maggie and having Maggie see me.

'I'm due to meet her in an hour. We're going to watch the fireworks together.'

Jade groans and shakes her head. 'There's no

other choice, Ryder. You're dead, she's not. That's all there is to it. Everything else is inconsequential. She has her life to live, you're just getting in the way and giving her false hopes of having this Charlie boy be interested in her. You're going to break her heart into a million pieces if you keep this up.' She looks at me sternly, the fire in her eyes telling me how much she really believes what she's saying.

The thought of breaking Maggie's heart is my undoing. I can't do this any longer. For her, I have to stop this no matter how much hurt and anguish it causes for me.

Jade smiles warmly. 'Listen, don't go tonight. Just cut off from her entirely. Come watch the fireworks with me instead.'

I imagine the disappointment on Maggie's face when Charlie doesn't turn up at the arranged time, her waiting for him fruitlessly, all dressed up with nowhere to go. She had been so excited when I'd suggested going to the display tonight. I know it means a lot to her because of her mother. I can't do that to her. 'I can't. I've already arranged it with her. I don't want to let her down.'

Jade punches me in the arm too hard to be playful. The frown on her face is stern as she speaks. 'Ryder, how let down do you think she's going to feel when she finds out the truth, or when Charlie suddenly stops seeing her? You need to stop this, Ryder, now! It's beyond obsessive.'

I let out a groan and nod. My eyes prickle with frustrated tears. My body feels like I have a lead weight on my chest as I slump back against the bench and cover my face with my hands. This would have to be the last time I used Charlie for my own personal gain. I would use tonight as my goodbye, tell Maggie I couldn't see her anymore, let her down gently. The thought of it was agony.

'You're right. Tonight has to be the last time. I won't do it anymore.' My voice breaks as I speak, the emotion of it escaping even though I try my best to keep it at bay.

Jade lets out a breath and runs her hands over her hair, smoothing it back into place. 'It's the right thing, Ryder. You're leading the poor girl on. She's probably falling in love with this guy right now, spending her lessons scribbling his name on her notebooks, fantasising about their first kiss.' Suddenly her eyes go wide. 'Wait, you've not kissed her, have you?'

'No!' I answer quickly, watching the tension leave her shoulders. *Not that I haven't thought about it…*

'Good. The first kiss shouldn't be fake like that. She doesn't deserve that. From what you've told me about her being a loner, it would probably be her first-ever kiss. That's the special one, the one you remember no matter how bad or clumsy it is, it's not to be taken by some stalker-ghost using someone else's body to cop a feel.'

I nod in agreement, but my mind is now stuck on wondering what Maggie's lips would feel like against mine.

I push myself to standing. 'I'm going to enjoy tonight and then tomorrow I'll tell her Charlie can't see her anymore.' Each word is like a punch to the gut, but there is no other choice.

CHAPTER TWENTY
~ RYDER ~

Outside Charlie's house, Jade's words reverberate in my head. This was the last time. It had to be. I sigh deeply. Tonight I would savour every second, commit it all to memory and then let Maggie go. It had to be done before I caused any irreparable damage. I just prayed I hadn't already.

I brace myself and pass through the double-glazed front door. Once I've verified Charlie's parents aren't home, I follow the sounds of music up to his bedroom and find him lying on his bed, eyes closed, foot tapping along to the beat.

This situation is perfect. I could bring him back to this spot and lay him down on his bed and he would just assume he'd fallen asleep ... no time loss involved. That would please Jade. I wouldn't even need to cancel the garden-party plans I knew he'd made with his friends. He would just not turn up and would have the legitimate excuse of falling asleep when anyone asked why he was a no-show.

Taking control of Charlie's body gets easier and easier each time. This time the transition is so smooth it's like sinking into a warm bath.

I don't bother to change Charlie's clothes, just spray some fresh deodorant and splash on some aftershave I find on his desk, before heading downstairs and grabbing his coat and scarf. I'm careful to lock the front door behind me as I step into the damp night air, my heart aching with every step because I know I'm that much closer to losing her.

Thankfully, I don't have to wait long before a bus arrives. I hop on, flashing Charlie's bus pass to the driver and spend the journey contemplating the end of mine and Maggie's so-called relationship.

I'm soon near to Maggie's house. As I wave a thanks to the bus driver and step off, nervous excitement builds in my chest, taking over the sadness that this is my last time with her. Walking towards her street, I vow not to spend the whole night wallowing, I refuse to let nostalgia ruin my last night with her, instead I decide to make it the best night ever, and to savour every last second of it.

It takes a few more minutes to get to her street and I stop, pulling back the sleeve of Charlie's sports coat to check the time on his expensive watch. It's ten minutes to five, I'm a little early but not too early that I have to wait so I head up the path to her house.

Almost as soon as I've knocked on the door, it swings open and a tall, overweight guy with brown hair stares over at me. Charlie is tall, we are almost the same height, but this guy's stature and girth makes me feel small. His stare is intimidating, his jaw is set tightly as his gaze slides over me from my head to my toes and back again.

This is Chris, the foster father I'd heard about. I swallow my nerves and politely hold out my hand. 'Hello, I'm here to collect Maggie. My name's Ry–' I catch my mistake and clear my throat quickly, 'Charlie.'

He grunts, his eyes searching mine as he puts his hand in mine and squeezes just that little bit too hard, making my fingers ache as my bones crush together uncomfortably. If a handshake could convey a message, this one would say you're-the-punk-that's-taking-out-my-daughter-and-I-already-don't-like-you.

'So you're taking Maggie to the fireworks?' he asks gruffly.

I nod, noticing he hasn't let go of my hand. 'Yes, sir.'

He glances behind me to the street and then back at me. 'You driving or what?'

'No, I came on the bus,' I answer, shying under his intense gaze.

Behind him, the door opens and Lorna pokes her head out. She sees me, takes in Chris's posture and the way he's blocking the door with his girth, and then shakes her head. 'Chris, leave the poor boy alone. You'll scare him off!' she scolds, setting her hand on Chris's shoulder and giving him a little tug.

Chris's eyes don't leave mine as he finally releases his grip. My hand throbs slightly and I drop it to my side.

'Come on in, Charlie. Maggie's almost ready,' Lorna says. Her tone is warm and soft – a million miles away from the icy stare her husband is shooting me.

I smile gratefully and watch as Lorna takes Chris's elbow and guides him inside, before beckoning me to follow. Holding my breath and praying Maggie really is almost ready so I don't have to make polite chit-chat with the parents, I step inside and shuck my shoes in the hall.

As I head into the living room, Chris and Lorna are having some sort of quiet, but fiery conversation. I stop just inside the door, feeling like I'm intruding, but then Chris turns to me, ignoring Lorna's warning glare. 'Listen, kid, you may have won over Lorna with your dimpled smile and manners, but you have a long way to go before you win me over. You take care of Maggie. She's not some plaything for you to use and then drop. She's a sweet and innocent girl, and I expect her to stay that way and be treated as such. Understand?' Chris's tone is warning, and we both know this is about sex. He thinks I'm going to take advantage of her.

Lorna gasps, her eyes wide as her hand shoots up to the side of her neck. 'Chris, seriously, stop embarrassing the kid!'

Chris's eyes don't leave mine as he shrugs one shoulder. 'Remember I was a seventeen-year-old boy once too. I know how you think, all raging hormones and fantasising about fucking. But believe me when I say you don't want to mess with this girl or else you'll have me to answer to. You keep your hands to yourself, got it?' He points one meaty finger at my face in warning.

'Got it.' I nod uneasily.

A squeaky step to the right makes everyone look up. Maggie is just walking down the stairs, a slight frown marring her beautiful face. Her fiery red curls bounce as she walks and almost hypnotise me. I long to bury my face into those curls and inhale her scent forever, I will never get enough of it. She's wearing a knee-length denim skirt with thick black tights underneath and an oversized jumper emblazoned with the slogan 'Okay, but Tom Holland though…' I swallow the wave of affection I feel for her.

How am I going to exist without talking to this girl ever again?

'What's going on down here?' she asks, looking from Chris to me and back again.

Chris smiles and shrugs his shoulders innocently as he replies, 'Nothing. Just getting to know Charlie. So, you guys are off to the recreation ground, huh? What time will you be home?'

Maggie looks to me again for confirmation and I try to force a smile that doesn't look too much like a grimace. Admitting that he just basically threatened me to keep my hands off her won't exactly curry me any favour with her foster dad, so I play along.

She seems to buy my act and she turns back to Chris and offers a small smile. 'Ten-thirty?'

His lips purse. 'Nine-thirty,' he counters.

One of her eyebrows rise. 'Ten?'

He rolls his eyes and nods. 'Fine, ten. But not a minute after.'

She smiles and takes the last couple of steps to my side, her cheeks colouring a cute shade of pink as our eyes meet. 'Hey,' she greets me quietly.

I feel the grin stretch across my face as her sickly-sweet orange Pez breath blows across my lips. I can almost taste it. 'Hey. You ready to go?'

She nods and turns to her foster parents who are watching us silently. 'See you at ten then. I have a key.'

'Have fun,' Lorna calls as we walk back into the small hallway.

'But not too much fun,' Chris adds quickly.

I flick a look over my shoulder in time to see a warning glare thrown in my direction just as Maggie closes the living-room door behind us, shutting us into the little entrance way. She smiles ruefully. 'I hope he didn't make you feel uncomfortable.'

I shrug and push my feet into Charlie's trainers. 'Nah, he was fine,' I lie, reaching for her coat and holding it out so she can push her arms through the holes, loving how my hands brush across her shoulders accidentally.

'So how was your day?' I ask as we make the short walk to the recreation ground. Maggie chats absent-mindedly, telling me about seeing her grandmother and how she bought her first Christmas present and I counter by lying about playing football with my friends.

By the time we get to the gate and I pay for our admission (ignoring Maggie's protests that she can pay) it's already hugely busy. Crowds of people swarm the stalls and the few fairground rides they've erected for the night.

'So, what shall we do first? We have about an hour before the fireworks start, I think,' Maggie says, checking her watch and then looking around, going on tiptoes in an attempt to see over people's heads. 'Want to get something to eat? I haven't had dinner and I'm starved.'

I nod quickly, stepping closer to her as a group of pre-teens bump into me from behind, laughing about something as they rush towards the bouncy castle. 'Sure, what'd you fancy?'

'They have jacket potatoes at that one.' She points to the longest queue I've ever seen in my life. 'Or if you prefer burgers or something—'

I cut her off quickly. 'Jacket potato is good if that's what you want.' She smiles happily and we join the end of the queue. 'You been to this display before?'

Shaking her head, she pulls up her coat collar and then pushes her hands into her pockets, ducking her head against the cold. 'No, last year me and my nan went to watch the fireworks at the castle.'

The queue moves slowly but we eventually get our food – jacket potatoes loaded with chilli and cheese, and a bag of sugared ring doughnuts to share

– and head off to one side to eat them where we won't be bumped by anyone. The food is amazing, though I'm not used to the amount of spice and struggle to finish the whole thing. The sugared doughnuts though: I could have easily eaten the whole bag myself.

When we're done, we both rule out the bigger fairground rides seeing as one of us might puke after eating. After walking around and seeing what's on offer, we have a couple of unsuccessful turns on the 'find the even number' raffle game. Maggie has a go on the coconut shy and then I spot a knockdown-the-cans stall.

'Oh, this one's my game!' I enthuse. Pulling out money, I step up confidently, a smug smile plastered on my face because back when I was alive I had a great throwing arm and it would be a piece of cake to win one of the stuffed animals hung on the sides of the stalls. 'You might as well pick out your prize now,' I tell Maggie, waggling my eyebrows as I'm handed three baseballs.

Maggie grins and shakes her head saying, 'You know, it's going to be really embarrassing for you now if you lose.'

'Lose? What is this *lose* that you speak of?' I joke, winking at her.

She and the lady running the stall laugh and watch as I roll my shoulders in readiness then get into position. Of course I've forgotten that this isn't *my* body; that isn't *my* throwing arm, it is Charlie's, and controlling it isn't exactly the easiest thing in the world.

The first ball flies through the air, hitting the back of the stall about three feet from where I'd been aiming. Maggie laughs and I glance at her, grinning sheepishly. 'OK, ignore that, that was a warm-up ball,' I joke, my confidence flailing now. The second ball is too short and hits the table the cans are stacked on and I wince, wishing I hadn't been so overconfident, when the lady running the stall shoots me a smug smile.

Maggie points at a fluffy duckling. 'Last ball, no pressure or anything, but I really have my heart set on that duck,' she jokes.

The third ball hits target but only one can falls. I grin sheepishly. 'OK, so I may have slightly overestimated my skills.' Without my permission my arm slips around Maggie's shoulder and I pull her closer to me while we walk away. She fits almost perfectly under my arm, just the right height that I could lean over and kiss the top of her head if I were brave enough. She grins wildly, her arm snakes around my waist and she grips the side of my coat; her cheeks are a dazzling shade of pink that has my finger itching to reach out and trace it. 'Shall we get a hot chocolate?' I offer, seeing there are only two people waiting at the hot drinks stall.

Maggie nods and we head over. With perfect timing, just as we're finishing up with our hot drinks, an announcement comes over the loudspeaker that the fireworks will commence in a couple of minutes. We move to one side, slightly away from the crowd and stand in companionable silence to wait. A cold wind blows, whipping Maggie's hair around her face and she quickly fights to tuck it behind her ears. Where she's standing so close to me, I feel her body shivering and see how she's jiggling on the spot, presumably trying to warm herself up.

'Cold?' I ask, and then mentally scold myself. Of course she's cold, it's five bloody degrees and her coat isn't thermal lined like Charlie's expensive one I'm wearing.

She nods, bringing her gloved hands up to her mouth and blowing on them.

'Here,' I mutter, reaching up to unravel my scarf and then lean over and begin to drape it around her neck.

'No, you'll be cold then,' she protests, shaking her head.

Rolling my eyes, I continue to wrap the scarf around her neck, pulling it up so it covers her ears a little and protects the back of her neck. 'Shut up and let me be a gentleman.'

She grins, the little dimple making an appearance. 'Thanks.' Her eyes catch mine and hold there and I forget the cold, forget the people around me, I forget everything as I fall into the two pale-green pools.

Suddenly, loud music starts booming and we both look towards the field as the first firework is launched into the sky. Dazzling colours explode, fizzing and hissing as more and more fireworks are sent up in time with the music, some of them booming so loudly it seems to make the ground shake. Maggie oohs and aahs beside me, gasping with delight as a Catherine wheel starts up across the other side of the field sending yellow sparks cascading from it as it whirls.

I turn to look at her, noticing now how her shoulder brushes my arm as she stares open mouthed at the sky. I can't take my eyes from her. The way the colours dance across her face, the expression of wonder that resides there, the way her eyes twinkle and sparkle with excitement, all of it takes my breath away. This is the most magical moment of my life, and I never want it to end. I want this night to last forever.

I memorise everything: her small gasps of pleasure, the way her body slightly jumps when a big bang goes off, the way her freckles seem to dance as she grins like a small child. The elation on her face is overwhelming.

Without my permission, my hand reaches out and closes over hers. I can feel the heat of her hand through the wool of her gloves as our fingers entwine. I gulp as she turns towards me and our eyes lock again; they still twinkle with pleasure as her teeth sink into her bottom lip. I long to be closer, to press against her, to feel her warmth surround me, to feel her soft skin on mine. Her hand tightens on mine and she doesn't look away, instead, she moves closer, pressing herself against me as she goes on tiptoes. Her eyes drop to my lips and I suddenly realise she's about to kiss me.

Everything I ever wanted is within touching distance, and my mind is racing. She's about to kiss me. This is real this time, it's not a fantasy, it's not my imagination, her mouth is just millimetres from mine and this is real!

But then it hits me…

This isn't real at all.

Nothing about this moment is real, because she thinks I'm someone I'm not. She's not about to kiss *me*, she's about to kiss *Charlie*. This whole thing, this whole night, is a lie.

Disappointment hits me like a sucker punch to the gut and I pull away before her mouth can meet mine. I'm disgusted with myself. Jade was right, I've just been leading her on, letting her fall for a person that wasn't real. Sure, it was my personality, that part wasn't an act, but I'm dead. We could never be together. She thought she was falling for Charlie – stupid, selfish, shallow Charlie who wouldn't look twice at this sweet and thoughtful girl if I hadn't taken his body to fulfil my own sick fantasy. It wasn't fair on her. I wanted to kiss her, I wanted to kiss her more than I'd ever wanted anything in my life, but not like this. Not built on a lie.

As I pull back, Maggie's eyes widen and her mouth pops open in bewilderment which quickly morphs into embarrassment as, even in the dark, I see her cheeks flood with colour and she steps back.

'Sorry, I misread the signals, I thought, now you aren't with Justine … sorry. I'm so stupid. I have to go,' she mutters, shaking her head in apparent horror as she turns to leave.

My heart lurches and I instinctively tighten my hold on her hand. 'Maggie, wait!' I plead. 'You didn't misread the signals,' I say, hating myself for the pain

I can see etched on her face. 'I want to kiss you, but it wouldn't be right, not like this.' I struggle to find the words to explain but I know there are none.

She turns back to me, her eyes inquisitive. 'What do you mean?' she croaks, chewing on her lip, unsure of herself.

I scowl down at the floor, shaking my head, I have nothing that could make this better.

My silence obviously speaks volumes to her as she huffs out a breath and tries to tug her hand from mine so she can attempt to leave again, but I hold fast.

'Wait,' I plead. 'I want to kiss you, really. Oh God, do I want to kiss you, it's just…' I gulp and reach up to grip a fistful of my hair, relishing in the small, burning prickling sensation it causes.

Tell her the truth, it's the only chance you have of still having her in your life! My mind is whirling, spinning through thoughts so quickly it makes me feel nauseated. Jade is right, she'll think Charlie is insane. But … it's the only chance I have. Surely any chance, even a slim one like this, is worth taking if it means I might get to keep her?

I swallow and square my shoulders, bracing myself. 'Maggie, there's something you don't know.' *Am I really going to do this?*

231

Her eyebrows knit together in a frown. 'What do you mean?'

Oh shit, I'm really going to do this…

'I mean…' I take a deep breath. The smell of hot dogs and doughnuts fills my nose. Around us the sounds of the funfair and fireworks cut through the air, the music still blasts from the speakers as I say the words I've been wanting to say for the last few weeks. 'Maggie, I'm not the person you think I am.'

CHAPTER TWENTY-ONE
~ MAGGIE ~

I gulp at his words. Not the person I thought he was. What does that even mean? I can feel my face flaming at the embarrassment of his rejection. I shift from foot to foot and look up at him expectantly, noticing that his grip hasn't loosened on my hand. He looks torn, his eyes flitting to the noisy crowd around us before coming back to me. He said he wanted to kiss me too – but was he messing with me? Was this all some sort of prank? Were his friends in on this the whole time, as some sort of sick bet that he could make me fall in love with him? Because it had certainly worked. I loved him. I'd fallen so hard it was more like a plummet from a great height than a simple fall.

'I can't tell you here,' he says quietly, leaning closer to me, so close I can see the pupils of his eyes shrink as the floodlights come on to illuminate the field so that people can find their way out now the fireworks are over.

I shake my head as the realisation hits me. He has no explanation; I just misread the signals and made a fool of myself. What would Charlie ever see in me? I'm a nobody, I don't compare to the Justines of the world, hanging on his every word during the day and not just when no one else was around. All this time we'd been seeing each other in secret, he said it was because I was in Year 11 and he was in Year 13 and that people would think him a cradle-snatcher, but he was just using me, leading me on so I would make a fool of myself exactly like I just had. It wouldn't surprise me if he and his friends had cooked this all up between them.

I duck my head and pull my hand from his, instantly missing the warmth of it. 'Forget it. I'm going home.' I shove my hands into my pockets as I turn on my heel to leave, anger now replacing the embarrassment.

'Maggie, wait, please?' he begs, rushing to my side as I storm towards the exit as fast as the dispersing crowd will allow. 'Please let me walk you home. I can explain, please?'

I scowl down at the floor, tucking my mouth into his scarf that he'd wrapped around my neck earlier. The scarf smells like him and I feel my eyes glaze over with tears. Blinking quickly, I vow not to let them fall.

The crowd bottlenecks at the exit forcing us to stop while the group files through a few at a time. Charlie steps in front of me, putting one hand on my shoulder, dipping his head so I have to look at him, at his pleading blue eyes, at the tension that's caused his forehead to crease. 'Just give me five minutes and I'll try to explain?' he says softly, sticking his lip out the way a child does when they're begging for sweets at a sweet shop.

And I don't know why, maybe I'm just a sucker for his pout and puppy-dog eyes, but I say yes and we head out of the field together, his hand still on my shoulder so we don't get separated.

We walk in silence for a few minutes in the direction of my house until he stops next to a bench. 'Can we sit for a minute? I just need to collect my thoughts and figure out how the hell I explain all of this,' he asks, sitting without waiting for me to answer and putting his head in his hands.

I frown down at him, my mind whirling, trying to pre-empt what he's about to say, but I have nothing. There's a ball of tension in my stomach that's growing larger by the second. The way he looks so rattled is unnerving me and I'm beginning to wonder if I should just leave, if I don't want to hear this after all, if I should run home now before he has the chance to

235

come up with some lie – or worse, confess the truth that this is all some sort of prank at my expense.

Charlie groans and looks at me pointedly before motioning for me to sit next to him on the bench. I can see the stress in his eyes and my knees weaken so I take the seat and wait.

He gulps noisily. 'My name isn't Charlie. It's Ryder, Ryder Edmonds.'

It's so unexpected that I snort a laugh and shake my head. 'Whatever, can you just get to the explaining part of this joke so I can go home?'

His eyebrows pinch. 'It's not a joke.'

I roll my eyes. 'So, what? You changed your name or something? Don't tell me, you're in some sort of trouble, or you're in witness protection or something?' My tone is harsh because what sort of idiot did he actually think I was?

He shakes his head, reaching up to rub at his temples. 'It's worse than that. I'm not even sure how to say it really because I don't know how to make you believe me and you're just going to think I'm insane or something.'

Now he's really starting to frighten me and the ball of tension inside is growing so large that it's making my stomach ache. I scoot back on the bench to get some space between us. When he's too close to me my senses seem to be off, my mind always gets a little fuzzy.

'You're making absolutely zero sense. Please just say what you have to say.'

He nods slowly, his eyes on mine. 'My name is Ryder and I died five years ago. I'm a spirit, or ghost, or whatever you want to call it.'

I recoil at his words. Whatever I had been expecting, it certainly wasn't that.

Oh, God, he really is *insane!*

He reaches out a hand as if to take mine, but I jerk it away quickly. 'Don't.'

He sighs. 'It's true, Maggie. I died in a rafting accident five years ago and I've been stuck here ever since, just wandering around. I first saw you three months ago, at the hospital, when your nan…' He trails off and gulps and my mind inadvertently slips to that day that I found my nan unresponsive on the bathroom floor when I got up to pee in the night. His eyes meet mine. 'I saw you there, and liked you, so I sometimes followed you around and watched you – I know that sounds really bad, but I'm not a stalker or anything. Well, maybe I am, but…'

My whole body stiffens and I'm torn between screaming at him or running away. He actually is insane. I'm sitting, alone, in the dark, with a crazy person who thinks he's a ghost. What the hell? You couldn't make this shit up.

He holds his hands up innocently, his eyes pleading. 'Don't freak out. Please, please don't freak out,' he begs. 'Remember that night Charlie saved you from being run over? Well, that wasn't Charlie; that was me, Ryder. I'd been with you visiting your nan and I like to walk home with you after. I saw the van coming and I knew I had to do something, so I jumped into Charlie's body and saved you. And after that I really liked being able to talk to you, finally, after so long wanting to, so I … I stole his body again and walked you to the bus stop, remember?'

As he speaks, a remarkable calm settles over me. This is the most ridiculous excuse for not kissing someone I've ever heard in my life and if he is expecting me to buy into this cock-and-bull story he has another thing coming. I may be naive enough to fall for the 'let's hang out in secret and not tell anyone' thing, but I'm certainly not dumb enough to go along with this crap. This was the worst practical joke I'd ever heard in my life. I almost felt sorry for him.

But he wasn't giving up yet.

'That's the reason why sometimes I'm so cold to you at school. Sometimes it's not me you're talking to, sometimes it actually *is* Charlie. He has no idea that sometimes I take over his body and hang out with you.' He grips his hair and groans in exasperation. 'I'm not explaining this right. It's not coming out right. I know this is hard for you to understand. God knows, I know how stupid it sounds. But it's the truth. I'm telling you the truth, I swear. I'd swear on my life but I can't because...' He shrugs, looking down at his hands in his lap.

I calmly stand and look down at him, determined not to let the hurt I feel inside show in my voice as I say, 'This is the most ridiculous bullshit story I've ever heard in my life. Your idea of a practical joke is way off the mark. This isn't even funny.' His mouth pops open at my words. The calmness is dissipating now and anger is replacing it. 'Why me? Did you and your friends pick me as a target to make a fool of: "Oh let's see how gullible the geek girl really is?".'

He stands, too, his whole posture defeated as his shoulders slump. 'It's not like that. I'm telling you the truth. I died, I'm a ghost, I've possessed Charlie's body because I wanted to talk to you. I'm crazy about you.'

He reaches for my hand again and I can't help my reflex. My anger flares, so strong that it takes me over. Before I can even talk myself out of it, I've pulled back my hand and slapped him across the face. The noise is muffled because of my gloves and but it still makes my fingers tingle from the impact. I can't hold back my tears anymore, and big fat droplets fall down my cheeks at the sheer humiliation of it all. I'd fallen for him, him and his lies. He'd made me feel special with all the attentive little things he'd said, all the time we spent talking, *really* talking. I've told him things I've told no one else. I am such a sucker.

'I'm leaving. Charlie, you're an arsehole!' What was the point in this? Making me look like a fool – but to what end?

'Ryder. My name is Ryder. Please, Maggie, please can you just open your mind and let me try to think of a way to prove this to you. I don't know how or what I can do, but please? I don't want to lose you. I don't have anything else!'

'I don't know what you set out to achieve here, Charlie, but if it was to hurt and humiliate me then, congratulations, you've succeeded.' I shake my head and reach up to swipe at the tears that continue to fall. 'Don't ever talk to me again.'

Before he can say anything else to hurt me further, I turn on my heel and run in the direction of my house, leaving him standing alone in the dark. I need to get home, I need to bury my face in the pillow and

240

cry myself to sleep, I need to be as far away from him as I can get.

'Maggie, please? I love you!' he calls to my retreating back and another part of my heart splinters off. My footsteps falter for a second but I don't stop. I've been so stupid. Why had I even dared to hope that someone like Charlie would like someone like me?

CHAPTER TWENTY-TWO
~ RYDER ~

I watch her run away and everything in me wants to run after her, to find better words, to make this right and explain. But I can't, because she doesn't want to listen. I've blown it. I've screwed up royally and worse, I've made her cry. That almost hurt more than the fact that I could never talk to her again. Seeing those tears on her face, knowing I'd caused them, was like The Hulk had smashed through my chest and crushed my heart.

But did she really mean it when she said I wasn't to talk to her ever again? My eyes fall shut and I sink back down onto the bench. All I can see is the hurt on her face. She thought it was a practical joke, that I was doing it out of spite. If only she knew, if only I could somehow make her see the truth. I don't know what possessed me to tell her the truth anyway. Of course that would be her reaction. Just like Jade had told me, Maggie had thought Charlie was unhinged.

And I couldn't even blame her. If someone had laid that bombshell on me when I was still alive, I'd have laughed right in their face and told them to stop behaving like a dick.

I groan in frustration and grip my hair, breathing heavily through my nose and trying to think how I could make this right. I'd have to watch her closely now. If she mentioned any of this to Charlie ... Oh, God, how had I got into this situation?

I longed to follow her home, to try and soothe her, to see if she was OK, but instead I had things to take care of. Namely, taking Charlie home so he was none the wiser that this little fireworks trip had occurred. I stand and angrily kick at a stone, sending it skittering away, before shoving my hands into my pockets and stomping off in the direction of Charlie's house, looking for a bus stop along the way.

When I finally make it back to his house after a long walk and twenty-minute wait for a bus, I'm seething with anger at myself for telling Maggie. I've been selfish, I should have thought more about her and what she would have felt hearing that and thinking I was blowing her off or messing with her, and not about my own selfish desires. I hate myself. And I hate Charlie, too, even though none of this is his fault. He is just the poor sap who was close to her when she was about to have her accident. He could have been anyone that night – and I wish he had been. At least then it would have been over, I wouldn't have been tempted into using his body again, and then none of us would be in this weird mind-fuck situation.

Luckily for me, Charlie's parents still aren't home when I get there so I slip in unnoticed, take my shoes and coat off and take Charlie up to his bedroom, laying him down on his bed before slipping out of his body and slumping to the floor a weak mess. Taking control of his body was getting easier every time, but leaving it always exhausts me. The longer I snatch his body for, the longer it takes me to recover.

As I sit on the floor, trying to regain control of my weak, wobbly body. Charlie sits up, a look of confusion on his face as he rubs a weary hand over his face. He looks around as if dazed for a few seconds, and then reaches for his phone which I've placed on his bedside cabinet. His mouth pops open in shock as he sees all the notifications that had been buzzing in my pocket all night – calls and messages from his friends asking where he was and why he hadn't arrived at Rich's house for the hot dog and fireworks night they'd planned.

He swings his legs over the side of the bed as he

puts his phone to his ear and checks his watch, uttering a swear word under his breath. 'Rich? Yeah, crap, sorry. I fell asleep, just woke up. My phone was on silent. Yeah, sorry, mate. Shall I come over now? Ah, really? Oh, no, OK I won't bother then if everyone's left. Yeah, gutted. Nah, I'm fine. All right mate, I'll see you tomorrow.' He disconnects the call and drops his phone onto the bed, his jaw clenching tightly, clearly angry with himself that he'd fallen asleep and missed the gathering, but at least he didn't suspect anything untoward. He never did.

He heads out of the room and a couple of minutes later I hear the shower turn on and I chance trying to stand up on my unsteady legs.

It takes me a long time to get back to my nightly meeting place with Jade – maybe subconsciously I am putting off the verbal bashing I know I am about to get from her, who knows.

The next day I watch Maggie like a hawk. I wait outside her house from seven in the morning, and when she finally emerges, I follow her to school and watch her during all her classes. She seems almost like a different person. Her shoulders are slumped and she hugs her books to her chest in a defensive way, but her eyes are the worst thing. They're constantly downcast, but when they rarely do leave the floor and I get a good look at them, they're red-rimmed and filled with pain.

One good thing is that she doesn't speak to Charlie at all. The dramatic unveiling or argument where he has no clue what she's talking about never comes. In fact, whenever she sees him coming down the corridor, chatting with his friends and acting like he doesn't have a care in the world, Maggie ducks into the nearest toilet or empty classroom to get away from him. It hurts to see her so upset. The fact that I've led her on was something I'll never forgive myself for. I've put that sadness in her heart. It makes me hate myself, and the selfish decision I made, even more.

After school I follow her onto the bus and to her grandmother's nursing home. As we go in, Maggie's body instantly becomes looser and a small smile creeps onto her mouth – the first I'd seen since last night at the fireworks before everything went wrong. While she signs her name and arrival time into the visitors' book, I head into the TV room where Doreen usually is at this time of day.

I spot Doreen over to one side. As I step in, it's clear that she's having some sort of coughing fit. She's sitting on one of the frayed lounge chairs, a

246

nurse next to her taking her pulse and another attendant kneeling in front of her holding a plastic cup of water. Great wracking coughs shake Doreen's whole body and they hold a tissue to her lips, her eyes glazed over with pain. I stop short, looking her over with dread washing over me. I fear the worst.

Seconds later, Maggie gasps behinds me and rushes to her grandmother's side, kneeling next to the attendant and immediately rubbing her nan's arm soothingly.

I hang back, not wanting to bump into anyone or inadvertently cause any trouble. I chew my fingernail, watching as Doreen's cough slowly subsides. Pain has made her features tight and her hands shake so Maggie has to help her hold the cup to her lips. I stand back to the side as Maggie smiles, her concern clear as she leans up and kisses her nan on the forehead before turning to the nurse with her face full of worry. The nurse explains that Doreen's cough has been getting worse at night over the last few weeks, and that the lack of sleep might be weakening her. Maggie frowns, her hand still stroking her nan's arm as she tells the nurses she's not happy with how Doreen sounds and that she wants a doctor to come in and see her. She's so forceful and decisive. Gone is the shy, demure Maggie. This one would fight through fire for her nan. The lioness protecting her cubs that I'd seen at the hospital when her nan was brought in after her stroke, the one that demanded better care, more help, was back. This was the trait that pulled me to her in the first place. She loved as my mother did: fiercely, bravely, all consuming. What I wouldn't give to have Maggie love me even a fraction of that much…

After the nurses agree they'll get the doctor called out tomorrow if Doreen isn't any better, they leave and Maggie turns back to her grandmother, her eyes softening again as she drops her school bag at her feet and pulls up a chair.

They don't talk much. Doreen is very quiet, coughing occasionally though not as badly as when we came in. You can see she's in pain when she breathes; she clasps her side and winces a fair few times. After a little while she falls asleep mid-conversation. I see a tear slide down Maggie's cheek as she holds her nan's hand in silence and watches her sleep.

I get an ominous feeling in my stomach, one I really don't want to believe in, but I know it's the sixth sense I've felt several times before. I know what it means. I glance over at Maggie, my heart aching.

At the end of visiting time, Maggie speaks again

to the nurses, her face stern and set. She looks way older than fifteen as she fights her grandmother's corner. I walk home with her, watching as she listens to her music and cries silently most of the way – even Frankie Valley and David Bowie can't lighten her mood. I was going to go inside and stay with her for a while, but as she opens the door Lorna takes one look at her face and engulfs her in a hug and Maggie's tears come full force, crying against her foster mother's shoulder. Lorna hugs her tighter, stroking her back softly even though she doesn't even know what's wrong. It makes me like her even more.

I slip outside the door and head to the end of their garden, perching on the wall. Leaving isn't an option, not tonight.

Before the sun rises the following morning, lights flick on in the Fishers' home, only one at first, then more and more until the whole house is illuminated. I close my eyes, feeling sorrow and grief settle in my stomach.

A little over five minutes later, Chris, followed by a distraught-looking Maggie, exits the house and rushes towards the car, with Lorna – who usually has immaculate hair and make-up, now with no make-up and her shirt on inside out – right behind, locking up the house before running to the car. I follow, slipping through the closed door and into the back seat next to Maggie. Her hand rests on the seat at my side and I can't help but place my hand on top of hers. Neither of us can feel it, but it comforts me at least.

I don't need to ask what's happening. No one rushes out of the house at this time of the morning, their faces ashen, their eyes shining with tears unless it's something bad. That ominous feeling washes over me again and I look over at Maggie, wishing I could help her through this. I was usually just an onlooker in this scenario, observing and intruding on other people's grief, now I'm in the thick of it.

When we get to the hospital, Chris tells Lorna to take Maggie inside while he finds somewhere to park. I follow the girls out, noticing the tight grip Maggie has on Lorna's hand. Her knuckles are almost white. After a brief stop at the reception, they're directed to the correct ward and I follow behind slowly, my feet feeling like they weigh a hundred pounds each.

Outside the room a doctor stops to speak to Lorna and Maggie. His face is grim and sorrowful as he tells them that Doreen has suffered another stroke, a severe one and that she has pneumonia. He tells them the prognosis doesn't look good but they've done everything they can to make her comfortable.

They are not expecting her to last much longer. As he speaks, Maggie doesn't look at him. Her gaze is firmly locked on the door to her nan's room. Her eyes shine with tears but, for now, they've stopped falling.

'Can I go in alone?' Maggie asks, turning to look at Lorna who rearranges her expression a nanosecond too late to hide the hurt the question causes.

'Of course. I'll be right out here waiting for you. If you need me, you just call and I'll be in.' She leans in and kisses Maggie softly on the top of the head, her eyes tight with concern as she watches her ward step away from her and over to the doors. Maggie's hand hesitates on the handle for a second, clearly steeling herself for what she'll see inside, before she pushes the door open and steps in. I follow behind, my heart squeezing with grief.

Doreen is lying motionless on the bed, the white cotton sheets tucked up under her armpits. She's not asleep, as I thought she would be; instead she stares at the ceiling through watery eyes as she rasps each breath, sucking in oxygen through a mask.

Maggie's whole body stiffens as she enters, her bottom lip wobbling. 'Hi, Nan,' she says softly, stepping to the edge of the bed and reaching out to take Doreen's non-IV laden hand in hers, stroking the back of it softly. Maggie's hands are shaking.

Doreen's eyes are the only things that move, settling on her granddaughter. I step closer too, seeing that the stroke has slackened the left side of her face so much that her lips are at a crooked slant giving her a sorrowful expression. She tries to speak, but all that comes out is a garbled mumble which makes a sob hitch in Maggie's throat.

'You don't have to speak, Nan. You just rest,' she says softly, leaning down to brush a kiss on Doreen's cheek.

'Ma ...I ... lo ...oh.' Doreen's slack eyes tighten as she tries to force the speech, a glob of spittle leaking from the left side of her mouth.

Maggie smiles warmly. 'I love you too,' she says, kissing her again. 'So much. So much.'

'Ma ... gee.'

Maggie nods, her tears flowing again now. 'Yeah, it's me, Maggie. I'm here. I'm here, Nan. You're OK,' she whispers, bringing Doreen's palm up and pressing it against her cheek, breathing in the smell of her grandmother. 'You're OK. You can fight this, you're tough. Please, Nan. You're the only one I have left. You can't leave me too. Please don't leave me alone.'

My heart is breaking watching them. Watching Doreen struggle for breath, watching Maggie's whole world fall apart in front of me when I can do nothing to help. There are an agonising few minutes where no one speaks, but they just look at each other, the love shining in their eyes as Maggie brushes Doreen's hair back from her face soothingly. And then Doreen's eyes flick to me and back to Maggie; they widen in shock and then flick back to me again.

I let out a breath I didn't realise I was holding and look down at her apologetically. It's her time. If she can see me it means she's at the end. I look up at Maggie and will her to get ready but Doreen is slurring again, looking at me intently.

That's when the understanding hits me: Maggie *isn't* alone, she has me; I just need to prove it, prove that I'll be here for her no matter how hard things get, that I won't ever leave her.

I lean closer to Doreen, seeing her fingers grip the bed sheets as she blinks rapidly. 'Doreen, can you say my name? It's Ryder. Please, can you please say my name? It'll help Maggie, I don't have time to explain but, please, it'll help Maggie if you say my name so she knows I'm here. Please?'

Her eyes flick from me to Maggie and back again, her slack lips moving but no sound comes out.

'It's Ryder. Ry-der,' I sound out the syllables, begging her with my eyes. 'Please do this for her. Please? It's Ryder.'

'Nan, are you all right? What are you looking at?' Maggie asks, looking at the spot above my head and back to her nan again. 'Nan?'

'Please, Doreen, say my name please? It's Ryder,' I beg again.

Doreen's lips part and her eyes squeeze closed with the effort. 'Bye ...dar,' she whispers.

'Ryder,' I prompt anxiously, looking at Maggie's confused face. 'Please, Doreen, it's Ryder!'

'Nan?' Maggie's voice is so small that I can barely hear it, her whole body is stiff.

'Ry ... ser,' Doreen manages to say it slightly more clearly, but it's still so slurred that I can see Maggie hasn't understood it at all and a single tear slides down Doreen's withered cheek and soaks into the pillow.

'Nan, what did you say?' Maggie asks desperately, pressing Doreen's hand harder against her cheek, looking down at her, her feelings laid bare on her face.

But Doreen doesn't respond. Her chest rises and falls one more time before the air leaves her lungs in a ragged puff and she's still.

Maggie blinks down at her nan, her mouth falling open before she makes a guttural groan that cuts through me like a knife piercing my very soul. That sound of her grief is raw and the last of the restraint that she'd held on to so well while she was saying goodbye to her nan falters and she breaks down, pressing her face into Doreen's stomach and crying so hard that the bed shakes.

My heart aches for Maggie and all she's lost. I close my eyes too, saying a silent farewell to Doreen Nichols, knowing she's in a better place even if it means her granddaughter is now more alone than ever.

CHAPTER TWENTY-THREE
~ MAGGIE ~

Last week was the longest of my life. I'd never felt so low, not even when my mum died. At least when mum passed I'd had my nan to hold me together as I, in turn, had held her together. Somehow we managed to scrape through it and out the other side. But this was entirely different. Now I am alone, trapped in my grief, feeling like a large part of me died in that hospital room along with my nan, and the part that is left is just an empty shell of a person going through the motions.

I stare into the mirror and hardly recognise the girl staring back. My red-rimmed eyes are empty, glassy, and cold, the skin around them sore looking where I'd dried and wiped them so much in the last week. My whole body feels tired and exhausted from lack of sleep. Night times are the worst. I just lie there in the dark thinking, or looking at pictures of my nan on my phone.

A soft tap sounds on my door and Lorna's soothing voice coos in, 'Maggie, the cars are here, darling. Are you ready?'

I don't answer. Was I ready? How could I ever be ready for this? I was about to say goodbye to my last remaining relative, the woman who had taken me in when my mother died, the one who made me smile again when I thought all was lost, the one who made the most amazing dippy eggs and soldiers on Sunday mornings. No. I wasn't ready at all.

I swallow and my gaze travels the length of me, over my black jumper, down over my black skirt and thick black tights. Lorna had gone out and bought the clothes for me a couple of days ago because I had nothing suitable and couldn't face shopping for funeral clothes. All black, likely the same colour my soul was stained now. This outfit needed something. It wasn't right to send Nan off in such a dreary way. She hated black. She was a colourful person in life so would want to be in death, too. I frown, thinking.

'Maggie? Can you hear me?' Lorna asks, tapping on the door again.

Suddenly an idea hits me and I race over to my chest of drawers, pulling open the one I keep my socks in and rummaging around for it. I find it right at the back – the Remembrance Day poppy Nan knitted for me. Remembrance Day was passed now, but the bright red, knitted poppy would add the splash of colour my nan would have approved of.

Behind me the door opens and Lorna peeks around it. My fingers are shaking. I hadn't noticed until I struggled to unclasp the pin. Lorna's smile is a sad, sympathetic one as she strides across the room and stops in front of me.

'That's beautiful,' she says, nodding at the poppy. 'A very lovely tribute to wear it.' Her eyes are glazed over and there are dark circles under them which she's tried to cover with too much concealer. I know she's found this week hard too, but she's been extremely supportive. I couldn't have done it without her. She helped me arrange everything for today; from claiming the over-fifties funeral policy Nan had been paying into for years, to the ordering of flowers and choosing the hymns we're going to sing. Everything.

'I thought a splash of colour,' I trail off, not wanting to say anything else.

She nods slightly. 'Here, let me help you.' She eases the poppy from my trembling fingers and expertly pins it to my chest, smoothing my collar down after. I don't look at her. Her sweet, flowery perfume fills my room and it makes me think of my nan again – how she always wore the same Elizabeth

Arden perfume and how different it smelt to Lorna's more exotic one.

'Thanks,' I say, my eyes firmly latched on the floor.

'Are you ready? The cars are here.'

Cars. The funeral cars we'd booked to take us to the crematorium. I shrug, still not knowing the answer, and she turns for the door, pulling it open and throwing me another kind smile. I close my eyes for a couple of seconds, trying to steel myself for what's to come, but I don't manage it. My insides tremble as I force myself to walk through the door. When we get to the bottom of the stairs, Lorna's hand rests on the small of my back, warm and comforting, but I try not to let myself enjoy it. I don't want to let this woman too far behind my defences. I can't lose anyone else, I just can't.

I busy myself putting on my shoes as Chris steps out of the living room in his black suit and tie. He doesn't say anything. He's not been as good as Lorna this week. Not that he's been bad, he's just not as adept at things as Lorna and always seems to be struggling with what to say to me. I get it. Death is hard, even on the outsiders.

At the funeral I don't shed a single tear. I sit there on

the uncomfortable wooden bench, in the too-warm room, wedged between Lorna and my social worker, Nicola, as the vicar talks about my nan and her life. I stare at the coffin they've carried in and placed on the raised platform at the front of the altar and at the beautiful white and red flower arrangement we'd chosen for the ceremony. I mouth along to the hymns without making a sound. My head isn't in the right place. It's like my body is here but my mind has fractured off somewhere. My hands are clenched into fists so tight that I'm beginning to lose feeling in my fingers, but I don't bother to move them, there's no point. They'll be just as numb as I am inside soon.

From the corner of my eye I see Lorna discreetly gazing at me, her arm too heavy across my shoulders, her grip that bit too tight to be comfortable, and I silently wonder if I am now too broken to feel emotion. I feel nothing. Just hollow. Maybe that was why I haven't cried again today – or maybe I've simply run out of tears. I've cried so much this last week that maybe my quota is used up. Does a person only have a limited supply of tears in their lifetime? If so, how sad was it that I had used all of mine in just fifteen years?

As the red velvet curtains close around my grandmother's coffin, I can hear some of Nan's old friends and ex-neighbours sniffing and snuffling into their handkerchiefs. It was nice of them to come, especially considering most of them were older than Nan was herself. I swallow down the lump in my throat. The room is stifling and I'm finding it hard to breathe.

'OK, Maggie?' Nicola asks, placing a hand on my knee and squeezing supportively.

I nod and stand, wanting to be out of here and get some fresh air. I feel nauseous.

Nicola is sitting at the end of the aisle so I have to wait for her to get up before I can make my exit. I shuffle forward, dipping my head and glancing around the room from under my eyebrows. At the back I spot a little group of people from the nursing home – a couple of nurses that I always liked, and next to them the snooty general manager who looks appropriately solemn in her power suit and sharp ponytail. I drag my eyes away from them as Nicola finally steps out of the aisle and I can get past her and make a break for the door at the back, shrugging off Lorna's arm, just needing this to be over.

The cold November air hits me in the face as I step outside, stinging my cheeks. Chris catches up with me, his hands shoved deep into his pockets, his eyes on the ground. We stop next to the flowers that the funeral directors have moved from the car to the back of the crematorium for display. I can see cards attached to some but I can't bear to read the words.

'So, what do you want to do now, kiddo? The plan was to have everyone back to the house for tea and cake, but if you're not up to it you just give me a nod and I'll tell everyone to take a hike. It's not a problem, you're the only one we need to be considerate of today,' Chris says kindly.

I shrug, appreciating the solidarity, but Lorna had gone to so much trouble yesterday baking cakes and making sandwiches and sausage rolls for the wake. I can't let her hard work go to waste. 'Tea and cake is fine. Whatever.'

'You're sure?'

I nod, forcing my eyes away from the flowers and over to the pretty grounds of the crematorium.

'OK, whatever you want,' he replies. Lorna steps to his side a few seconds later and they share a fleeting look and a nod. I look away and wonder if she had sent him over here to ask the question about the wake because she knew I wouldn't want to tell her to cancel it. If so, I appreciate that solidarity, too.

I wrap my arms around my midriff. 'Can we go now? I don't want to stand here anymore.'

'Sure, darling, come on,' Lorna answers immediately, smiling kindly as she motions with her head for me to start walking towards the car park at the front. She falls into step with me as I march down the path, rubbing my hands together to try to warm them up. My feet feel like lead weights.

I stay quiet on the ride back to the house, looking out of the window. There's nothing left to say. Lorna and Nicola talk quietly about the lovely service and how many people might come back to the house for tea. Nicola jokes that we'll have to set a time limit for the wake because, in her experience, the old codgers don't like to leave until the last crumb of free food was eaten.

Back at the house, Lorna takes charge, ordering Chris to get out a few fold-up chairs from the garden in case there aren't enough inside already, while she and Nicola head into the kitchen to boil the kettle and fill the coffee and tea urns that Lorna has borrowed from her café. I stop next to the table at the back and set to work pulling the cling film from the cheese sandwiches and the sweet treats, just for something to do.

The wake feels even more stifling than the funeral itself. I've managed to get myself stuck next to my old next-door neighbour, Beryl, who brought along her son to help push her in her wheelchair. She's prattling on about old times and reeling off stories of years gone by.

In the midst of it all, Lorna brings me a steaming mug of tea and a cheese and cucumber sandwich with some crisps on the side of the plate, eyeing me knowingly. 'You should eat something, Maggie. You haven't eaten all day.'

Ah, so she noticed my untouched toast in the bin in my room, did she? Damn it. I stare down at the plate and my stomach churns. I'm just not hungry, my stomach is already full of knots, I couldn't possibly fit anything else in there. 'Thanks,' I mutter quietly, which brings a smile to her face and she saunters off to refill people's cups, endlessly circling the room like a shark with a coffee jug.

Instead of eating, I pick up my spoon and stir my tea listlessly as Beryl continues to prattle. This time she's talking to the elderly gentleman on her other side. I stir my tea slowly, in large circles, teasing the spoon around the edge of the mug. The sound makes me think of Nan, and how she always liked her tea in a china teacup and saucer. The sound it made when being stirred was different, more of a clink than the scraping sound of the mugs Lorna and Chris have.

My eyes prickle at the sound. I miss it. It's such a silly, small thing that I didn't even know I knew until now.

I can't do this anymore. I can't sit here and pretend I'm OK when I'm dying inside.

I stand without speaking and go over to where I can see Lorna chatting with Chris. He smiles awkwardly at me as I approach. 'OK, kiddo?'

'I want to go to my room.' My voice is flat, emotionless. 'Is that OK?' I direct my question at Lorna.

She smiles, her eyes ablaze with sympathy, and reaches out to brush my cheek with one finger. 'Of course it is, darling.'

'Sorry to leave you here with all of this…' I wave my hand around at the old people milling in her lounge and spilling into the kitchen, dropping flakes of sausage roll onto the carpets.

Lorna shakes her head. 'Don't be silly. Off you go. I'll save you a slice of cake.' She reaches out and gives my hand a supportive squeeze and I smile gratefully in return.

As I trudge up the stairs and into my room, pulling my curtains closed to block out the sunshine, I silently wish I had someone here I could talk to. I feel so alone that it hurts. My mind wanders to Charlie but a surge of anger at him and his lies surfaces again – as it does every time I think of him – so I push the thought away and flop on my bed, burying my face in the soft pillow.

For the thousandth time this week, my mind wanders to Nan and the last moments I got to spend with her in that hospital room. How frail she looked, how she struggled to breathe and her lungs seemed to crackle with each inhale. The memory of it makes my heart ache and I press a hand over my eyes, willing the thoughts away. Why was that always how I saw Nan when I thought of her now? It was like all my nice memories of her, all our fun times together, her kind smile and the crinkles around her eyes, had faded from my memory and all I had left was her pain-filled dying moments. When I closed my eyes all I saw was her agonised face and the tear that slid down her cheek as she slurred her last words. I hate it.

As the wake goes on downstairs and people drink the tea and talk about old times, I let my eyes drift closed and I replay the last moments with my nan over and over. How she slurred so much I could barely understand her when she said she loved me. How she'd looked frightened and tried to say goodbye but her slack mouth struggled to formulate the words.

How she kept looking at one spot and then back to me again as if trying to work something out, her eyes wide and slightly fearful, her fingers tightening around the bed sheets. I replay it all, over and over and over again, my brain whirling with it, my heart heavy because of it, and just as I'm about to fall asleep, I remember her last words and the desperation of trying to work them out. Her last words and I couldn't understand them. That would probably haunt me forever. Her last-ever words, and I don't know what they were.

Bye … Dar – maybe, bye, dear? Or maybe pig's ear, buy beer. I sigh in exasperation.

And Ry … ser.

I say them over and over in my head, the words swirling, formulating, and smashing apart again, like waves breaking on rocks.

Suddenly an idea hits me like a bolt of lightning and I sit up, ramrod straight on the bed.

Ry … ser. My nan was slurring with her slack mouth, could that S sound have meant a D? Was my nan trying to say … Ryder?

CHAPTER TWENTY-FOUR
~ MAGGIE ~

I wake with a sort of renewed sense of purpose. After my epiphany last night that *maybe* Nan had said Ryder's name, I had to know, I had to find out. It was important, my grandmother's last words are *the* most important thing to me.

And what if she *had* said Ryder's name? What did that mean? I wasn't sure if I believed in stuff like that – ghosts, the afterlife, reincarnation, heaven – I didn't know what was right or what to believe ... but I had to at least open my mind enough to look. My nan had said his name, for goodness sake, I owed her the time it took me to look.

Unfortunately, I had no way of investigating myself, with my laptop on the blink, and my phone screen still smashed, I was limited on options. I lay awake for hours last night thinking about it, and finally decided at 3am to use the library computer. And once I'd decided that, I fell into a dreamless sleep for hours. It had been the most sleep I'd had all week.

When I head downstairs, fully dressed and of my own free will instead of having to be cajoled into it, Lorna looks up from her coffee and her eyebrows rise in surprise. It's Thursday, but I know I'm not expected at school again today because it's after ten and Lorna hasn't woken me. I'm glad for that. I'm not ready for school yet, I'm not ready to pretend to be OK or to plaster on a fake smile and pretend I'm not broken inside.

'Morning,' she says, shooting me a smile and getting up from the table. 'Want a cup of tea and some toast? Or, if you fancy, there's some cake left. I won't tell if you don't,' she offers, shooting me a conspiratorial wink.

'No thanks. I'm not hungry.' I walk to the fridge and select a bottle of orange juice. 'I don't have to go to school today, do I?' *Please say no, please say no.*

Lorna's head tilts and her lips press together in a sympathetic pout. 'No, dear. I told them you wouldn't be up to it today after yesterday.'

I stare down at my socks and nod gratefully. 'Good, thanks. I was wondering, would it be all right if I go to the library for a little while this morning and get a couple of books to read?' I say it casually, hoping my voice doesn't betray me. I've never been good at lying.

'Oh right. Yeah, sure, that's fine. But let me make you some breakfast though, OK? I don't like the idea of you leaving the house without some food in your belly. You need to start looking after yourself, Maggie. Or, at the very least, let me look after you.' Her gaze is probing as she watches me closely, looking for signs of depression no doubt. I know she's reporting everything back to Nicola. I see her sometimes scribbling things down in her little notepad ready for when she sees my social worker and can blab all about me.

I hold in my groan and shrug. 'OK, sure, if it'll make you feel better.'

She grins triumphantly. 'It will, actually.'

'Fill your boots then. Let's go for the cake.'

She grins at my choice. As we settle down at the table, two huge slices of Victoria sponge between us, I look up at her. 'Thank you, for yesterday.'

'You don't have to thank me.' She smiles as if it was nothing and reaches out, giving my hand a little squeeze.

Knowing I need to make the effort after what she did for me yesterday, I don't pull my hand away this time. I still feel dead inside, so this is all I can offer her for now. Her smile tells me it's enough.

When I walk into the local library, the sweet old librarian looks up at me and smiles warmly. I force a smile in return and head over to her desk, knowing I am going to have to do some sweet talking if I want to use one of the computers. I haven't booked so am crossing everything that one of them is free. Luckily for me, I usually come in here at the weekends for a little bit of peace and quiet, so she knows me.

'Good morning, Maggie. No school today?' she questions, her eyebrows knitting together.

I shake my head. 'I have an inset day today,' I lie. 'How are you? Is your cold any better?'

She holds a hand to her chest and shakes her head. 'No. I got rid of it but I think it's making a comeback again. My whole family has it now.'

'That's not good,' I say sympathetically. 'Um, Lyn, is there any chance I can use one of the computers to get online? I haven't booked, but my laptop at home is broken and I have a few things I need to research for a school project I'm doing.'

She doesn't even question my lie, instead she turns to her own computer, tapping the keys with vigour before turning back to me with a small smile. 'You're in luck. There's one free right now, but there's someone coming in to use it in about forty minutes. Can you be done by then?'

I grin and nod. 'Definitely.'

She points to the computer room off to the left. 'Station two.'

I shoulder my bag and take a step backwards as I speak, 'Thanks so much, Lyn. I'll be quick.'

Three other people are already sitting at their stations. None of them look up as I walk in.

I didn't know where to start. How would I find anything when I didn't know what I was looking for? I stare at the screen for a few seconds and decide to try searching his name, but then I stop. What did he say his last name was? I close my eyes, thinking back to that night on the bench when he broke my heart.

It was something beginning with an E: Edwards, Eddleton? I groan in frustration. I simply can't recall it.

I abandon that line of inquiry, I only have forty minutes, I don't have time to sit here and think about it for too long. Instead I try typing in: 'Rafting accident'. After pressing enter, page after page of links come up, varying dates and places. I need to be more specific. I try again: 'teenage rafting death' and press enter. More links come up but fewer this time, more manageable. I scroll down, reading the little previews, dismissing the ones that are too recent or too long ago. And bam, one of them jumps out at me. It's a headline from the *Eastern Daily Press*.

'Norwich schoolboy, 17,
dies on family rafting trip'

A lump forms in my throat and I drag the mouse, letting the arrow hover over it. Did I want to open it? Before I can decide if I want to, my finger acts of its own accord and clicks.

Up pops the article, with a grainy black-and-white photo of a boy in a rugby shirt holding a large trophy, his grin almost as big. Under the photo is a tiny caption: Ryder Edmonds after winning player of the season.

I look at the photo. Even though it's grainy and pixelated, I can tell the boy was very cute, a good-looking lad that I bet all the girls fancied, especially since he was a sporty guy. His hair looks dark and messy, like this was at the end of a game of rugby rather than the beginning. His grin is wide and cheeky. I study him for longer than necessary. I don't know what I'm looking for, maybe some sign of recognition, I don't know, but whatever it is I don't find it.

I go back to the article. It's short, just a description of how he died, how he was a promising student and how he leaves behind a beloved family. There are a couple of quotes from people saying how much they'll miss him – one from a boy described as Ryder's best friend who says how shocked and upset he was to hear the news; another quote is from the PE teacher who talks about Ryder's dedication and how he'll be sorely missed on the team following this tragedy. Then there's details of the funeral for anyone wanting to attend.

I'm confused.

Clearing the search, I type in his full name. More hits. I scan them quickly, most are irrelevant, but when the Facebook page jumps out at me, I click.

The page is in memorandum. I click the profile picture, enlarging it and lean in to get a better look. I was right, the grainy newspaper article didn't do him justice. He's gorgeous, his brown eyes twinkle with mischief and his smile could break hearts. He's tanned, his dark hair shorter than in the newspaper, strong jaw, straight nose, just gorgeous. This is a professional school photo, complete with obligatory grey background.

I click off the photo, scanning the page, reading posts that span the last five years, from his family, friends, teachers, neighbours, all saying how much they miss him and what a special boy he was.

The wall is punctuated by photos of him, most of them posted by his mother with heartfelt messages. I examine them all: he's various ages, with his friends, alone, blowing out birthday candles, pulling stupid faces, in family holiday photos. There's even one that his father has posted from the day he died. He's wearing a wetsuit that's only on up to his waist and I can't help but focus in on his chest. He's very athletic, clearly all the sports were good for him! I feel a blush grace my cheeks so I keep scrolling. There are lots of posts from a guy called Ben Raddish over the years, the most recent is one is a status from July that he has tagged the page in, saying how he had just had his University degree results and how he was feeling sad and reflecting on his best friend who should have been celebrating alongside him and how much he still missed him. The emotion and heartfelt sadness in the posts made my heart ache. Ryder was loved and is missed, that is extremely clear.

I read all the posts, look at all the photos, scanning for clues, for help, for answers, but there are none.

I'm no more the wiser than I was this morning. Yes, he's died, that is clear, but none of this proved that he was a ghost or that he possessed Charlie's body or that this whole thing wasn't bullshit or a joke that I didn't understand. After all, there was no reason

Charlie and his friends couldn't have looked this up to give their joke more credibility.

But there was a niggling feeling at the back of my mind. My nan had said his name. We were alone in that room and she'd tried to say Ryder, I was sure of it. How would she know that name? Where would she have got that from, if he hadn't told her to say it? Plus, all the times I'd tried to speak to Charlie at school and he looked genuinely perplexed as to why I was talking to him, and the fact that he said he had no recollection of saving me that night and looked so shocked and worried when I told him. Was anyone that good an actor? I wasn't sure.

What if this *was* the truth? What if it really was this dead guy and he really had taken control of Charlie's body to get close to me. *What if?* What was I supposed to do now? The thought scared me a little. It made me question things I thought I knew about life. I wasn't sure I believed in ghosts, but here this person was, perhaps, questioning everything I thought was true.

I needed to find out. But how? I'd told Charlie – or maybe it had been Ryder – to never talk to me again. What if I never got the truth and there was always this lingering doubt? What if I never had the answers?

The only thing I could think of was to speak to Charlie. I could sound him out, see what he knows about it – or if he knows anything at all – and if this is a prank of some sort. I had to try because I couldn't just leave everything unanswered and up in the air like this. It was confusing, and if it was true then that meant that this boy, this one from the photos, was trapped here on Earth forced to use another boy's body just to speak to anyone. I felt bad for him. How lonely must that be? I couldn't imagine.

And … and he'd shouted that he loved me.

I gulped and forced that thought away. I couldn't even think about that now, there was too much else to deal with first.

I needed answers. Once and for all. Tomorrow I'd go back to school and would try to find some.

CHAPTER TWENTY-FIVE
~ MAGGIE ~

The next day I tell Lorna I'm ready to go back to school. She tries to resist, attempting to convince me to have one more day off seeing as it's Friday anyway, but I refuse and explain I need to get some normality back and have some noise around me to keep my brain occupied so it doesn't keep returning to my nan. It's only a half lie. It *will* actually be nice to think about something other than her for a while.

My morning is uneventful, nothing ever changes really. The teachers have obviously all been apprised of my situation and all take pains to give me sympathetic smiles and, on a couple of occasions, a friendly, encouraging pat on the arm. But the students are no different, just as I had expected, no one knows and even if they did know, no one cares.

I don't see Charlie all morning even though I've been keeping my eye out for him, but everyone goes to lunch so I know this is my best chance to speak to him.

I hang around in the hallway, near the entrance to the canteen, my stomach in knots every time a boy in non-uniform walks around the corner, my eyes straining to see if it's him. By the time he turns the corner and walks towards me, I'm a nervous wreck. I've bitten my thumb nail so short it's actually bleeding.

I watch him approach and I hold my breath, my heart thumping erratically. All day I've been trying and trying to think of a way to start this conversation but nothing is coming to me. There is no right way to start, so I'm just going to go for the head-first tactic and hope it evolves from there.

Charlie is with his mate, George, and they're deep in conversation about weekend plans so he doesn't even glance at me as I push away from the wall and smile tentatively over at him. In fact, he doesn't even break stride until I step directly in front of him and hold up a hand in a halting gesture. He looks up then, a confused expression crossing his face as he flicks a glance over my shoulder before his eyes travel back to me.

'Is the canteen closed or something?' he asks, annoyance lining his forehead.

I gulp and shake my head. 'Um, no. I... Can I talk to you for a minute, please?' My face is burning as they both look at me as if I'm something they stepped in. A lowly Year 11, talking to them, how dare I?

One side of Charlie's mouth pulls up into a distasteful sneer that I try not to let hurt, but fail. 'Who, me?' He gestures to himself before looking at George. I nod in confirmation and his eyebrows pinch together with a frown. 'Oh, right, er. OK, sure.' He turns to his friend and shrugs, his expression saying 'I have no fucking clue' to George who snorts a laugh.

When George makes no move to give us any privacy, I decide to just do it. If this was a prank then George would know about it anyway so no point in hiding it. I swallow my nerves and take a deep breath. 'I wanted to talk to you about the other night.'

One of Charlie's eyebrows rises as he takes a step back from me, his stance wary. 'The other night?'

I nod quickly, taking in every movement of his body, every tiny expression that crosses his face. He looks cautious, and slightly perplexed. I try to find the hidden meanings in it all but, so far, I'm still unsure what it all means. 'Yeah, fireworks night.'

Now he looks downright puzzled as he brings up a hand and rubs the back of his head, his eyebrows pinched as he looks over at George before turning back to me. 'Fireworks night?'

His repeating my questions without answering them makes my frustration build and I struggle not to snap at him. 'Yes, fireworks night,' I say, exasperated, waiting for him to tell me it was all a prank, that he was just winding me up because I'm a gullible cow, and that him and his friends have been making fun of me all week about it.

But he doesn't.

He huffs out a breath and clenches his jaw. He doesn't want to be here talking to me, that much is clear. 'I didn't do anything bonfire night. I fell asleep and missed a sick party by the sounds of it.' He frowns. 'What's it to do with you anyway?'

I recoil. His words hit me like a punch in the stomach. He fell asleep. He wasn't with me that night. What did that mean? Did that then tie up with what Ryder was saying about him stealing Charlie's body? Or am I just letting myself get way too carried away with this crazy scenario?

He snorts sarcastically. 'Look, whatever your name is, this isn't a good time for idle chit-chat, OK? I'm hungry, I'm gonna go grab some food.' He moves to step around me but I cut him off.

'Please Charlie, this is important.' He shrugs dismissively and walks to the canteen door, George following in his wake. My determination flares. I decide to change tactic because this line of questioning isn't working. 'Have you had any more superhero blackouts?' I blurt loudly.

That makes him stop. His hand stills on the door handle as he slowly turns around to face me, his eyes wide.

George looks between us both. 'Superhero blackouts, the fuck is that?'

Charlie swallows, his throat bobbing before he turns to George. 'Um ... look, mate, I'll catch up with you in a minute, all right.' He pulls the canteen door open, the noise and chatter growing as he motions for George to go inside.

I watch George walk in and head towards the hot food queue, glancing back over his shoulder for a couple of seconds, his eyes curious and questioning, before he shakes his head and lets it go, now more interested in food than his friend's conversation with an insignificant girl. My mind is whirling.

If this were some kind of joke or prank like I'd envisioned, wouldn't Charlie have kept George around as a witness? Someone else to mock my gullibility and stupidity? They both would have bust out laughing by now, wouldn't they?

Charlie lets the door swing closed and steps towards me, his eyebrows pinched together, his hand kneading the back of his neck roughly. I have no idea what he's about to say so I try to brace myself, but my insides are a mass of nerves and my hands are starting to tremble in anticipation.

'I have actually had a couple of blackouts,' he admits.

'Oh,' is all I can manage as my heart thumps wildly in my chest.

He steps closer to me again, his eyes piercing into mine, searching for answers that I just don't have. 'Like, sometimes I'll just get home late from school and my mum will ask me where I've been and why I'm late, and I just can't think where I've been at all. Or I'll just get home and not have a single memory of the journey. At first I thought it was nothing, but the more it happens, the more I'm starting to get a bit worried about it actually.'

I chew on my lip so hard that I can taste the metallic tang of blood. I don't know what to say. He almost looks scared, and it frightens me a little too. Is this real? Is what he said to me the other night true ... that he wasn't himself, that this guy I'm talking to now is Charlie but the other times he's been someone else? Is it even possible? Did I believe it now? Ghosts? Possessions? That a dead boy is in love with me?

I can't process it all. I don't know what to think anymore. My mind is a mess.

Charlie's still looking at me, waiting for a reaction, some words of advice, something to make him feel better. But I have nothing.

His eyes bore into mine and in the depths of them, I see something. Something different but unexplainable. These aren't the soft, tender, probing eyes I've been staring into, fantasizing about, dreaming of, there is something ever so slightly different, but I can't pinpoint exactly what it is. The shade is the same, there's nothing physically different, these are definitely Charlie's eyes, but there's something missing. Some spark or depth to them that isn't there anymore. The emotion and interest that I'm so used to seeing there, is gone.

I gulp as realisation hits me full force.

It hasn't been Charlie that I've been spending my days with.

And now that I've noticed the eyes, I notice other subtle little differences too. Like the way he stands: it's too straight, his shoulders pulled back, his chest puffed out with an air of arrogance that isn't usually there. My mind flicks back over all the times I've spent with him, and the other times when I've seen him at a distance with his friends. He held himself differently.

There was an air of loftiness and arrogance that wasn't usually there when we were alone. Now that I realise, it's so easy to see. This is a totally different person from the one I usually hung around with. Body language experts would likely pick up on it immediately, I had been so blind to not even question it. But then again, who in their right mind would even think about stupid stuff like that? No one.

Charlie is waiting, his gaze growing impatient as I stand there, mute.

I swallow, knowing I need to tread very carefully here. I can't just explain what Ryder had said. I couldn't understand it myself, let alone even begin to try to explain it to Charlie. Besides, he would never believe me in a million years. He would be just as closed minded as I had been on fireworks night. More so even, because he'd just blacked out with no recollection, he hadn't witnessed the subtle changes I had. And I hadn't believed a word of it. It had taken my nan speaking his name for me to even entertain the possibility of it all.

I couldn't tell him anything. Besides, the last time I'd spoken to 'Ryder' I'd told him I didn't ever want to see him again, so there should be no more blackouts for Charlie anyway. He can just move on with his life as if nothing had happened. I wish I could do the same.

'I'm sure it's nothing,' I lie, shrugging one shoulder dismissively, willing my tone not to betray the uncertainty I feel inside. 'Maybe you've just been distracted or something. I know sometimes I zone out on the bus ride because it's so monotonous and the time goes like that.' I click my fingers on the word that.

His frown deepens. 'I don't think it's that.'

'Maybe a concussion?' I suggest. 'Did you ever go get checked out after you banged your head?' I know he didn't, but I play along as if I don't know anything about him, as if I haven't spent almost every day after school with him. Technically, I guess I haven't spent any time with *him* at all.

I take a step back. Wanting this conversation to be over. I shouldn't have done this here. Maybe even at all. I need to go before I open up a can of worms that I'll never be able to close.

His expression turns to annoyance as he grinds his teeth. 'Concussion?' he says irritably, shaking his head. 'I've had a concussion, that isn't like this. Anyway, that was weeks ago.' Suddenly his eyes narrow in accusation as he reaches out and grasps my elbow. 'What do you know about this? Why did you ask about it?'

I go cold, my mind goes blank as I shake my head

slowly, searching for a lie to placate him. 'I just … I was curious. I wanted to check you were OK after saving me.'

His head tilts to the side as he considers my answer. 'But you specifically asked if I'd had any more blackouts. And you asked about fireworks night too.'

Shit. I had. Think, Maggie, think. 'I just wanted to talk to you. I was making conversation, that's all.'

'But you said it was important, that you wanted to talk to me alone,' he presses, not looking convinced.

I feel my face flood with heat at what I am about to say, but I know it's the only way out of this awkward situation. 'I … I like you. I wanted to talk to you and maybe see if you wanted to go to the cinema with me one time? Like a date? I didn't want to ask in front of your friend.'

Understanding washes over his face. He immediately lets go of my elbow, recoiling at my words. 'Oh. Oh, right.' He steps back raising himself to his full height as he glances up and down the corridor to make sure we're alone. I can see the slight revulsion at the idea on his face but he's trying to hide it. He's not doing a very good job.

I know then and there, from that one expression, that Charlie has no idea we've been hanging out. No idea that he almost kissed me a week ago. No idea that he shouted that he loved me as I ran away from him in the dark of the night. No idea that he's broken my heart. Because none of those things were Charlie. His expression now makes me certain of that.

'Look, uh…' He clenches his jaw, clearly trying to think of my name, and I stay silent, not helping him. He finally gives up. 'Look, sorry, but I'm not interested.' He doesn't even try to offer up any excuses, and I'm surprised to admit to myself that I hadn't even expected him to. This Charlie doesn't care if he hurts people's feelings. Unlike the Charlie I'd grown to know.

'It's OK,' I squeak, my face growing hotter. I try to school my expression so it doesn't show the unreasonable hurt I feel inside, but I can tell by how uncomfortable he looks that I've not managed it very well. I sidestep away from him and grip the strap of my bag tightly, forcing a smile. Every part of me wants to run away and find somewhere quiet I can think about this and what it means, but I force myself to stay and really drive the point home that it was just a normal run-of-the-mill conversation, nothing to be suspicious of. 'It's fine. It was just a thought, I thought it might be nice to hang out but it's OK. Never mind.' I glance up the hallway at the door at the end of the corridor. 'I should go and let you get back to your lunch and your friends.'

Just as I'm about to turn and make a swift exit, his entire body seems to stiffen. His hands clench into fists, his eyes squeeze shut and his shoulders hunch over as if he's just been punched in the gut. 'Wait,' he grunts. I frown, watching the scene play out. It only takes a second, or maybe two, but as Charlie straightens again and his eyes meet mine, my skin breaks out in goosebumps.

A small, insecure smile tugs at one corner of his mouth. 'Hi, Maggie.'

Air rushes out of my lungs and my school bag drops to the floor.

I know. Somehow, I just know.

It's him.

Ryder.

CHAPTER TWENTY-SIX
~ RYDER ~

'Ryder?' she whispers, her eyes sweeping over me from my stolen head to my stolen toes.

I nod slowly, feeling a huge thrill caused by my name coming from her lips. It sounds better than I thought it would. We stare at each other, me in Charlie's body that I couldn't help but steal yet again even though I vowed I wouldn't subject him to it anymore, and Maggie, still as a statue, her eyes wide and her mouth slightly agape.

Her eyes betray a small amount of fear, and that she knows who I am. Who I *really* am. She knows I've taken Charlie's body again.

I can't help the small smile that creeps onto my lips because she's starting to believe me. I never even considered this would happen, wasn't prepared for this at all today. Yes, I'd followed her to the library yesterday, watched her google me and read about how I died, but I didn't know what to expect.

On instinct, I'd followed her to school today because I wasn't sure what she would do with her new-found knowledge. Now, seeing her see *me* for the first time, I am enormously glad I did!

She's still staring at me, her lips slightly parted, her school bag all but forgotten where it fell on the floor in her shock.

'Are you OK?' I ask, eyeing her worriedly. Only a few seconds have passed, but it feels like an eternity.

She gulps and opens her mouth to answer, but two students enter the hallway, heading towards us and the canteen doors to our right. They glance at us, taking in our awkward posture and Maggie's bag on the floor then one whispers something to the other and they both chuckle.

I step closer to Maggie but don't reach out to touch her, I'm not sure if she's ready for that yet or what her reaction would be. 'Do you want to go somewhere so we can talk? Maybe the park?' I suggest.

'OK.' She nods, seeming a little shell-shocked, and watches as I bend and pick up her school bag, slinging it over my shoulder and motioning for her to walk up the hallway towards the exit. We walk out of the school in silence and thankfully, no one stops us to question why we're leaving the school during lunch.

By the time we reach the park down the road, the silence is almost deafening, and I feel my palms growing slick with sweat as nerves build in my stomach. We've been stealing little glances at each other on the short walk, but it seems neither of us know how to start this conversation.

She takes a seat on one of the benches, pulling her coat tightly around her before reaching into her pocket and producing a knitted cream bobble hat that she slips on, pulling down over her ears and hiding her red curls. Her cheeks flush as she notices me watching, captivated by how cute it makes her look.

I purse my lips and decide to just jump right into it. 'So, I guess you believe me now?'

Her gaze drops to her lap. 'Um … I'm not sure. I don't even know…' She shakes her head slowly. 'I know there's something weird going on. After speaking to Charlie just now I know there's something not right with his blackouts, and he's so different a lot of the time, like a split personality. I mean that's the more logical answer than ghosts and dead boys. What you're suggesting is so…' Her lips press into a thin line as she searches for the right word.

'Out there?' I offer.

She nods and the corner of her mouth hitches up.

'Yeah. Just … I want to hear it all. Tell me everything and then I'll decide if we're both bloody nuts.' She laughs, but it's humourless and holds more fright than anything else.

I nod and lean back against the backrest, settling in for the long haul.

Over the course of the next half an hour or so, I explain everything, I don't leave out any small detail. I tell her how my family and I went on the rafting trip when I was seventeen, how I was thrown from the boat, how I don't really remember dying but I can remember watching as they tried to revive me. I tell her about the light that came to collect me and how I ignored it. I tell her how lost I felt, and still feel, and about how I followed my family and friends for a long time, watching them grieve and try to move on with their lives without me. I tell her how, after it became too much to bear, too excruciating to watch them fall apart and blame each other, that I eventually left and met Jade. I explain about how the dying can see us, just for a few seconds before they leave.

She sits there, still as stone the whole time, her face expressionless, as if she's schooling it deliberately, afraid to betray what she's thinking in case I stop talking. But when I get to the part where I explain where I first saw her – the night her nan was brought to hospital following her first stroke – her back straightens and her breathing becomes shallow.

I smile apologetically, longing to reach out and take her hand that's balled into a tight fist, but knowing it's not appropriate. I need to let her process it all, and until then, until she knows everything, I have to stay at a distance and let her take it all in.

I swallow awkwardly before continuing, knowing this is the part that makes me sound like a total stalker that she should probably get a restraining order against. 'I was there at the hospital that night, seeing someone else, wanting that validation from someone actually seeing me,' I scowl down at my lap, hating how it makes me sound, 'when your nan was wheeled in on the gurney and you came trailing in behind her. Your eyes were all red rimmed, your face streaked with tears, and you had snot on the cuff of your pyjamas.'

She snorts a laugh beside me and I offer her a flash of a smile.

'When you argued with the nurse to be allowed to stay with your nan even after visiting hours finished, I thought you were the bravest, cutest, most fascinating thing I'd seen in ages.'

She scrunches her eyes up, shaking her head, smiling in disbelief. 'Covered in snot and tears? That's the kind of thing you're into?' she jokes, her cheeks burning pink.

I shrug one shoulder. 'What can I say, a guy likes what he likes.' I grin sheepishly before continuing. 'After that I kept tabs on you. I'd tag along for your visits to your grandmother, listen to you talking, and then walk home with you after each visit. It made me feel less alone, like I was part of something. I guess I kind of crossed a line a little.'

One of her eyebrows rise in question. 'Kind of?'

I shoot her a lopsided grin and raise my hand, holding my thumb and forefinger an inch apart. 'Just a little.' I scrunch my nose in admission. We both know it was more than just a little crossing of a line.

I kick my toe in the grass, digging up clumps of earth to avoid looking at her as I say the next part. 'While I was spending time watching you, I … um … fell head over heels in love with you.'

There's a sharp intake of breath from her, but I can't look at her, I keep my eyes firmly latched on the mud at my feet. My insides are swirling with sheer terror. It's the first time I've ever told anyone I love them – well, other than my parents, or me screaming it at her the other night as she ran away from me thinking I'd lost my damn mind.

I quickly push on, not allowing her time to say

anything in case she shoots me down, I need to get this all out there, not get stuck on one point. 'Then one night you walked out in front of that van. I couldn't just do nothing. I couldn't let you die.' I grind my teeth at the thought of losing her. 'I didn't even really think. Charlie was there and I just acted. I stole his body and I saved your life. I hadn't ever done anything like that before, wasn't even really sure I could. But I wasn't expecting you to know him,' I admit. 'That made things awkward because I was worried you'd say something to him about him saving you and things would get weird because obviously he didn't know anything about it.'

I glance up at her for her reaction. She's watching me with a mixture of shock and understanding on her face. I gulp. 'So I started following you even more, to make sure you weren't shouting your mouth off about the guy who saved you while he didn't have any recollection of it. I guess that facilitated the rest of this mess really.' I shake my head at myself and the situation. 'Once I'd stolen his body and talked to you, I started to really realise what I was missing out on, so I figured one more time wouldn't hurt … but once turned into twice and–' I groan and put my head in my hands. 'And then this whole mess came about where I was leading you on, you thinking I was someone that I'm not, while poor Charlie didn't even have any clue what was happening. I'm sorry, Maggie. I really am. I never meant to hurt you. I just wanted to know you, properly, and for you to know me. I got so swept away with it and it all escalated so quickly that I couldn't find a way to stop. But then when you went to kiss me at the fireworks, I realised how truly wrong it was. You didn't think you were kissing *me*, you thought you were about to kiss *Charlie* and I couldn't let that happen. But I also didn't want to lose you by just breaking it off.' I sigh and look over at her. 'I don't have anything else in my life. I just wander through the days with nothing to look forward to other than you; so I knew that the only chance I had to keep you in my life was to tell you the truth and see what happened.'

Her face flushes a deeper shade of pink as she chews on her lip. There's silence as we both take in what I'd just said. 'I'm glad you told me the truth,' she says eventually.

'Yeah? Even though you thought I was completely crazy?'

She laughs and nods. 'Well, yeah. I didn't believe a word you'd said, I thought you were just trying to pull some elaborate prank or something. But then...' Her voice breaks and I see her eyes glaze over with tears. 'Then my nan…' Her body heaves with a giant sob and she can't finish the sentence.

I turn in my seat and smile sadly. 'I know. I'm sorry,' I say. 'I was there, you know. When your nan died. I get a sense of these things when they're about to happen. I knew that day she was going to die, so I hung around so I could be there for you. I know that sounds stupid because you didn't even know I was there, but I wanted to be there to support you.'

Her head bobs a fraction. 'She said your name.' Her voice is barely above a whisper as a tear slides down her cheek.

'Yeah. I asked her to. Right at the end, she could see me so I asked her to say my name so you'd know I was there and that you weren't alone.'

She sniffs, swiping the tear from her face but it's quickly replaced by another.

I can't help myself, seeing her cry is making my heart ache, so I scoot closer to her on the bench and tentatively slip my arm around her shoulders. 'I'm sorry, Maggie. She was a lovely lady. But I strongly believe she's in a better place now. She went into her light, she's better off there than here. I can't explain it, it's just a feeling. The light, when I felt mine it was so warm, so welcoming and felt like home. She's definitely in a better place.' I can still remember the feeling of my light glowing on my skin, how incredible it felt, how the warmth spread through my whole body, calling me into that safe, soft place, wherever it may be. There wasn't a day that went by that I didn't wish I'd gone into mine, even if it meant I never would have met Maggie.

Maggie's full on crying now and leans her body against mine, resting her head on my shoulder, her face pressed into my neck. I close my eyes and realise that the light I was just thinking of feels very much like the feeling of a loved one in your arms.

We sit like that until her tears subside and then she edges away from me, looking up at me through damp eyelashes, her eyes pink. 'So ... I guess this is real then. You really are dead?'

I nod and shrug one shoulder. 'Yeah.'

She sniffs and looks at me thoughtfully. 'So why are you still here and not moving on? Do you have unfinished business or something?'

'This isn't *Casper the Friendly Ghost*.' I snort a laugh and nudge her shoulder with mine.

We both sit there, chuckling at my lame joke for a few seconds before she turns to me. 'Seriously, though, why are you still here?'

I frown. 'I don't know. When the light showed up to collect me, I was terrified. I thought maybe if I ignored it, it would just not be true. I wanted to stay with my family. I was too scared to go on my own. But then the light went away and didn't come back. I guess I missed my chance at moving on.'

'That's so sad.' Her eyes have filled with tears again.

I watch as a lone tear rolls down her cheek. I want to wipe it away, to press my lips to her skin and feel the warmth of her. Her eyes meet mine and there's a shift in the air. My breath catches and my insides fizz and crackle as the longing to kiss her becomes overwhelming. Before I know what I'm doing, I slowly lean forward and gently press my lips to hers. The kiss is softer than a butterfly's wings and barely lasts a heartbeat, but I feel the sensation of it throughout my entire body, right down to the tips of my toes. I suddenly realise that the kiss was the closest I'd come to describing what the light felt like. Like home.

When I pull back, my eyes meet hers for a second, assessing, trying to see what she made of it, afraid of what I'd see there. But under the shock that I'd kissed her, I see joy too.

The corner of her mouth twitches with a smile as she leans in and presses her lips to mine, harder this time, more insistent. My body sags with relief as my hand comes up to cup the side of her face, my fingertips touching her hair. The heat from her body seeps into me, warming my very soul. The kiss is disorientating and dizzying, but at the same time it's the best thing I've ever experienced in my life. I never want it to end.

When she finally pulls away, I watch colour bleed across her face as she grins and reaches up to touch her lips with her fingertips, her eyes sparkling with happiness. I know my soppy grin matches hers as we both stare at each other dumbfounded and in a happy bubble.

She looks away, across the park at nothing and gently leans her body against mine. As if I've done it a thousand times, my arm slips around her shoulders, holding her to me as we sit in companionable silence like that. It's the happiest I've felt since I died.

Without moving from her position, nestled under the crook of my arm, her fingers tangle with mine as she speaks. 'Do you ever see your family and friends?'

I gulp, a wave of emotion crashing over me, swallowing me up as I think of the day I decided to leave my home. I'd had to do it. Watching my best mate isolate himself and barely scrape through the last year of his A-levels, seeing my parents' marriage crack under the pressure of grief, my brother falling behind at university and losing his dream of becoming a doctor, my dad crying when he thought no one was around, and then my little brother just up and leaving. It was all too much. I couldn't watch it for a moment longer. But leaving them had been the hardest thing I'd ever done.

'Occasionally I go back, just to check in on them all. But leaving was definitely the right decision for me. I couldn't have stayed there long term, just on the fringes of their lives, clinging to something I could never have back. Seeing the devastation it caused when I died. The guilt of it, it still crushes me. I know it's not really my fault, but it feels like it is. I stayed with them for almost two years, witnessed them just spiralling out of control. The hardest part for me was watching my older brother lose himself. He had always been the one that had dreams and aspirations, he just lost his drive and will after I died. He gave up. He lost everything. I took everything away from him. In the end, I just had to detach from it. Leave. Think about something else instead of being consumed by it every day. That's selfish of me, I know.'

She shakes her head adamantly. 'That's not selfish. It's self-preservation. I can't imagine how hard it would be to watch someone you love crumble but not be able to help or comfort them. I don't think I could have stayed as long as you did. It's like watching life play out through a window or on TV.'

I close my eyes, appreciating her solidarity.

Wind whips through the field, causing her to shiver against me. 'Your friend Jade that you told me about. Is she here now?' Maggie asks, changing the subject as she glances around furtively.

'No, she's not. We don't usually hang out in the day, but we always meet up in the evenings.'

'There are more, like you? Or just you and Jade?' She turns her head, looking up at me inquisitively.

I smile and am unable to stop myself from reaching out and brushing one finger across her cheek. 'There are more. Quite a few, actually. But Jade and I tend to stay away from them if we can help it. Some of them are a little crackpot. Maybe they've been wandering for too long. Loneliness can break you.'

She gives me a small smile and a gentle nod of agreement. I see the pain in her eyes. She is lonely too. In a way, we're the same. Both ripped away from our families, forced to survive in a whole new world. Alone. If anyone understands loneliness, it's Maggie.

Her fingers tighten in mine and she settles back against my side. 'So, what happens now then? Now that I know who you are. What do we do about it?'

I smile sadly. That's the million-pound question. 'I don't know. There's nothing we can do about it. I'm dead, you're not. I don't have a body. You can't see or hear me. And after your discussion in the hallway and how paranoid he seemed about his blackouts, I don't think I can use Charlie again.' I scowl out over the park as I say the words. They hurt to say but they're the truth.

We're just two lonely souls, destined to be apart.

'No, you can't use him again. He definitely thinks there is something wrong. I think while we were speaking he finally admitted it to himself that there was a problem. It wouldn't surprise me if he goes to the doctors and asks for a CT scan straight after school. Especially after he realises he's lost time again here.'

I sigh and concentrate on the feel of her fingers, on the warmth and softness of them, knowing this will be the last time this will happen. It's heaven.

She tilts her head up, looking at me quizzically. 'When you're being you, can you, like, touch things?'

Touch things. My mind instantly goes to places it shouldn't, and my face must betray my dirty thoughts because she makes a strangled choking noise in the back of her throat and her eyes widen as her whole face flushes with colour.

We both laugh and she shakes her head quickly before I have a chance to answer. 'I meant, like, can you move things, knock things over or something?' she clarifies.

I grin sheepishly. 'Very rarely. I'm not very good at it. Jade, my friend, she's great at it. She even does it by accident sometimes when she gets pissed at something. She's tried to teach me a bunch of times, but it's still more miss than hit.'

'Why can she do it, but you can't?'

I shrug in answer. 'I honestly don't know. Jade always says it's because she was always an emotional person when she was alive, she says it's the same passion that she uses to make things move – like anger, or frustration, or desperation, the same sort of feeling she gets in her stomach when she does it. Or maybe it's just as simple as, she's been wandering longer than I have. We've tried to work it out but…' I shrug again. 'I've seen a couple of other wanderers do it too. Once I saw a guy go into a full-on rage and throw stuff across the room, smashing glasses, breaking tables. I guess, to the living, wanderers like that would be called poltergeists.'

Maggie draws in an uneasy breath, her body tensing against mine.

'So the honest answer is, I just don't know. I can

do it a little, like maybe if I concentrate hard enough and long enough I could move something small and light, like a piece of paper but that's about it.'

'Ah, I kinda hoped you were going to say you could pick up a pen and write a note or something,' she replies. I shake my head and she purses her lips, thinking. 'I guess, for a while, until we figure things out, maybe when you want to let me know you're there you can attempt to knock something over or something. It's not ideal, but neither is stealing someone else's body to talk to me.'

'It's just not fair,' I grumble. 'It's like we're destined to be apart. I wish I'd met you when I was alive.' I reach out and trace the side of her face with the back of my finger, loving the soft feel of her.

She smiles sadly and settles back against me. 'We'll have to keep thinking. This can't be the end. We've only just officially met. It can't be over before it's even had a chance to begin.'

Sadness washes over me at her words and the truth of them. 'For now, let's just make the most of this time we have together,' I suggest, gripping her fingers and bringing them up to my lips, planting a gentle kiss on the back of her hand. A warm glow spreads across her face and my insides feel just as toasty.

CHAPTER TWENTY-SEVEN
~ MAGGIE ~

My days seem to be blurring into one another. Has it really been just over a week since Ryder confessed everything to me? It feels like a year has passed already.

I walk around like an emotionless zombie. I can't help it. It feels like I've nothing left. First I found an epic love, then I lost him just as quickly, and then I lose my nan. Everything has gone to shit in the matter of a few weeks. It feels as though there's nothing left for me anymore and I'm just going through the motions of human life.

I've tried to keep positive, but I feel so lonely inside. Ryder and I haven't found a way to communicate; sometimes I just talk and hope that he's there, but he's not given me any signs so I can only assume that he either can't or he simply isn't there.

Charlie seems to have gone back to normal. I'd

heard through the grapevine that he'd visited the doctor for tests but that they'd found nothing physically wrong that would cause the blackouts. He doesn't like to talk about it to his friends, apparently. I personally think he just wants to put it behind him, and now that Ryder has vowed never to use him, he can get his life back on a normal track again. I see him in the corridors some days, his high jinks around the school haven't changed; he's still the big man and living it up as the most popular kid in school. Only now, he avoids me like the plague. Before I asked him out, he ignored me because he simply wasn't aware of my presence, now he ignores me because I clearly make him feel uncomfortable. Whenever he sees me he'll deliberately walk the other way or start a conversation with someone and get the heck out of there like a bat out of hell. I don't blame him really.

I sigh and pull on my woolly hat, tugging it down over my ears, sticking my head into the living room. 'I'm going out for a walk,' I tell Lorna.

'OK, what time will you be back?' she replies, glancing up from the book she's reading.

I shrug and wrap my scarf around my neck. 'Not sure. I've got my key.' Before she can answer or pin me down for a more certain time, I throw her a wave and open the front door, heading out and immediately ducking my head against the cold. The Fishers are nice, they've been great trying to support me since my nan passed, but they're not my real family and I can never forget that. I have no one, not really. No friends, no family, no boyfriend. Nothing.

I sigh and begin walking down the street, crunching on lemon Pez, unsure where I'm heading but just needing to keep busy. I'm so lonely it's like a cold stone has settled where my heart used to be, all heavy and impenetrable. Knowing that Ryder is real wasn't the weight off my mind like I'd hoped it would be. Since our talk and his confession, it's just made me feel worse, knowing he's lonely too, stuck here, wandering around with no purpose, just like I am now.

I miss him so much my stomach aches.

I reach up and touch my lips. The essence of the kiss still lingers there; when I think about it, I can almost still feel his mouth against mine. I think about that kiss all the time. My first and only kiss from the boy I'm in love with. How tragic.

I know I've succumbed to a bout of depression. I've let it take over, eat me up and spit me out the other side broken and bruised, but I can't seem to shake myself out of it.

It doesn't really surprise me when a while later I

arrive at the entrance to the woods where Charlie/Ryder and I once walked his dog. Subconscious or not, I just like to feel close to him. I've tried other things we did to make myself feel better too – like buying a hotdog from the same vendor we once went to, but the taste of it was like cardboard, I'd walked the same streets we used to walk together and replayed our conversations in my head. I listened to some of the music he said was his favourite and sat for hours on the park bench we shared our kiss on. It did all make me feel slightly closer to him, but the uncertainty of not knowing if I'd ever be able to see him again weighs heavily on my heart and my state of mind.

The day is quite cold, but there's not a raincloud in the sky, so I decide to venture into the woods for a while and enjoy the peace and solitude. Being here makes me feel close to Ryder. I need it. I'm so lonely my whole body aches.

CHAPTER TWENTY-EIGHT
~ RYDER ~

She's come to our woods. I had wondered where she was headed when she set out this morning, but even she hadn't seemed to know where she was going. For a while she had wandered in circles ... until she ended up here.

I smile as she looks up at the sky before pulling her coat tighter around her and steps onto the dirt track, deliberately kicking up the crunchy, frost-covered leaves in front of her with each step.

I wish I could tell her I was here.

I concentrate with all my might, the way Jade has been teaching me all week, and attempt to snap a branch to get her attention, but I fail. I simply lack the strength or the skill to do it. I've tried all week to move something, knock something over, to give her any signal that I've been with her, anything to lift the dark mood I can see has settled over her, but to no avail. I feel like a failure.

I'm frustrated. I can see she is too. I've been there a few times when she's had one-sided conversations with me, wishing I was there, asking me to let her know I was there. I've seen her cry. I've seen her mood sink lower and lower, I've seen her sob herself to sleep and push food around her plate instead of eating it. All of it hurts my very soul.

We're alone, there's not another soul around as far as the eye can see and the only sounds are the chirping of birds and the rustling of wind whipping through the trees as we make our way deeper inside the woods, winding around trees because she's stepped off the trail and is just walking aimlessly into the foliage now.

It must be at least an hour before we come to a clearing. There are some large rocks covered in moss and grime at the top of a steep hill. Maggie stops and looks up at them, shading her eyes against the glare and craning her neck to get a better view, before beginning to climb the hill, digging her toes in and hunching over almost to all fours to give her more purchase as she ascends. I frown and follow her up.

When she gets to the top, she takes off one glove, running her hand over the stone. The rock is massive from up here, taller than she is. Maggie shades her eyes with the other hand and looks out at the view.

It's pretty: blue sky as far as the eye can see and the tops of trees. A small smile graces her lips, it's one of the first I've seen in a long time.

Suddenly, her lips purse and her eyebrows pull together as if she's thinking about something. She pulls off her other glove, shoving them both in her pocket before she reaches up and grips the top of the rock, beginning to hoist herself up.

'I'm not sure this is a good idea,' I warn, even though I know she can't hear me.

She's got her foot in a little crevice now so she can lift herself higher and hook her elbows over the top. I grin. It looks extremely undignified as she swings one leg up to the top and pulls with all her might, making grunting noises from the effort until she's managed to shimmy her body onto the rock. I roll my eyes and do the same, finding it easier than she did because ... hello ... I am a wanderer after all.

The climb has obviously worn her out a little because she just stays on her back for a minute, catching her breath before she tentatively gets to her feet. 'Eww,' she groans, grimacing at the mud and grime that clings to her coat and jeans in clumps. She brushes them off as best she can, taking off her hat that's now smeared with mud and shoving it into her pocket with her gloves before standing and looking out over the view again. Her smile returns, this time it's bigger and reaches her eyes.

Now I know why she came up here. The view is much better from higher up. It's serene looking over the tops of the trees, the sky all dusky blue, the spire of the cathedral way off in the distance. It's spectacular.

'Not sure if you're here or not,' she says, her eyes still roaming the view, 'but if you are, this is a pretty romantic spot. If we ever figure out a way to talk again, we should come up here and bring a picnic.'

I grin, reaching out and brushing my hand down the side of her hair, wishing we could both feel it. 'Deal.'

She stays there for a long time, just silently looking out over the horizon, her phone resting on the rock next to her, quietly playing Queen's greatest hits through the speaker. The sky begins to darken before she finally looks at her watch. She lets out a heavy, resounding sigh, picks up her phone and shoves it into her pocket before turning on her heel, readying to climb down.

I see what's going to happen before it does, but this time, I can do nothing about it.

As she moves her foot to take a step closer to the edge, she steps in a clump of damp moss and her foot slides out from under her. My breath catches as I watch, frozen to the spot, as her eyes widen in surprise. I see the fear cross her face as her foot goes over the edge of the rock, her other foot losing balance too as she begins to fall backwards.

'Look out!' I scream, my warning echoing the one Charlie had shouted all those weeks ago. My useless hands shoot out to catch her but my grasp ghosts straight through her body.

And then she's falling. Falling. Falling.

And I can do nothing but watch in horror, my heart in my throat.

CHAPTER TWENTY-NINE
~ RYDER ~

She doesn't hear my desperate cry as she slips, her head striking the rock with such a sickening force that the sound, the dull thunk of skull on rock, reverberates in my ears. Her eyes lose focus, her body slackens. But then she's falling again, slipping over the side of the rock and smashing into the ground six feet below. Even in her dazed state, her arms come up to brace for impact. A scream pierces the air, but she's still not done. The momentum pushes her forward and she's spilling and sliding down the hill, building speed, her body being thrown around like a rag doll. She tumbles and smashes down the hill over and over, for what feels like forever, before finally hitting a tree at the bottom and coming to an abrupt stop.

I'm stuck to the spot for a few seconds, watching her motionless body. I can't see if she's breathing from up here and my panic has taken over. Seconds pass and I'm still stuck to the spot, staring at her, waiting for any sign of movement.

My eyes drop down to the rock where Maggie was moments before. A red, wet trail there makes my heart jackhammer in my chest, and that thaws me out.

Jumping off the side of the rock and half running, half stumbling down the steep hill, I fall to my knees at her side.

'Oh God, no,' I groan. There's blood everywhere, on her face, on her coat, plastering her hair to her face. 'Maggie, please.'

I reach down to turn her over, forgetting that I can't touch her and my horror builds as I see her arm is bent at an unnatural angle. 'It's OK, it's just a break, it's OK,' I tell myself, feeling my tears begin to fall. I manoeuvre myself to her other side to get a better look. There are scratches all over her face, cuts oozing with blood, dirt everywhere on her. Nothing that can't be fixed … but that's when I see the puddle of blood that's building around her head, slowly seeping into the earth, colouring the dry leaves in sticky crimson. 'Oh shit.'

I jump up, looking around for someone, anyone that can help, anyone that can put pressure on the wound and call 999. But there's no one. No one at all.

I drop back to my knees at her side, concentrating with all my might, willing my hands into action as I attempt over and over to reach into her pocket and pull out her mobile phone. I manage to move the material of her pocket, but that's all. I'm totally and utterly useless. 'Please, please, please,' I mumble over and over.

As I panic, her eyes open and my hope builds. *She's going to be OK. She can call an ambulance for herself, or someone will come.*

But then the air changes around me, becomes heavier, thicker somehow and my heart sinks. Resignation seeps into my bones. 'No!' I beg. 'Please no.' I lean over her, continuing to try to get her phone, but I already know it's fruitless. You can't fight fate. Jade had been right. There was no escaping death, after all.

Maggie's lips pop open as her watery, pain-filled eyes latch onto me. Almost instantly, her eyes widen in shock and recognition. 'Ryder?'

My heart swells in my chest, fit to bursting as bittersweet emotion washes over me in droves. I've always wanted her to look at me, to see me, to acknowledge me … but not like this.

'Hi,' I croak in response, unable to think coherently given the circumstances.

'I – I see you,' she stutters before her eyes scrunch up tightly and she sucks in a sharp breath.

'Maggie, no,' I whisper, shaking my head and reaching out to smooth down her dirt-encrusted curls even though I can't actually touch her. 'Please, no. Just hold on. Don't die, please?'

An agonised smile twitches at the corner of her mouth as she raises a shaky hand as if to touch my cheek but, of course, she can't touch me either. A sad smile graces her lips. 'It's OK.'

But it's not OK, nothing will ever be OK again because she's moments from death. The mere fact that she can see me proves that there is no hope. Gritting my teeth and ignoring the tears that wet my cheeks, I look around for someone to help again, some person that can staunch the blood flow that seems to be trickling at an alarming pace from the side of her head. But there's no one.

No help.

No hope.

She's going to die and this time there is nothing I can do but watch as she walks out of my life to begin her next.

'Maggie, please hold on. Help will come,' I whisper.

But it doesn't come. No one comes and within

seconds her body shuts down and goes limp before my eyes.

As she takes her last breath, my heart fractures, splintering into a thousand pieces.

'You look just like your pictures.'

At her words, my grief builds in my chest, strangling me, choking me. Slowly, I turn away from her body to see her standing behind me. The blood is gone now, her skin is radiant, her hair wilder than ever.

I choke out a sob and she shakes her head, her eyes sad and sympathetic as she looks at me. 'It's OK, really.' Her voice is almost a whisper and I push myself up from my knees and stumble over to her, wrapping my arms around her tightly, crushing her against me, my hands stroking her back. Her arms wind around my waist and we stand like that as I grieve for her, I grieve for myself, I grieve for our lost relationship that can never be now.

When the hug breaks, she pulls back a little so she can look at me, but I can't take my arms from around her, not yet. I'm not ready to say goodbye to her. She looks up at me, her green eyes meeting mine. I can see wonder there, and curiosity. I hold my breath as her hand reaches up to my face, cupping my cheek before softly tracing one finger along my jaw line until her hand slips into my hair. A small smile plays on the corner of her lips and everything in me is screaming to close the distance, to press my body against hers, to claim her mouth with such a ferocity that I would always taste her even after she leaves to move on.

Her eyes are locked on mine. She's seeing me, all of me, all that I am. I'm laid bare to her in that moment, just willing her to know how much I love her.

'I've always preferred brown eyes,' she says.

I can't help but chuckle at that. 'Maggie,' I begin, but she shushes me with a finger against my lips.

'Don't say anything. It's happened. It can't be undone,' she says, and I notice she's deliberately not looked down at her body, not once. 'Let's just enjoy this right here,' she continues, pressing her hand against my chest, feeling my heart thump wildly against my chest, her teeth sinking into her bottom lip.

'I love you, Maggie.' It's the only thing I can think of to reply.

It's enough.

A beautiful smile breaks out on her lips. 'I love you too, Ryder.' At the sound of my name from her lips, I lose all control and dip my head, pressing my lips to hers. Her hands slide up my chest, one looping around my neck, the other gripping the back of my hair as she kisses me back with everything she has. The kiss is wonderous and bittersweet, an all-consuming passionate kiss that I feel all the way down to my toes.

Suddenly she pulls away, her eyes squinting as she turns her head behind her.

My heart sinks. It's time to say goodbye.

Her mouth drops open as she reaches up with one hand to shield her eyes, blinking rapidly. I let my arms fall from around her and step back, my stomach tightening with sorrow.

'You should go. You only have a few minutes,' I encourage, slipping my hands into my pockets, watching the awe and amazement on her face.

She gulps noisily and there's a slight shake of her head. 'I'll stay here with you. Now we can be together.'

I gasp. My first split second reaction is to scream YES, but then the selfish part of me is under control. 'What? No way. You're not staying here, Maggie. Not for me. Just go.'

A frown lines her forehead as she looks from me to where her light is again, an agonised expression on her face. I can almost feel how torn she is. Tears well in her eyes. But I refuse to let her stay here. I would never wish that for her, even if it meant it made my so-called life more bearable. 'Go,' I encourage, forcing a smile. 'Please go. You don't want to stay here. I won't let you suffer this for me. Go!'

She's full on crying now and I call feel my tears wetting my cheeks again too. 'Can't you come with me?'

I shake my head. 'I … I … can't.'

She takes a step towards me and I step back, keeping the distance between us. I need to stay strong. I have to let her go. I have to *make* her go.

'Have you ever tried?' she asks, looking from me back to her light again.

I gulp. 'No.'

'Then try,' she whispers. 'Come with me.' She reaches out her hand. I look down at it, not knowing what to do. She's wasting time. She needs to be quick before her light gives up waiting and abandons her here like mine did.

I step forward, slipping my hand into her smaller one, my heart aching in my chest.

As soon as my hand is in hers the world explodes with light, so bright it feels like I'm blinded. It bounces off every surface, illuminates everything and makes it ten times more beautiful. Its warm glow slides over my body, bathing me in joy. I can feel the safety and protectiveness of it.

My breath comes out in one long gust as I blink rapidly, looking back at Maggie. She's grinning at me, the most radiant, beautiful smile I've ever seen in my life and everything feels like it's fallen into place.

'Do you see it?' she asks, squeezing my hand.

But I'm dumbfounded, I can't speak. So I just nod.

'Come with me,' she whispers again.

The light is so warm, so soft and welcoming, it fills my whole body, calling me, pulling me towards it, promising unseen things, things like acceptance and happiness.

I'm finally leaving. It's finally over. No more wandering, no more endless days and nights by the river just begging for someone to acknowledge my existence. Maggie and I could be together forever and move on from this place.

But then my mind flicks to Jade. *If I leave, she'll have no one, she wouldn't even know where I was. I can't do this...*

As if sensing my hesitation, Maggie squeezes my hand, bringing me back to her. She's smiling at me and it's so radiant it makes my breath falter; the light, it frames her face, bouncing from those curls in such a way I'm almost dazzled by it.

'It's your choice. Either you come with me or we

both stay. Either way we'll be together and that's all that matters,' she says, her soft green eyes holding mine, showing me the truth in her words. She really would stay here, wandering, forever trapped amongst the living with me.

But it's the word *together* that makes up my mind for me. I can't pass up this opportunity. For years my only regret has been not going when my time was up, I couldn't make the same mistake again, and I refuse to let her give up her chance for me.

'Let's go,' I whisper, throwing up a silent 'I'm sorry' to Jade. But I know she would understand, she hates being stuck here as much as I do. If the roles were reversed, I'd want her to go and to not even spare me a second thought. Now I can only pray she somehow gets her happily ever after, too.

'Together,' I say, my voice hoarse with emotion, and I step towards the light, pulling her along with me.

'Together,' Maggie agrees.

Always together.

EPILOGUE
~ JADE ~

It takes me a long time to realise what's happened – well, to partially figure it out, anyway. As a wanderer we can't just jump on Google, so old-fashioned detective work it was. Finally, after a week of not seeing hide nor hair of Ryder, I started investigating and found out about Maggie dying. It hit me like a ton of bricks, but I can honestly say I wasn't that surprised. After my mum and what happened to her, I am a firm believer that when someone's time is up, it's up. And Ryder shouldn't have intervened and saved her in the first place. It gave them both false hope.

That knowledge doesn't make me feel any better though. Poor Ryder is somewhere, consumed with grief, suffering on his own instead of letting me help him.

When he hadn't come back to any of our meeting places, I'd left it a while before trying to find him, hoping he'd come back when he was ready, but almost three weeks have passed now since Maggie died and there has been no word from my best friend.

Walking through the cemetery slowly, I glance around, reading the names on the little plaques in the urn burial garden as I make my way to the one which I've found belongs to Maggie. They've buried her ashes in the plot next to her grandmother. She would have liked that.

I've taken it upon myself to sit here for the last three days, thinking that maybe Ryder would show up here to hang out with her or pay his respects. So far, he hasn't. I'm getting extremely frustrated by the fact that I have no other way to contact him and help him. For the last five years we've barely gone a day without seeing each other.

Stopping at the foot of Maggie's freshly mounted plaque, I sigh and sit cross-legged, tipping my head back and letting my mind whirl. I wonder when he'll come back. Once he's got his head straight, probably, but how long does that kind of thing take? I'd been a mess for a year after my mum passed. I secretly and selfishly hope he doesn't take much longer. I don't let my mind think about the other possibility – that he may never come back. He wouldn't do that to me. He knows he's all I have left in this world. No, I won't go there. One day he'll be back and everything will be just like it was.

As I sit there, soaking up the sun, wishing I could feel the rays and the warmth, I spot a funeral procession coming in through the gates. The flowers inside the hearse spell the name *Sarah* in white and pink carnations. They park up near the crematorium where a crowd of people wait; some are already crying, some start as they see the coffin through the glass of the car.

A man steps out of the lead car, his black suit worn and shabby-looking. He doesn't look at anyone or meet anyone's eyes as he reaches behind him and takes ahold of a woman's elbow, helping her from the car. The woman is crying hysterically as she emerges from the car. She wears a black dress and coat and in her hair there's a black headband with a bright blue satin flower attached to it. Her eyes are red and puffy, she holds a tissue to her nose as her knees buckle and the man has to catch her and prop her up as she cries on his shoulder.

Movement from the corner of eye catches my attention. I turn and see a girl, maybe just a little younger than me, standing at the back of the row of cars, watching the woman in black. Her arms are wrapped tightly around her midsection, hugging herself. There's something off about her, a shimmer, the edges of her body not quite sharp enough. I know it can only mean one thing. I look from her to the coffin and sigh deeply.

She's Sarah, those are her parents, she didn't cross over and is now stuck here alone too. A wanderer, just like me.

I keep my eyes on the girl as I push myself to standing and walk towards her. She hasn't noticed me; her wide eyes don't leave her grieving parents. Her face is deathly pale and I see her fist clenching and unclenching, gripping the side of the hospital standard pyjamas she wears. Tears slide down her cheeks relentlessly, though she doesn't make a sound.

I clear my throat and her head whips around in my direction, her red, puffy eyes widening with shock.

'Hi,' I say.

Her eyes dart around, her whole body turning in a full circle to see who is behind her. When she sees no one, she turns back to me, her eyes so wide it's almost comical. 'Are you talking to me?' Her voice is barely above a croaky whisper.

I nod. 'Sure. You're the only ghost standing there, aren't ya?'

I see her throat bob as she looks down at herself then back at me. 'You see dead people?'

I snort a laugh. 'Oh, come on, this isn't *The Sixth Sense* movie.'

Her forehead creases with a frown. 'The what?'

I roll my eyes at her rubbish movie knowledge. '*The Sixth Sense*? It's only the second best Bruce Willis movie ever. Don't you know anything?' I joke, keeping my tone light and friendly because I remember like yesterday what my first encounter with a wanderer was like. I don't want to frighten the poor girl; she's been through enough already recently.

She watches me wearily, her eyes darting back to the crematorium and the mourners who are now heading inside the building, someone I assume is her mum is hanging back, looking through the glass of the car at the coffin that lay inside.

'Why can you see me? No one else...' her voice breaks and her shoulders hitch with a sob as she stops talking abruptly and shakes her head.

I shrug, trying to keep my mood up because being here reminds me of my own funeral and my own mother breaking down into hysterics when they carried my coffin into the church. 'I'm dead too,' I say simply. She gasps in shock and I shrug again. 'So, what got you then?' When she blinks and doesn't answer, I clarify. 'What did you die of?'

330

'Oh,' she says softly, looking down at her bare feet amongst the grass. 'Cancer. Leukaemia.'

'That sucks.'

'Yeah. What about you?'

'Car accident.'

'Sucks.'

'So, your name's Sarah, I'm guessing?' We both look up as the coffin is carried inside and her mother follows behind crying endlessly. 'I'm Jade.' She doesn't answer so I find myself speaking to fill the void as Eva Cassidy's 'Songbird' begins to play inside. 'Was that your mum with the flower headband?'

'My poor mum. That was my headband,' she sobs.

I glance down, now lost for words as my own memories surface. Loneliness and sadness overwhelm me. I need to go. I need to get back into a routine. Life *must* go on … so must death. Ryder will be back soon. I can't stand around here and put my existence on hold for him if he doesn't want to be found. I need to keep busy or the sadness will overwhelm me and I'll start down a hole I may never be able to get out of.

'Well, I'll see you around. Maybe.' I start to walk away but then an image of Ryder pops into my head – not Ryder as he was now, but Ryder when I first met him. How lost he'd been, how sad, and I thought about how we've stuck together and propped each other up when we were down. About how much I miss and need him back … and that small niggling feeling I have in the back of my mind that I don't dare acknowledge, that he may never come back.

I don't want to do this alone.

I stop and turn back to the girl. 'So, what are your plans now then, Sarah?'

She sniffs; her sad, tear-filled eyes turn to me. 'I … I don't know. I don't know what I'm going to do.'

'Well, you can't go with them,' I nod towards the mourners, 'not anymore.'

Her chin wobbles and as she bites down on her bottom lip, her eyes filling with tears again. My heart aches for her. She's too little to be here alone.

'Want to come with me for a bit?' I offer.

She thinks about it for a few seconds and I realise in that short space of time how much I need her to say yes. Maybe I'm too little to be alone here, too. Maybe we all are.

'OK,' she says quietly.

I smile reassuringly and motion with my head for her to come along. 'I know just how to make you feel better,' I tell her confidently, eyeing the groundskeeper as he pulls weeds from a nearby flower border, humming to himself.

'How?' Sarah asks.

Instead of answering, I focus all my energy on my hand, reach out and knock over the nearby rubbish bin. Litter spews everywhere and the plastic bin makes a resounding crash as it strikes the ground. The groundskeeper jumps and makes a loud girlish screech, then cries, 'Jesus, Mary and Joseph!'

I laugh and look back to Sarah, seeing the first blossom of a smile tugging at her cracked lips.

I grin and do a little theatrical bow which makes her smile grow a little bit larger. I crook an elbow and her arm loops through mine, holding on to me tightly.

She sniffs and we walk slowly out of the grounds; she glances back only once at the crematorium, and I reach down and pat her hand softly, smiling reassuringly.

Her throat bobs and then she asks, 'So what's the best one?'

I frown in confusion. 'Huh?'

'You said *The Sixth Sense* was the second-best Bruce Willis movie, so what's the first?'

I smile broadly. '*Die Hard* of course; coincidentally, it's also the best Christmas movie of all time.'

One of her eyebrows rise incredulously. '*Die Hard* isn't a Christmas movie.'

I stop walking and eye her, wondering if we can

actually be friends after all, but then one side of her mouth hitches up and she gives me a little shove. 'Kidding!'

'Phew!' I breathe, mock wiping my brow. 'For a moment there I thought I was going to have to dump you back where I found you,' I joke, before tipping her a conspiratorial wink. 'Come on, Sarah, let's go see how much havoc we can cause, shall we?'

Her red-rimmed eyes crinkle with a smile and I already know we're going to be great friends.

ACKNOWLEDGEMENTS

My first thanks must go to my family for always being there and cheering me on. In particular, my husband, Lee. You've always believed in me and love me more than you should – I'm glad you don't realise you deserve better than me! I love you all to the moon and back.

To my bestie, Kerry. You're both the one who keeps me grounded and the one who lifts me up. Thank you for always encouraging me to keep going. You're my person, and I wish you lived closer (but, I suppose, if you did, we'd probably never get anything done!)

To the wonderful team at Firefly. Thank you for taking a chance on this unconventional romance novel, and for loving the story and characters as much as I do. A special thanks goes to Rebecca and Leonie for their passion for the book from the get-go, and to the design team for the gorgeous cover, it encompasses Ryder and Maggie so well. It has been a pleasure working with all of you.

Lastly, to Lorella and the team at Lorella Belli Literary Agency, thank you for always championing me and my words. Your support and belief mean everything.

At Firefly we care very much about the environment and our responsibility to it. Many of our stories, such as this one, involve the natural world, our place in it and what we can all do to help it, and us, survive the challenges of the climate emergency. Go to our website www.fireflypress.co.uk to find more of our great stories that focus on the environment, like *The Territory*, *Aubrey and the Terrible Ladybirds*, *The Song that Sings Us* and *My Name is River*.

As a Wales-based publisher we are also very proud the beautiful natural places, plants and animals in our country on the western side of Great Britain.

We are always looking at reducing our impact on the environment, including our carbon footprint and the materials we use, and are taking part in UK-wide publishing initiatives to improve this wherever we can.